# TWILIGHT ROAD

Also by Michael J. McCann

Project Changeling
The Long Road Into Darkness
A Death in Winter
No Sadness of Farewell
Persistent Guilt
Burn Country
Sorrow Lake
The Rainy Day Killer
The Fregoli Delusion
Marcie's Murder
Blood Passage
The Ghost Man

# TWILIGHT ROAD

A Maddie Hubbard Novel
of Supernatural Suspense

## Michael J. McCann

A Solar Salamander Book

The Plaid Raccoon Press
2022

TWILIGHT ROAD
Copyright © 2022 by Michael J. McCann

The Plaid Raccoon Press supports copyright, which protects creativity and the right of authors to profit from the fruits of their considerable labour. Thank you for buying an authorized edition of this book and for complying with copyright laws by not reproducing any part of this book, paperback and/or e-book, without permission from the publisher.

ISBN: 978-1-927884-23-2 (paperback)
          978-1-927884-24-9 (e-book)

Cover images: Pete Linforth/Pixabay; Enrique Meseguer/Pixabay
Maddie portrait: cipella/Thinkstock; Michael J. McCann
Author photo: Michael J. McCann

Visit the author's website at www.mjmccann.com

This is for you, Sandra,
because you wanted me to finish it

*Maddie Hubbard*

# FAMILY HISTORY

Gabrielle + Jean-Louis
Proulx    Fournier

|

Lisette + Gilles
Fournier    Hamelin

|

Marie-Claire + Claude
Hamelin    Desormeaux

|

Joelle + Mark    Robert   Nicolette
Desormeaux   Hubbard

Maddie     Quinn
Hubbard    Hubbard

DEVLIN

# 1

The moment she walked into the room, Dr. Dennis Devlin knew that something was different.

It began with her eyes, which glanced around the consultation room as though seeing it for the first time, taking in the steam radiator below the window, the fireplace with its row of white candles on the mantel, and the open doorway into his office.

It extended to her mouth, which, although not smiling—never smiling!—was relaxed, almost amused. An expression new to their relationship.

It included her clothing, which consisted today of a dark blue, ankle-length dress with small grey flowers and four white buttons on the front, a slender navy belt around her waist, and black shoes with thick, low heels. Although she'd occasionally worn a dress or skirt to previous sessions, her preferred wardrobe over the winter had been jeans and a pullover sweater. Simple and to the point. But here they were, on the first Tuesday in March, and Maddie Hubbard had chosen a dress from her closet that he'd never seen before.

"How are you feeling today?" he asked as they sat down, each in their usual brown armchair. Between them was a glass coffee table with a stack of books on pottery, Dutch art, and French rural gardens; a platter of wicker balls painted gold and green that his cats occasionally knocked onto the floor when the room was otherwise unoccupied; and a bowl of dried rose petals that Devlin liked because they had come from the bushes in his garden.

Her eyes found his. "I'm well, thanks. How about yourself?"

He smiled, pleased with her willingness to make eye contact. "Not bad. Happy to see the snow beginning to go away."

"I agree. I don't like the winter much, either." She looked out the window, distracted by a bird passing in her peripheral vision. She frowned, a very brief crease at the bridge of her nose that quickly smoothed out, and turned back to him, ready for his next question.

Devlin crossed his legs. It was his practice to conduct what was called a mental status examination at the beginning of each session with a client. Based on a generic model commonly used in clinical treatment, it was a quick series of observations regarding the person's mental condition. His exam covered about nine different categories, including such things as appearance and grooming, facial expression, behaviour, compulsive movement, speech patterns, thought processes, and that sort of thing. This morning she seemed to be checking off all the boxes with noticeable improvements from her previous sessions.

"How's your Aunt Brigitte doing?"

"Fine. I drove myself today."

"You did?" Devlin was unable to hide his surprise.

She nodded. "I got my licence back last Wednesday."

"That's wonderful, Maddie." He was pleased. After her release from the hospital in November, her doctor had recommended the suspension of her driver's licence while she underwent treatment. She'd shown very little progress over the course of the winter, and her aunt had assumed the driving chores so that Maddie could attend her various appointments.

Last week she hadn't said anything about trying to get her licence reinstated, and he suspected she'd been worried about being turned down. As well, judging by her expression as she watched him process the news, she'd probably held it back in the hope of being able to surprise him.

She'd succeeded.

"How do you feel about being able to get around on your own again?"

She thought for a moment. "Satisfied."

"It was a good week, then?"

"Yes. A very good week."

When she'd first started seeing him on the first Tuesday in January, she'd said very little. Almost nothing, really. It had taken a while for her to trust him enough to speak in complete sentences, and after that to express thoughts complex enough to require at least a paragraph or two.

Verbally she showed frequent hesitation despite her increased willingness to talk, as though she were having trouble finding the right word. He briefly worried about a speech disturbance of some kind until he realized, with something of a shock, that she was trying to dumb down what she was saying to him. Once he began to elevate the level of his own diction, he saw that her comprehension didn't misfire and her vocabulary expanded accordingly.

She was incredibly bright, he surmised, and like a tall youth who stoops so as not to draw attention to themselves among shorter people, she'd developed a habit of hiding her intelligence when in conversation with others.

Thinking of a word, but taking a moment to search for a simpler substitute so as not to alienate her listener.

The discovery delighted him to no end.

Today Maddie obviously had something on her mind, and he was very interested to hear what it might be.

"I've made a decision," she said.

Devlin watched her eyes shift to the window again, where a tree branch moved back and forth in the wind. When she'd finished thinking about what she was going to say next, he saw her nod microscopically to herself before returning her attention to him.

"I've made up my mind to talk to you about what happened."

"I'd love to listen."

"You're not judgmental. Like the others. That's why I come back here every week."

"I'm very glad that you do." He was aware that she'd seen several psychiatrists after her crisis last October, in the hospital in Kingston and after her release in nearby Smiths Falls, driven back and forth by the saintly Aunt Brigitte. He knew that the experiences had not helped her, other than to provide a new set of prescriptions each time that soon proved ineffectual.

Finally, when her family doctor had suggested a psychologist, her Uncle Robert hesitated. After all, he would be footing the bill for it, as Maddie's finances had been placed in escrow, and while psychiatrists could be consulted free of charge in Ontario, their services being covered by provincial health insurance, psychologists expected to be paid for their time by the client.

Devlin suspected that Aunt Brigitte had put her foot down. Not only was it she who'd brought Maddie around to his office in rural Kilmarnock every Tuesday, but she was also the one who paid for the sessions using her own credit card.

Their first three meetings had been hopeless. Nonetheless, Aunt Brigitte persistently brought her back, and Maddie doggedly sat through the hour each time, no doubt honouring her aunt's wishes while staring at her hands and saying almost nothing.

The next few appointments, however, showed incremental improvement, as though she were slowly climbing out of the deep, dark well into which she had fallen. Until now, today, on the first Tuesday in March—Maddie finally seemed willing to trust him with what was on her mind.

"You'll have to stay that way," she said. "Not judgmental. You'll have to suspend disbelief and not jump to conclusions."

"I promise you, I'll do my best."

She raised an eyebrow. "You'll have to do better than that, Dr. Devlin. Are you up to it?"

"Yes, of course."

"It's going to take time. I know you're expensive, but Aunt Brigitte said she wanted me to keep seeing you until I feel better. And anyway, I'll pay them back later."

Devlin nodded, not particularly liking the part of his job that involved receiving payment. Although he was human enough to enjoy having a healthy bank account, the expectation of remuneration, and the necessity of asking for it, always made him feel uncomfortable. Which was why he was glad his wife handled that part of the business.

"I have to do it my way," she said.

"What do you mean by that, Maddie?"

"I have to tell it my way. And you can't be jumping in and announcing that I'm psychotic or delusional or whatever."

"I see. Well, I certainly want you to tell it your way. And at your own pace."

"You've been wondering all this time what's been going on in this strange little head of mine."

He smiled.

"Well," she said, "now you're going to find out."

# MADDIE

# 2

I've never been the kind of person who thinks too highly of herself.

Oh, I suppose you could say I have a reasonable amount of self-confidence and a decent understanding of who I am and what my place in the universe might be, but I don't think anyone would ever say that I come off as egotistical or pompous or self-important.

At least I hope not.

I bring this up right away because I think it's necessary to stress that I have a solid awareness of myself, and I'm not trying to dramatize things in order to appear like a young superhero or something. Because I'm not.

Far from it.

I'll have to go back here and there to explain things that occurred in my life which caused me to end up where I am right now, but I don't want it to come off like some kind of *Bildungsroman* by Goethe or Mann or something, because that *would* be self-indulgent. Just the same, there are things you need to know, things you need to hear about, in order to understand what happened and *why* it happened.

The trigger event, as they like to call it, happened last

fall. To be specific, September 26. A Monday.

I was driving Stephen back home from his doctor's appointment in Smiths Falls. We were talking—well, he was mostly talking and I was mostly listening—about his upcoming trip to Spain, which he was pretty excited about.

Stephen didn't drive. He didn't have a licence, although I had no idea why he never went for it. His mother wasn't able to take him into town on this particular afternoon because she was getting ready for a baptism at her church, so I volunteered to give him a lift in my little eggbeater Toyota. I grabbed a few things at the grocery store and picked him up when he was done.

Stephen wasn't my boyfriend. Don't get the wrong impression. We were very good friends, former high school classmates and, of course, next-door neighbours. We got along very well and had a number of common interests.

One difference between us, though, was that he was very religious and I wasn't. At least not in the conventional sense. The trip he was going on next week was a four-month sabbatical to Spain that was being put together by a church group based in Kingston. Apparently there was an entire organization that arranged for Protestant missionaries to go over and help people who were living in poverty and in desperate need of help. The fact that they were predominately Catholic also gave the missionaries a chance to convert a few souls along the way at the same time, I suppose.

Stephen finally ran out of steam as we made the last leg of our drive from Bennett's Corners to the end of Twilight Road. I watched the sun flicker in the trees as I drove. The leaves were beginning to turn colour, and the thought that summer was over so soon made me feel a little sad.

Even sadder was the thought that I would miss having Stephen as a friend once he was gone. The plan was that he'd come back after Christmas and resume his coursework at Carleton University in January, but I had a feeling that once he left, I wouldn't see him again. Something would come up that would keep him in Barcelona for the foreseeable future, and that would be it. I couldn't say what; I just knew it would happen.

Let's please not talk about clairvoyance right now.

I slowed at the mailbox with NORTHROP spelled out on the side in metallic letters and turned into the driveway. Stephen had been a little sheepish when he admitted that his mother had been told to put her name on the mailbox herself. I'd have thought it was something the sexton should have looked after for her, but Stephen said that each new pastor was expected to peel off the name of their predecessor and put on their own.

Sort of a ritual, apparently. Installation with a Canada Post twist.

I shouldn't be so cynical.

"Come on in and we'll grab a Coke," he said, getting out of the car.

"All right."

I shut off the engine and unbuckled my belt. On the left, between his house and mine, was the decrepit hulk of the original church. Behind it was a graveyard that was still in use. For burials, I mean. I got out and stared over, as I always did.

Built in 1901, the church was a small frame structure with a tower and steeple at the front. The wooden clapboards had originally been painted white, but they'd been steadily looking worse each summer since I'd lived here. According to Reverend B, the trustees were trying to decide whether to sell it, tear it down, or wait for it to be struck by lightning and burn to the ground so they could collect the insurance and have done with it once and for all.

She was only half-kidding when she said it.

(I should explain that I always called her Reverend B instead of Reverend Northrop, which sounded too formal to both of us, or Belinda, which sounded too familiar to me. One day "Reverend B" just popped out while I was talking to her, and she smiled when I said it, so it stuck.)

Anyway, a new church had been built at Bennett's Corners nine years ago. It was smaller than the old one, but it had a finished basement, a propane furnace, and air conditioning. All the comforts of God's home away from home.

Behind the old church were neat rows of headstones, some of them going back a hundred years or more. About two-thirds of the way in, the grass had begun to grow over the surface of the grave that had been dug in June.

Reverend B had presided over the burial of Mrs. Theresa Pollock, an old woman I'd only met once. The wife of one of the church trustees, she hadn't liked French people very much. Although I was raised to speak English as my first language and French as a second language at home, and my family name was about as Loyalist as you can get, Mrs. Pollock knew my grandmother's surname was Desormeaux and her maiden name was Hamelin, and that she was a Québécoise through and through. Not to mention a Catholic, God forbid. As a result, Mrs. Pollock had apparently thought it was important to extend her dislike of the French to me.

I attended her burial as a courtesy to the family, since I was right there next door anyway, but I didn't shed a tear.

You can bet the farm on that.

Stephen led the way into the parsonage and through a doorway on the right into the kitchen. He grabbed a couple of cans of Coke from the fridge and gave me one. He knew I didn't like drinking from a glass, so he didn't offer one or take one from the cupboard for himself. We sat down on high stools at the island.

"What are you reading, Maddie?"

"*A Portrait of the Artist as a Young Man.*"

He swigged his Coke. "Joyce? What course?"

"Twentieth-century fiction. Sort of a survey course."

"What's it like?"

"Not bad. Interesting. I'm reading an annotated edition, so that helps. I know absolutely zip about Irish history, so it gives me a fighting chance with all the references to Parnell and the Catholic Church and that. Plus the literary allusions, which were Joyce's specialty."

He grinned. "I've always said you're the intellectual in the crowd, Maddie. You just love to take on all the hard stuff."

I tried to match his smile, knowing he liked using my name to allude to the novel by Thomas Hardy whenever he could work it into our conversation, but I couldn't quite do it. I was once again experiencing the horrible feeling that had lately been coming over me whenever I set foot inside the parsonage. It felt like a weight pressing down on my head, forcing all the blood out of my brain. I was having trouble breathing, and my thought processes were a little messed up.

I'd begun to make excuses not to come inside when he invited me, because of the way the place was making me feel these days. It wasn't a bad-looking house, as far as that went, although it was almost as old as the church next door. An L-shaped brick structure, it had a living room and dining room, a large kitchen, four bedrooms on the second floor, and an extensive third-floor attic filled with stuff left behind by previous pastors. It was like many of the old farmhouses built in the early 1900s that you could see while driving around the back roads in this area. The story I heard was that the trustees thought a nice parsonage would not only attract a good pastor but keep them there for a long time.

In Reverend B's case, it had been five years since she and Stephen had moved in, a year after my brother Quinn and I had come to live at the far end of Twilight Road with our grandmother. So far, I hadn't heard her express an opinion about the parsonage one way or the other. If she found it as creepy and oppressive as I did, she hadn't said.

Stephen got up and went to the cupboard. "I'm going to have some oatmeal. Want anything?"

"No thanks."

He filled a bowl with water and took a packet of instant oatmeal from the box. He preferred to nuke the water first, then add the oatmeal, then nuke it again to finish it up. As he was about to put the bowl of water into the microwave, his cellphone rang. Without thinking, he put the bowl down in front of me and answered the call.

"Hello? Yes, this is he. I'm well, thanks."

It happened so quickly and so unexpectedly that I was caught completely off guard. The water in the bowl rippled and caught the light from the window above the sink.

I couldn't help it. The glittering drew my eyes. It was an involuntary thing, and I couldn't stop myself from looking.

Before I could turn away, I saw a woman's face in the

water. Her mouth opened and her eyes pleaded with me.

*Help me, please! Help! Oh God, please help!*

I screamed and pushed at the bowl. It flew off the island onto the floor, shattering and spilling water everywhere.

"Maddie!" Stephen whirled around. "What's wrong? Are you all right?"

I was already off my stool and halfway out of the kitchen.

"Maddie! Where are you going?"

I ran out of the house, jumped in the car, started the engine, backed out onto the road, shifted gears, and raced past the church to the safety of home.

# 3

That evening I was putting the supper dishes into the dishwasher when Quinn looked up from his cellphone.

"Do you believe there's such a thing as the third eye?"

I closed the dishwasher door and punched the buttons. "Do you have homework tonight?"

"Yes. Well, no. I did it when I got home." He pushed away from the kitchen table but didn't get up. "This post says that it's a reference to the pineal gland, whatever that is, and that the third eye in humans shrank down over the millennia until it was just that. The gland thing."

"I don't know, Quinn. Shit." I found a drinking glass he'd shoved up against the backsplash on the counter, between the paper towel dispenser and the can opener. It still had juice in it. Turning my head away, I tipped it out into the sink.

"Jeez, I'm sorry, Maddie. I forgot."

"Well, don't forget next time, all right?"

"I won't. Did Maman ever talk about the third eye?"

"No."

"It's supposed to be, like, right here." He pointed at the middle of his forehead. "It says that people with highly developed abilities, like clairvoyance, use their third eye to see beyond the normal plane. To see stuff, I guess, like you and Maman. And Mémère."

"I don't know anything about it, Quinn." I turned the glass upside down and left it on the counter. It would have to wait until the next dishwasher load. Unless Quinn wanted to wash it himself.

Like that would ever happen.

"Are you okay, Maddie?"

"Yeah."

He put down his phone. "You seem upset."

Quinn was twelve years old, but sometimes he acted like he was thirty. He looked a lot like our father, Mark Hubbard, with his wavy hair, chubby cheeks, and pale grey eyes. I, on the other hand, looked like our mother. And my grandmother. And my great-grandmother. And thereby hangs a tale, no doubt.

Along with his looks, Quinn had inherited a certain amount of our dad's calm pragmatism, which Mark had used to great advantage during his career as a criminal defence lawyer. In Quinn though, I have to admit, it could get a little annoying sometimes.

Because he was eight years younger than I, he still referred to our mother as Maman, while I'd called her Joelle from the time I was ten. The same way that our grandmother had always been Mémère to him, while I called her Marie-Claire. Different relationships; different terms of reference.

"I'm not upset," I fibbed.

He picked up his phone and resumed reading. "Is there a problem with Steve?"

"No." I snapped the lid on a plastic container into which I'd scraped the leftovers from supper—fish and chips—and put it into the fridge.

Quinn had his own challenges, given his unique situation as a male child in a predominantly female family, but he always seemed able to work through them. He'd learned to control his fear by the time he was eight or so, not long after Joelle was murdered, and he was always willing to talk to me about *my* fear.

The problem was, I wasn't.

I didn't want to have anything to do with any of it after Joelle died. Not after what I'd seen when I tried to contact her.

I was out. Finished. Done.

At least that's what I told myself. Over and over again.

Careful habits and the avoidance of open water, either in containers or in rivers, lakes, pools, gutters, or mud puddles, had kept me safe. Along with a strict adherence to the mental routines I'd taught myself to keep my mind focused and attentive and out of trouble.

Until today.

I'd been inexcusably careless.

I opened my mouth to tell Quinn about it, hoping he might have something to say that would make me feel better, but he was already absorbed in whatever he was reading on his phone.

I closed my mouth again and went upstairs to do some reading of my own.

# 4

The following afternoon, I was sitting at the kitchen table, organizing my notes from the online class I'd just finished. It was a second-year Canadian history course, and the lecture had focused on the construction of the Rideau Canal and its economic and military objectives. The professor, Dr. Hoffman, had a way of making things interesting that were normally as boring as day-old toast, so I'd enjoyed the class.

This was the off week for the seminar portion of the course, and my Thursday schedule would include two hours of research on my term project, which was the decline and fall of the seigniorial system in Quebec. There were a couple of books I had to read, one I'd ordered online and the other I'd borrowed from the Smiths Falls library, and I was looking forward to getting into them. I'd declared English lit as my major, but I was seriously thinking about Canadian history as a minor.

During the pandemic, Queen's University had ramped up their distance learning program and I'd taken advantage of it to enrol as a first-year student doing my coursework online. It was ideal for me because I could continue my education from here without uprooting Quinn at a time when he was nicely settled in at school in town and content with our current life.

I was just about to shut down my laptop when there was a knock at the door.

I may not have made it clear that Quinn and I lived out in the middle of nowhere. Twilight Road was a narrow stretch of gravel that ran from Bennett's Corners, a crossroads hamlet northwest of Smiths Falls, into the wilderness. There were a few farms along the road, but nothing else until you reached the parsonage, the old church, and my grandmother's house. After that there was a little cul-de-sac turnaround, and after that about six hundred acres of bush.

Buttcrack, Ontario.

Plus, I was it for an adult presence in the house. Joelle was murdered when I was twelve, and Mark had died in a car crash in Ottawa six years ago, after which we'd moved in with Marie-Claire out here in Nowheresville. She was our guardian until last year, when she'd died after suffering a massive stroke. Uncle Robert and Aunt Brigitte were our only living relatives, at least that I knew of, but I'd already turned nineteen and insisted that I could look after Quinn and myself just fine, thank you.

Uncle Robert had inherited the house, being Marie-Claire's only surviving offspring, and at first there'd been talk of him selling it and pocketing the proceeds. Apparently after hearing from a real estate agent that the place wasn't worth much, though, he'd hesitated long enough for me to appeal to Aunt Brigitte to let us stay here. When I promised to pay a modest amount of rent out of my student loan, sufficient at least to cover the property taxes, he relented. So here we were, all alone in Marie-Claire's house on Twilight Road.

All of which to say that whoever was knocking on the door was either Stephen, Reverend B, Aunt Brigitte, or someone who was really, really lost.

I went to the door, peeked through the curtain, and opened it up.

"Hi, Reverend B."

She held up a casserole dish and smiled. "I have to run down to the church for an hour or two, but I wanted to drop this off first."

I swung the door back. "Come in. That's so sweet of you."

"My pleasure." She stepped into the hallway.

I took the casserole from her. The dish was still a little warm. "Can you stay for a few minutes?"

She followed me into the kitchen. "No. I wish I could, but the trustees are meeting about the old church. Again. I wish they'd make up their minds, but that would be too much to hope for." She leaned her hip against the door frame. "Anyway, I have to be there."

I peeled back the tinfoil and sniffed. "Mmm. Tuna."

She smiled. "My culinary skills are not what they could be, I admit, but when I put it in front of Stephen it manages to disappear pretty quickly just the same."

I laughed. "I'll bet." I opened the fridge door and put it in.

Reverend B was somewhere in her late forties. She was short and slim, soft-spoken and very kind, intelligent and well read. She wore her hair in a careless pageboy cut, and in the five years since she'd moved into the parsonage, I'd watched it grow steadily greyer until it was pretty much half brown and half silver streaks, with the grey about to move into the lead on a permanent basis.

One of the things I liked about her was that she wasn't

evangelistic in the least. We'd talked about religion once, in the early going. She'd heard that my grandmother was Catholic and wondered if I was, too. I said that I wasn't. In response to her follow-up questions, I explained that I could probably be best described as a deist, someone who believed there was a God somewhere but He or She was either very distracted these days or just didn't give a flying crap.

"Okay. Well, any time you want to talk about it, you know where to find me, Maddie."

And that had been it.

Instead, we talked about other things. One of her favourite subjects was literature, coincidentally. She'd done a bachelor's degree in English at Wilfrid Laurier University, formerly known as Waterloo Lutheran University, before getting her Master's and Doctorate of Divinity at McMaster, and she liked to talk about poetry when we visited. That was her thing. I was all about fiction, nuts about twentieth-century novels in particular, but Reverend B was a lover of poetry.

Which is why I wasn't surprised now when she took a slim volume out of the pocket of her sweater coat and handed it to me. It was an old Penguin edition of the poems and prose of Gerard Manley Hopkins.

"You can keep it," she said. "I have another copy."

"Thank you." I was touched.

"Stephen said you were talking to him about the reading list for one of your courses, and he mentioned to me that Hopkins was on it because he knows how much I love his poetry."

I laughed. "Yeah, it's coming up in the spring term."

"'Margaret are you grieving/Over Goldengrove unleaving?'"

"We took that in Grade Twelve," I said, recognizing the first lines of the Hopkins poem "Spring and Fall." Then I felt foolish, because of course Stephen had taken it with me, and she would have known that. So to cover my embarrassment, I finished the poem for her: "'It is the blight man was born for,/It is Margaret you mourn for.'"

She nodded, smiling that sad little smile of hers. "I know he was an Anglo-Catholic, and I'm not trying to influence your thinking in any way of course, but I just spotted it on the shelf this morning and got a little enthusiastic, seeing that I have a kindred spirit next door. A lover of literature."

"Thanks, Reverend B. I really appreciate it." Since Stephen had his sights set on becoming an architect and had very little time for the literary arts, she was probably grateful to have someone else around who shared her interests.

She slapped her hip. "I have to get going. While I'm driving down to the Corners, I have to make up my mind which side I'm going to take on the old church. Frankly, I think it's a safety hazard and should be torn down, and I'm not as sentimental about local history and what not as some other people are. I think the main debate will be whether or not they have the money in their budget this year to at least make it safe enough to go inside and fix up."

She went out into the hallway and opened the front door. "If I were a betting woman, my cash would be on 'Do nothing until next year.' But that's so obvious it's not really a serious bet, is it?"

"I hope it goes well."

She paused on the verandah. "Stephen said there was something yesterday that upset you. Over at our place."

"It was nothing. Really."

She sighed. "The place sometimes bothers me a bit, too. It's so old, it makes a lot of noise at night when the wind blows. 'Old bones, that creak and groan.' Anyway, I hope it's nothing that will keep you from coming over to visit. Once Stephen's gone, I'm going to be a little lonely over there by myself."

"Don't worry. We'll see a lot of each other."

"I hope so. Give my love to Quinn."

"I will."

As I watched her get into her car and drive away, I wondered whether she was just being polite, or if she actually did feel that something was off about the parsonage. Could she be sensing the same sort of bad vibrations I'd been getting from the place for the past several months?

I closed the door and went back into the kitchen to shut down my laptop.

# 5

That evening, Stephen called to ask if I'd come over to watch a video with him.

For some reason, instead of calling me on my cellphone, he dialled Marie-Claire's landline, which Aunt Brigitte insisted on paying for, even though it was almost never used. I was walking by the phone on the kitchen wall when it rang, and it scared the absolute crap out of me.

I didn't want to go, for the reasons I've already explained, but he was insistent in that polite, irresistible way of his. It was some kind of promotional thing about his upcoming sabbatical, and he wanted me to see it.

It started off with a profile of Spain that must have been borrowed from a travel agency's TV commercial. Stuff about the scenic mountains and Mediterranean coastline and that sort of thing, calculated to appeal to the restless tourist in all of us. Then it got down to business, switching to shots of poor people sitting in doorways and little kids in dirty clothes playing with dogs in the street. Poverty is as real in the cities and towns of Spain as it is in any other country of need, the narrator explained in his calm, sad baritone. A situation complicated by the large influx of poor immigrants who have resettled in the country over the last decade.

What about the Catholic Church? you might ask. Weren't they doing everything they could to help? Barely suppressing a sigh, the narrator explained that while more than two thirds of the population of over 50 million people are Roman Catholic, only one quarter of Spaniards overall declare any religious affiliation whatsoever.

I could almost read his mind right through the screen: *Goose, what we have here is a target-rich environment.*

The rest of the video described the outreach work being done in the living rooms of everyday Spaniards to bring the gospel into their homes and to share the love of Christ in meaningful, personal ways. By the time it was finished, they'd used pretty much every cliché in the book, and then some.

I sat through it with a fake smile on my face, and when it was done I told him it looked like a really wonderful opportunity, knowing that was what he wanted me to say.

I glanced at Reverend B to see how she was reacting to it, but her mind seemed elsewhere. Stephen, on the other hand, had been totally absorbed from beginning to end. It was as though he'd been trying to memorize landmarks in the background so that when he was handing out loaves of bread and bathing blistered feet, he'd know he was in the right place.

Again, I shouldn't be so cynical.

When it was over, he brought out a movie and asked me if I'd stay to watch it with him. I hesitated. Quinn was on his own, but I'd left him playing a video game in his room, and I knew he was perfectly capable of staying out of trouble. If anything came up, he'd call.

The movie was a recent Tom Hanks film, and since I'd never seen it—and who didn't love Tom Hanks, anyway?—I said I'd stick around. Surely to goodness if anyone could ease the constant sense of dread I got from the parsonage, it was Tom Hanks.

I excused myself to visit the washroom while Stephen was loading the disc into the DVD player. God bless Reverend B, she was strictly old school when it came to electronics. Quinn and I usually streamed stuff on our phones or the laptop. I guess it was part of her charm to prefer outdated hardware.

The washroom was upstairs, at the end of the hall. A small water closet had been added downstairs just off the kitchen during the residence of the previous parson, but the toilet down there didn't flush very well and Reverend B had asked me not to use it until it was fixed. Upstairs was a full-sized bathroom with a tub and shower; a large commode with a sink and modern faucets; and a cupboard. It was actually pretty nice. Reverend B had fixed it up with crocks, stacks of towels, and a little captain's chair in the corner.

I feel silly and rather embarrassed to mention this, but over the years I'd developed a simple routine with toilets. When I was finished, I would flush, stand up, rearrange my clothing, and then reach behind me to lower the lid on the toilet seat. It sounds awkward and stupid, but it was my way of making sure I didn't look at the water inside the toilet bowl at any time. As I say, it was something I'd done for years.

The reason for it will become obvious in a moment. Unfortunately.

As I sat there, I realized I was starting to get a serious migraine. I got them from time to time, either at the beginning of my period or when there was a rapid change in the weather, and I had medication I took for the pain.

Unfortunately, I didn't have it with me; it was in the kitchen cupboard next to the refrigerator at home.

I was thinking I would just beg off on the movie for tonight and head back. The migraine seemed to be worsening by the second, accompanied by a sense of dread that was almost suffocating. I was really starting to feel very crappy.

I finished up and flushed the toilet. I got to my feet and pulled up my underwear and jeans. I was just about to reach behind me to drop the toilet lid when pain lanced through my head like a hot knife. I think I must have screamed. I remember it was incredibly painful.

As I struggled to stay on my feet, I heard feet coming up the stairs, and a pounding on the door.

"Maddie!" It was Reverend B. "Is everything all right?"

"Yeah!" I managed. The pain had diminished slightly to the level of a burning, boiling sizzle.

I turned around and groped for my little handbag on the rack above the toilet.

The toilet lid was still up.

I looked down.

The woman's face stared up at me.

Middle-aged. Reddish brown hair, matted and filthy. White, white skin streaked with dirt. Obscenely red lips. Pale blue eyes.

I shrieked again, this time from fear.

"Maddie!" Reverend B shouted, on the other side of the door.

"What do you want from me?" I screamed.

*Please! I know you can see me. Cold! So lonely!*

Behind me, the door flew open.

"Maddie!" Reverend B rushed into the room.

"I need to leave!" I yelled. "I need to get out of here!"

She grabbed me in a bear hug. "Maddie, what is it? What's wrong?"

I twisted around in her arms and looked down into the toilet.

The face was gone.

I leaned against Reverend B and started to cry.

# 6

That evening Quinn and I went outside to sit in the backyard before bedtime.

Marie-Claire had built a little patio behind the house with a burn pit and a grill for cooking food, and there were Adirondack chairs and other outdoor furniture back there as well. It was a nice, comfortable spot.

In the summer, the bugs tended to get very bad. Persistent visitors included mosquitoes, black flies, and my least favourite, deer flies, so Quinn and I didn't go out there much.

Thankfully, though, they'd all gone off to wherever annoying insects go in late September, sparing us their torment until next spring, and we could now sit outside without being driven crazy by them.

It was a mild evening, and the stars were out. I wore a zippered sweater, and Quinn had thrown on a hoodie. We sat in the darkness, staring up at the night sky.

My mind wandered back to when Quinn and I had first come here, six years ago. Mark had just died in the car accident that had also killed two other people, leaving us orphaned. We were living in Ottawa at the time, in the big house in Barrhaven, and needless to say, we were both in shock when we were told what had happened to our dad.

Marie-Claire immediately stepped in to take control of everything. Mark had had the foresight to name her the executor of his will, his own family being scattered to the four winds and not easily tracked down, and she met right away with Mark's lawyer, a fellow partner of his in the firm, to iron out all the details.

He'd left the bulk of his estate to me and Quinn, divided equally. The assets, including the house, cars, summer cottage in the Gatineaus, his equity in the law firm, and an extensive investment portfolio, were all liquidated. The proceeds were placed in trust funds for us, not to be accessed until we turned twenty-one. Marie-Claire was given power of attorney for the funds, and she was appointed as our legal guardian.

I was fourteen at the time, and Quinn was six.

Her house in the country was not much to look at, certainly a long step down from the mansion in Barrhaven. It had three small bedrooms upstairs and an unfinished basement, no garage, no air conditioning, a crappy oil furnace that had to be serviced each fall or it wouldn't work, and a small hot water tank that often ran out right in the middle of my morning shower.

But boy, were we glad to be there.

Of course, we'd come down to Twilight Road a few times with Mark to visit Marie-Claire, so we knew the place. She always made us feel right at home, but the entire concept of leaving the city for good to be transplanted into the middle of nowhere, and the idea of leaving behind our friends and switching to small-town schools, shocked our sensibilities, to say the least.

Marie-Claire understood this very well, though, and I don't know how we would have survived without her patience and kindness. And her understanding of what made Quinn and me unique.

One afternoon shortly after we moved in, at about this time of year, she and I were sitting back here together. I'd just gotten off the school bus, and Quinn wasn't home yet. Coals were glowing in the burn pit, and a cast iron pot sat on the grill. Nearby, a tray of stuffed potatoes wrapped in foil waited to be dropped into the coals for slow roasting.

"How was school?"

"Not the worst." We spoke in French, as was her preference when it was just the two of us. Quinn's French, it should be noted, was only so-so.

I looked at the pit. "Smells good."

"Lamb stew. I know how much you like it."

When it came to food she was very old school, following methods and recipes passed down from her mother and grandmother in the traditions of rural Quebec and French Ontario.

"We don't need to talk about this," she said after a long silence, "but let me just say one thing and we'll leave it at that. Don't try to reach out to Joelle any more. Do you understand?"

I didn't say anything. What was there to say? I was still reeling from my last attempt.

"She must deal with what has happened to her in her own way. You cannot help her."

"I understand." I looked at her. "I've given it up. Completely. For good."

She nodded. "I think it's for the best."

We never spoke about it again.

Now, sitting here with Quinn, I stared at the cold burn pit with its long-dead ashes, an indistinct shape in the gathering darkness. Oh, how I missed her. We'd been close, almost as close as I'd been with Joelle, and I felt her loss almost every day.

I knew Quinn had something on his mind because he'd kept his cellphone in his pocket instead of dragging it out to do on it whatever it was he did for hours at a time. I waited for him to get around to what he wanted to talk about.

"It's so quiet," he finally said.

"Mmm. Last night I heard the coyotes. It's probably time for them to be on the move."

"They're hunting," he said.

"I guess so."

He went quiet for a moment, and then shifted in his chair. "I read something interesting about coyotes and ravens."

"Oh?"

Quinn was a big fan of ravens and crows. There was a whole community of them in the woods around our place. They flew back and forth over the house, cawing and croaking, and during nesting season you'd see them being chased around by smaller birds trying to protect their eggs and young. Ravens in particular, the larger of the *corvus* clan, were carnivorous raiders and not popular among the other sky dwellers, but Quinn loved watching them.

He'd read once that they were so intelligent they could distinguish one human from another and could carry a grudge for years if you happened to throw a rock at them or otherwise treated them badly. Quinn, being Quinn, tried to talk to them. When he was outside and one flew over the house, he would call up to it, "Hey, crow! Hey, crow!"

Hopefully ravens didn't hold a grudge if someone called them a crow. Quinn swore it was the same bird each time, but I had no idea whether it was or he was just hoping it was. They might be able to tell us apart, but to me one crow looked like every other crow. Or raven. Or whatever.

I wasn't sure what that might have said about my level of intelligence compared to theirs, but anyway.

"There's a lot of co-operation between them when they hunt," Quinn said.

"Between coyotes and ravens?"

"Yeah. When ravens find a dead animal first, they make a lot of noise to get the coyotes to come around. They do this so the coyotes will start pulling the carcass apart, which lets the ravens get at the insides more easily."

"Maybe it's the coyotes who are smart, listening for dumb ravens to tell them where to find supper."

He shook his head. "Ravens even play with coyotes. They fly over them with sticks to get the cubs to jump for them, and they play tug of war. They even pull on their tails with their beaks to tease them. They make friends with them."

I waited, knowing that this wasn't what Quinn really wanted to talk about.

"I'm not sure if I told you before about Benedicta," he finally said.

"Who's that?"

"I meet her sometimes when I travel."

"Oh?" I looked over at him. His head was tilted back, and he was staring up at the black sky.

"I think she's an angel, but I'm not sure. She's mostly just light, kind of a glowing, pale blue light, but I can see her face and hair. It's long and wavy and brown."

"Where do you meet her, Quinn?"

"Just around. On one of the astral planes. I don't always go there, I mean to that particular place, but when I do it's usually her I see."

I should explain that Quinn is a night traveller. When he falls asleep, his spirit often leaves his body and moves around on another plane of existence in what's known as astral projection. The idea is that there are a number of spheres between Earth and Heaven that are populated by angels, demons, and other assorted spirits, and a few rare individuals like Quinn have the ability to separate their astral body from their physical body and travel to these otherworldly places.

I know, I know. I sound like a complete wackadoodle. As though my brother were some kind of junior Doctor Strange or something. But astral projection was a part of metaphysical philosophy in ancient Egypt, in Chinese Taoism, in Indian Hinduism, and even in Inuit culture, and Quinn had experienced it since he was small.

A few times he bumped into entities on the astral plane that were less than benevolent, shall we say, but he learned to avoid those places. His night travels were mostly positive experiences, according to what he told me about them afterward.

This was the first time he'd mentioned this particular spirit.

"Does she talk to you?"

"Sometimes. At first she just stared. You know, checking me out. Hanging around a bit until I moved off. Then after a while she started asking me questions."

"Oh?"

"About myself. But it seems almost random. It never goes anywhere. I don't stay around very long."

"At least she sounds nice."

"Last night she asked me questions about you."

"Oh?" I was surprised. "What kind of questions?"

"I don't know. General stuff. Like she was trying to

figure you out."

"Did it upset you?"

He took a moment to think about it. "A little. Oh, she's an okay spirit. She wouldn't do anything bad. That's why I'm pretty sure she's an angel. But she's, I don't know. Got something on her mind."

We didn't say anything for a while. Quinn was exceptionally bright for a twelve-year-old, and I didn't have to tell him what to do or how to handle himself when he was travelling. He knew that he'd either find out what she wanted from him or he wouldn't. She might just drift away and never reappear, her inscrutable curiosity satisfied. Or she might come right out and explain what their meetings were all about. Only time would tell.

"Are you scrying again, Maddie?"

Again he surprised me. "Why do you ask?"

"I can tell something's bothering you. Are you looking for Maman again?"

"No. God, no."

He was silent for a while. Then he stirred. "I think Benedicta knows something about her. Knows where she is, maybe. That's why I thought she asked me about you last night. Because you'd started looking for her again."

"I haven't." This time I was the one who hesitated. I wanted to talk to him about what was happening to me, but I wasn't exactly sure what was going on, what I was being pulled into, and I didn't want to upset him. I'm just as protective of him as he is of me, more so I guess because I'm the big sister and he's the little brother, but he understands what I do, my special ability, and he's a good listener. After going back and forth on it, I finally relented.

"I'm seeing faces again. People. Women. Well, the same

woman, I think."

"On purpose?"

"Good lord, no. But it's happened twice now, over at the parsonage. Stephen and Reverend B must think I'm batshit crazy."

He snorted softly. "Well, you are. Face it. But then, so am I."

"Once in a bowl of water, and today in the toilet. I got careless."

"That's why you were pissed at me last night for leaving that glass of juice on the counter."

"Yeah. Sorry about that."

"Who's this woman? Wait, what does she look like?"

"Middle-aged, maybe late forties. Reddish brown hair, almost curly, matted and filthy. Pale white skin streaked with dirt. Red lips, like someone put too much lipstick on her. Her eyes were blue. Pale blue, like a husky dog."

"Doesn't sound like Benedicta."

"No, it wouldn't be her. It's someone connected somehow to the parsonage."

Silence.

"There's something wrong over there," I finally said.

Quinn grunted. "It looks okay to me."

"You never go inside."

"True. Even if I did, I couldn't tell. That's your thing."

Silence.

"I miss Mémère," he said.

"Me too."

"And Maman. She'd know if something was going on."

"Yeah."

"Too bad you couldn't ask her."

"No. I'm not doing that again. Ever. I'll go insane if I try."

"All right. I'm sorry."

Silence.

"Something's really bothering you, Maddie."

"I know."

He leaned forward. "I think it started when they buried that old woman. That's what I think."

I thought about it. He was talking about when they buried Mrs. Pollock in the cemetery next door, back in June. "You may be right. But it's not her I'm seeing. Thank God."

"Just the same." He sat back again. "That's the first time they buried anyone over there since we've been here. Maybe it disturbed something."

"I don't know," I said. "Could be."

Silence.

# 7

I remember very clearly when we figured out what was going on with Quinn.

He was about four years old when it started, and it caught Joelle off guard, because males in our family—by which I mean my mother's family, because that's the one that counts for the purposes of this story—normally didn't possess any sort of special ability. None of them ever displayed the slightest inclination toward unusual behaviour along psychic or paranormal lines.

Until Quinn came along.

I was about twelve, just beginning to endure my own mental chaos and the physical joys that went along with the onset of puberty, so I didn't pay a lot of attention at first when Quinn started babbling about the strange people he saw and the strange places he visited in his dreams at night. It was typical little brother stuff, I figured. Annoying and dumb.

Mark and Joelle humoured him, pretending to show an interest in his stories of flying through the air and chatting with weird people and bizarre, friendly animals and all the rest of it. But after a year or so of this, his fantastic tales began to settle into patterns that alarmed Mark enough that he took him to the doctor, who referred him to the children's hospital for a brain scan and a bunch of psychological tests.

Quinn was an exceptionally bright kid, as I've already mentioned, and he quickly figured out it was probably a good idea to shut up about the ladies in golden robes and the beasts with cat heads and snake bodies that got him to answer clever riddles and recited poetry to him and so on. Everyone was reacting a little too weirdly to it, and some internal survival mechanism in him soon kicked in—zip the lips and just stay cool.

Mark was puzzled when the only thing the children's hospital came up with was a prescription for glasses to address the myopia they'd diagnosed while testing his eyesight. No tumours or cysts, no chemical imbalances, no anomalies whatsoever. Just an apparently normal four-year-old kid. And once Quinn stopped talking about it, Mark kind of went to sleep on the whole thing for a while. His life was busy enough as it was, and since the doctors all assured him there was no crisis, just odd, kiddish behaviour, he kissed Quinn on the top of the head and went back to his other, more pressing, priorities.

Joelle, however, had done some serious thinking and thought she knew what might be going on. She brought up an occasional chair from the basement and left it in Quinn's room, telling him he could put his clothes on it when he changed into his pyjamas at night. After he fell asleep, she crept in and sat in the chair for hours, watching him.

You must remember, of course, that Joelle wasn't a regular, everyday housewife and mom. I guess I'll have to talk about that a lot more as we progress with this autobiographical confession or whatever you'd like to call it, but for now let's just say she was watching for things a typical mom couldn't see.

Ever.

One night she came downstairs late and found me watching TV in the living room with all the lights out. I was struggling with menstrual cramps, one of the latest novelties I'd begun to experience, but by the time she came in I'd finished crying and was more or less calmed down.

"What are you doing up?"

"You know." I kept my eyes on the TV, although I didn't have a clue what I was watching.

"Did you take ibuprofen?"

I nodded. "A few minutes ago."

"It should help."

"Yeah. Were you sitting with Quinn again?"

She dropped into her recliner and pushed back so that her feet went up. "He's travelling, Maddie."

I frowned, not understanding.

"I thought that's what it must be, but how could it be possible? Boys in our family are always normal."

I snorted.

"You know what I mean, silly. They can't do the things you or I can do."

I'd recently begun seeing the faces of strange people and hearing their voices in my head, plus I knew, vaguely, about the sorts of things she did, so I nodded.

"It's called astral projection. His spirit leaves his physical body and travels to other planes of existence."

"Yeah, right. And you know this, how?"

"I saw him leave, dear. A faint golden glow around his body that lifted up above the bed, and a very slender, very pale, silver cord that kept him tethered. The glow rose up through the ceiling and was gone. I knew right away what was going on, because it's a concept I'm familiar with, even though I've never actually seen it with my own two eyes before."

"You were in his room for a long time."

"I waited. Eventually the glow came back and re-entered his body. His breathing quickened for a moment, then smoothed out. He was home again, and just asleep." She sighed. "Only asleep."

She explained to me what she knew about astral projection, which included some of the things I've mentioned, and then she got up and said she was going to bed. I could see the relief in her eyes as she bent down and kissed me goodnight. Both cheeks, and the top of my head, as was her way. A French thing, I guess.

Quinn's strange behaviour had become something she understood. Something she could help him with, something they might be able to learn how to control so that he could do it safely and she could stop worrying about it so much.

She was that kind of a mother.

And I'm going to leave it there for now, because I miss her terribly. She never got a chance to help me and Quinn the way she wanted to, and I'm not going to be able to keep myself from crying if I go any further right now.

# DEVLIN

# 8

On the second Tuesday in March, Dr. Dennis Devlin's nine o'clock session was cancelled, so it gave him a little time before his appointment with Maddie Hubbard to do some extra reading.

After skimming through his notes from last week to refresh his memory, he went to his bookshelf and pulled out a book by Robert Monroe on astral projection. Sitting down behind his desk, he opened it to the yellow sticky note where he'd marked his place the night before. Monroe had popularized the term "out-of-body experiences" when discussing travels to other planes of existence, and Devlin had to admit he was rather fascinated by the whole concept, in a Charles Fort/science fiction/vivid imagination kind of way.

He was looking for parallels between what Maddie had told him last week about her brother's "ability" and what could be found in the literature on the subject. Quinn sounded quite precocious, and it was possible he'd read an article or two about astral projection and decided it was the thing for him. Something to lift him up above the common herd, to make him appear special and different from other twelve-year-olds. It was impossible to say for sure right now, of course, since Devlin was only getting second-hand reports from Maddie.

Which was not only pertinent, since Maddie was his client and not Quinn, but also more interesting. She'd been quite matter-of-fact when telling him about her brother and his alleged "night travels," just as she'd been completely forthcoming when relating her own alleged experiences of having seen a woman's face in water on two different occasions.

It was possible they were merely illusions, tricks of reflected light that, in her agitated state, she'd mistakenly misinterpreted. It was more likely, though, that they were hallucinations, false sensory impressions that she believed to be actual, particularly where she also reported auditory hallucinations at the same time.

It presented him with a logical progression he was reluctant to follow. Last week she'd shown major improvement in her mental status, right across the board, and he'd originally been prepared to work with her on a plan for complete recovery. However, as she'd begun to tell him her story, the background behind the crisis that had sent her to the hospital in a severely withdrawn state, as well as her beliefs about her brother's vivid dreams, he'd reminded himself not to jump to conclusions before all the information was available.

During the week, as he thought through what she'd confided to him, he'd left open the possibility that Maddie suffered from psychotic delusion. A final diagnosis would have to be delayed until she'd disclosed everything she was prepared to tell him, of course, but Devlin couldn't see at this point how any other conclusion would be possible.

As far as her brother went, astral projection and other out-of-body experiences were hallucinations, most likely connected to problems in the temporal lobe. He remembered an article he'd read several years ago in which instability in this part of the brain was seen to have led to an increased number of perceptual anomalies reported by subjects of the study. Out-of-body experiences were apparently connected to body-distortion problems often seen in epileptics and schizotypes. Oddly, though, they also seemed to occur in psychologically normal individuals.

Maddie's calm acceptance of her brother's hallucinations as factual was what concerned Devlin because it reinforced her belief that her own hallucinations were also real experiences. The whole business of psychic abilities and so on bothered him because he wanted to see her make a full recovery, and this stuff was standing in her way.

At five minutes before ten, he closed the book and went out into his consultation room. The weather was messy this morning. Rain pelted against the window, and the bare branches of the wild apple tree outside the window moved intermittently back and forth.

He thought about lowering the blind, but preferred to leave it open for whatever natural light was available. It also gave clients something to look at when they didn't want to make eye contact with him. While eye contact was very important, Devlin understood that too much of it could make people feel intimidated or overly pressured. They needed an alternative, a safety valve, so to speak, when they wanted to reflect on what was being discussed, or simply retreat into their own thoughts for a moment or two.

He heard sounds in the outer room that told him Maddie had arrived. There was a side entrance clients used when arriving for their appointments, a beautiful old walnut door at the end of a stone path leading from the parking area, and he could hear his wife closing it and hanging up Maddie's raincoat.

He stood in front of the fireplace, which was never used but looked very charming, and he smiled as she entered the room.

"Good morning, Maddie." He gestured to her regular chair. "A wet day today, isn't it?"

"Yes." She sat down and crossed her legs. She was wearing a grey pleated skirt that reached the middle of her shins, a cinnamon-coloured blouse, and dark brown shoes. It was a very fashionable look, and he was quite pleased. It indicated that the gains she'd shown last week were likely continuing this week.

He sat down. "How are you feeling today?"

Her mouth took on that amused look he'd seen for the first time in their previous session.

"Good. I had a decent week."

"I'm very glad to hear it."

"How about you, Dr. Devlin? How was your week?"

"Busy."

"Lots of reading?"

"Some." He knew what she was driving at. Once again, he was impressed by her marked improvement. Everything in the silent mental status exam he was running through was once again getting green check marks, except of course for item number six—"perceptual disturbances, including hallucinations and/or illusions"—in which he anticipated continuing problems. Unless there was a change for the better today.

She was guessing—accurately, of course—that his reading had centred on the psychic phenomena she'd talked about last week and whatever he could get his hands on that connected such patient reports to psychotic states.

"Any tentative conclusions?" She turned sideways and looked at him from the corner of her eye, as though baiting him to come right out with it.

"Your tests came back fine, as I expected they would," he temporized. Every week he ordered a full panel of blood and urine tests for her, to screen for the presence of drugs, including the ones currently prescribed to her. Each week they told him that she was taking what she was supposed to take and not consuming anything illegal or ill-advised, including cannabis.

"So they're not drug-induced hallucinations, then?"

"Likely not. Only one of your meds lists them as a possible side effect, and I made a few calls. I think we can probably rule out pharmaceutical causes."

"So then, do you think I'm a psycho?"

Devlin winced. "Let's not use terms like that, Maddie. We need to talk a lot more about this before we can decide what exactly happened and what it means. Are you still willing to work through everything with me?"

"That's why I'm here. Are you still sure you're up for it?"

"Yes, of course."

"I have a couple of ideas." She clasped her hands in her lap.

"I'm all ears."

"I think . . . one thing I guess I'm going to have to talk about is Reverend B. Once you see how she handled what happened, a sane and well-balanced woman of faith like her, it might give you something to think about."

Devlin nodded. Once again, of course, anything she reported about the actions and responses of Reverend Northrop would be filtered through the subjective recollections and impressions of Maddie herself, and therefore must be taken with a grain of salt. But he did think it sounded like a good idea for Maddie to verbalize what she was feeling about her relationship with the older woman.

"First though, before that, I think it's a lot more important to explain about my family. The women in my family. Who *they* were. What *their* lives were like."

"Of course, but I'm not sure—"

"It's *important*. Before you judge me. For some of it, there's documentary evidence you can Google, if you think I'm totally delusional. Believe it or not, 'There are more things in Heaven and Earth than are dreamt of in your philosophy,' Dr. Devlin."

"Of course, Maddie. By all means."

Family of origin issues, as they were referred to in his profession, were always an important area to discuss, even if only to obtain an overview of a person's upbringing and possible unresolved family problems that needed to be addressed. Devlin had only been going to say that he wasn't sure it was necessary to spend a great deal of time on it right now, but the fact that she'd interrupted him in mid-sentence—which in his experience so far was quite unlike her—and her insistence on talking about it now, convinced him to shut his mouth and let her take the lead.

"It's going to take some time" she said. "I know you're anxious for me to talk about what happened, the thing that put me in the hospital, and God knows I'll get there. Eventually. But like I said last week, you have to let me do this my way. *My* way, Dr. Devlin."

"Of course. As you wish, Maddie. As you wish."

He saw in her eyes that she recognized the allusion to *The Princess Bride* and wasn't offended by it. She was no doubt thinking that he might soon reconsider his assumption that the story she told him would be a fairy tale, a fantastic adventure, with no actual basis in reality.

Time would tell.

MADDIE

# 9

As I've already mentioned, the women in my family were different. We were all born different, we grew up different, and we did things as adults that were so different most people either wouldn't understand them or else just plain wouldn't believe they could possibly happen in real life.

Which is fine with me. I don't really care what other people think, when it comes right down to it.

Nevertheless, I'm going to explain some of this stuff now, as well as I can, because it's important for me to get it out there, to talk through it, to verbalize not only the concepts but the feelings behind them that I've experienced over the years.

Where to start?

At one point, when I was in high school, I tried to do some research on the subject, approaching it from a scientific angle. I borrowed books from the library on genetics, hunted around online for simplified explanations, and even annoyed my biology teacher during lunch period asking questions that she answered with terminology and concepts I struggled to understand.

I was an English lit geek, remember, and not a science

nerd.

Just the same, I was able to digest some basic information about genetics that at least gave me a clue about what must have happened in my family to produce strange little me.

It all seemed to involve what was called mitochondrial DNA. Mitochondria were tiny doodads that lived in our cells and were involved in the production of energy in our bodies. They were passed on by mothers to their children, generation after generation. Within these mitochondria were chromosomes that got passed down at the same time, and they contained the code for specific proteins that drove the aforementioned energy production.

My theory, which I formulated in complete ignorance and have never mentioned to anyone before now, was that some kind of mutation occurred at some point in our matrilineal past that created a protein that generated energy to unlock certain portions of our brains where special abilities otherwise would lie dormant.

Now, while I was fumbling through my research on this subject I also tried to read a few articles related to neuroscience and psychic abilities. It was pretty much all a bunch of hoo-haw, but a few things stuck out. First, the notion that we only used about 10 per cent of our brains was clearly considered a myth within the scientific community. Apparently almost 100 per cent was active at one point or another, but the interesting part was that we had no idea where in the brain our consciousness lived. It was believed that it didn't have a specific location, like, say, the parts that controlled speech or vision or taste, for example. It seemed to be the synergetic product of a number of different areas of activity. And also interesting was the admission by prominent neuroscientists that, while the brain as a whole was almost continuously working hard on something or other, we only understood about 10 per cent of what it was actually doing. Which is where the 10 per cent notion comes from, I guess.

One thing my mutation theory didn't explain, though, was why the mitochondria passed down in our particular haplogroup, a.k.a. our wacky family, only affected the brains of female children and not males. If asked, I would say it was probably a side effect of the aforementioned mutation. Apparently mitochondrial DNA was more susceptible to mutation than regular DNA, so it was a plausible theory, I suppose, that the particular protein I was talking about was active in females but not males. I didn't really know for sure, though. Sorry.

I'm not very comfortable talking about things I know next to nothing about, so all I ask is that you not yell at me if you actually know about this stuff and I've gotten something wrong or mixed up. As I say, I'm not a scientific type.

One other thing I'll mention, though, is that the literature also talked about something referred to as Mitochondrial Eve. As you could probably guess, the theory was that if you traced back the mitochondrial DNA through enough generations, you'd eventually arrive at the woman with whom the whole thing started.

Eve, or a reasonable facsimile thereof.

So within my family line, then, there must have been a Mitochondrial Eve whose chromosomes mutated in the way I'd theorized, producing generation after generation of women cursed with some kind of paranormal ability they didn't ask for and couldn't get rid of. Or blessed, depending on your point of view, I guess. It's definitely up for debate, as far as I'm concerned.

Anyway, you can imagine that I've given a lot of thought to the question of who our Mitochondrial Eve might have been. Unfortunately, my family didn't include any competent historians or genealogists along the way, and so the question has gone unanswered to this point.

As I think I said before, Marie-Claire didn't like to talk about this subject. She was completely close-mouthed about her own ability, and she said very little to me about Joelle, or her own mother, or anyone else. They might not have been anything other than completely normal and boring women, as far as she was concerned. Most of what I know came from Joelle, and most of what she knew she got from *her* grandmother.

So let me run through what I've learned. I can't go all the way back to Eve, of course. But I can go back to Gabrielle.

That's my starting point.

# 10

The morning after Quinn told me about Benedicta, the angel spirit he'd been meeting during his night-time travels, was a quiet Wednesday for me. Quinn was at school and I had the day off, my next online seminar not scheduled until the following morning.

After breakfast, I wasted a bunch of time searching the house for a set of pastels Quinn wanted to use for an art project coming due on Friday.

Although he wasn't particularly talented when it came to drawing or painting, he enjoyed it as an activity that relaxed and amused him. He thought the pastels were in his bedroom but couldn't find them.

After coming inside last evening we'd spent at least an hour hunting around for them. We looked in the basement. Not down there. We looked in the living room, dining room, and the kitchen, searching every piece of furniture that had a drawer or door or hatch, every cupboard, every closet.

Nope.

Whenever Quinn couldn't find something, he got whiney. He'd talk about a science fiction story he once read in which some guy discovered there were unseen dimensions into which everyday things disappeared just when you went looking for them. He also liked to complain about me moving his stuff when I was tidying the house, which I'd learned over time not to do more than minimally necessary to restore order in the face of Quinnian chaos.

It got on the nerves after a while.

So I decided to try again. I went through the kitchen and the hall closet with the same results as last night—zip. I was about to tackle his bedroom one more time when I suddenly realized we hadn't looked in Marie-Claire's room.

I only went in there once a week, to dust and vacuum, and otherwise I stayed out. It had been her private place. It also was the room in which she passed away. Out of respect, and maybe also out of fear, I avoided opening that door and stepping inside any more often than absolutely necessary. Quinn, I should mention as well, never set foot in there. Ever.

This morning, though, I figured I might as well steel myself and take a look.

It took me about a minute flat to find the pastels. They were sitting right there in plain sight, in her closet, on the shelf. Don't ask me how they got there because I have no clue. Every now and again, strange things happened in Marie-Claire's house, and I knew better than to ask too many questions.

Before closing the door, I ran my eyes around the interior of the closet to see if there was anything else in there that should be somewhere else instead. Almost all of her clothing had been given away after her death, but there were still a couple of sweaters on hangers that I couldn't bear to part with. There were shoes, an empty suitcase, and a few other odds and ends.

God, how I missed her.

On the shelf were several photograph albums I'd forgotten about. They'd been offered to Uncle Robert after the funeral, but he hadn't wanted any part of them, so they'd been stuck up here. I'd never looked through them all before, because they'd been Marie-Claire's, she'd kept them in here, and I figured it might be best to keep my nose out unless she invited me to check them out.

Next to the photo albums was a shoebox that was supposed to be in my closet, but wasn't. What did I say about this house? The box contained letters that had been written to Joelle by her grandmother. After Joelle's murder, when Mark was going through her things, he'd offered the box to me and I took it. I glanced at a few of the letters, started crying, and put them back in the box, which immediately went under my bed.

At the time, it was too painful to experience things directly connected to Joelle, so I never went back to them. But after Mark's death, when I was packing up for the move to Twilight Road, I made sure to grab the box and shove it into my knapsack.

I carried the pastels, the shoebox, and the photo albums into the kitchen, remembering to close Marie-Claire's bedroom door behind me with respectful care.

Tossing the pastels on the counter next to the sink where Quinn would find them when he got home, I sat down at the kitchen table with the other stuff and started going through it all.

Other than a brief break for lunch, I spent several hours reading everything.

The letters began when Joelle was eight. Curious about her grandmother in "faraway Quebec," whom she'd never visited, Joelle asked Marie-Claire if she could write to

Lisette. Marie-Claire gave her permission, and so little Joelle wrote a lengthy missive asking her grandmother a thousand questions about herself. Lisette responded right away, and they began a pen-pal relationship that lasted throughout the final six years of Lisette's life.

The letters were written in French. Joelle told me once that Marie-Claire had learned English after moving to Smiths Falls and had made sure her children were all fluently bilingual but that Lisette was a unilingual francophone. Fortunately, Joelle and Mark had made sure that my French was as good as my English, so I was able to read Lisette's letters without a problem.

As I worked my way through them, I realized they were a treasure trove of family history that I'd neglected for far too long. I won't quote them verbatim to you, because I've always disliked epistolary narrative (think of Samuel Richardson's *Pamela* and *Clarissa*, for example, and try not to shudder), but I'll pass on what I learned from them to justify my insistence that genealogical roots are very important to me.

After finishing the letters (I'll refer back to them here and there, I promise), I returned to the photo albums. The first one I opened happened to be the one with the oldest stuff in it. On the first page was a newspaper clipping. Taken from the *Eastern Ontario Review,* a very old local paper published in Hawkesbury at the beginning of the previous century, it was the obituary of my great-great grandmother, Gabrielle Sabourin Proulx.

Born in Rigaud, Quebec, in 1874, Gabrielle married a Franco-Ontarian named Jean-Louis Fournier and lived the rest of her life in Hawkesbury, a small town on the Ontario side of the Ottawa River. She died on December 1, 1923, at the age of 49, after a battle with tuberculosis. She was predeceased by a son, Jean-François, and survived by two daughters, Fleurette (Tremblay) and Lisette, living at home.

Unfortunately, the obit failed to mention who her parents were, or brothers or sisters. I looked online for documentation connected to her, such as her death certificate or birth certificate or the like, but without luck. My awareness of our genetic line stopped with her, for the time being. The identity of Mitochondrial Eve continued to remain a mystery.

But the clipping was important to me, very important, because it included a brief reference to Gabrielle as a "well-known local fortune teller." Her fame, it would seem, rested in part on having read the Tarot cards of Mrs. W.J. Duncan, wife of the newspaper publisher, and having accurately predicted that a rich relative would soon die and leave her a handsome legacy. A week later, the obit reported, her maternal uncle passed away in Montreal and left her half a million dollars.

Sure, fortune telling was a lot of bunk. Only, what if it wasn't always fake? What if some people *did* have a strange and inexplicable power to anticipate the future?

> "**Precognition** n. Knowledge of something in advance of its occurrence. [Late Latin *praecognitio*, from Latin *praecognoscere*, to know before." *The American Heritage Dictionary of the English Language,* William Morris, Editor, 1969.

Sorry. Couldn't resist.

I leafed through the letters in the shoebox, which I'd arranged in chronological order as I read through them, until I found the one in which Lisette described her mother to Joelle.

Gabrielle was, Lisette wrote, a genuine "Gypsy type." She ran a tea room and social salon in downtown Hawkesbury that was, for many years, very popular with the ladies of the upper social stratum. She vividly remembered her mother leaving the house in the morning dressed in a billowy white blouse, colourful full-length skirt, Romany-style scarf, silver bangles, and hoop earrings. The full costume, it would seem. I would dearly loved to have seen a picture of her, but none had ever made it into the photo albums.

As a nineteenth-century woman, she would have taken advantage of the stereotypes of the day to give herself a familiar vehicle through which she could express her special ability. Tea leaves, Tarot cards, crystal ball—all the paraphernalia and rituals of a French-Canadian version of a larger-than-life Romany woman.

I really wish I'd known her. I have an image in my head of a tall, slender, raven-haired woman with a ready laugh, dark eyes, and a world of troubles that she kept to herself.

Someone I could easily identify with.

# 11

I was interrupted by a call on my cellphone from Reverend B. She said she was taking Stephen to the airport to catch his flight, and she wanted to know if I'd like to come along. Stephen would have called, she explained, but he was so busy packing and fussing over last-minute details that his head was in a thousand different places at once, and it hadn't occurred to him yet to ask me to see him off.

"I understand," I said. "I'd love to."

I liked airports. I liked the excitement of travel to distant places; people with suitcases on wheels walking down long, high-ceilinged concourses; the soft, calm, muffled voices announcing arrivals and departures over the public address system; the low thunder of jets taking off in a joyful defiance of gravity.

I'd never flown on an airplane before, though. Mark's idea of a vacation was a week at our summer cottage, out on the lake pretending to fish, his nose in a best-selling thriller. For her part, Joelle usually preferred to stay at home, so as a family we'd never travelled outside the country or any farther than somewhere we could reach by driving.

I'd like to. Fly somewhere, I mean. I'm not claustrophobic, so I wouldn't mind sitting in an enclosed place for several hours. I'm not afraid of heights, so I'd love to sit in a window seat to watch the landscape slowly pass by down below, and the clouds, and the lakes, or even the ocean.

Travel costs money, though, so I'd have to wait until the trust fund was released into my bank account, because as it stood I could never afford tickets for Quinn and me, let alone pay for accommodations and all the additional costs that went along with it.

Stephen's expenses, fortunately for him, were being paid for by the evangelical group arranging his mission, so he didn't have to worry about where the money was coming from. It was, basically, a free trip abroad. I felt happy for him because he was so excited, and when he shook my hand at the security gate instead of giving me a hug I forgave him, although I was a little disappointed. I know I've said he's not my boyfriend, and I hadn't had any well-formed romantic thoughts about him at any point along the way, but I thought a handshake was, well, a little too businesslike.

Wouldn't you think?

Because it was Wednesday, it was sermon day for Reverend B: the day she wrote her homily for the upcoming Sunday service. As we drove back home from the airport, she told me she was thinking about something centred on losing a loved one and the importance of remembering that death is not necessarily a permanent separation for those who accept Christ into their hearts as their saviour.

I thought maybe she was drawing a little bit on the sadness she was feeling over Stephen's departure, which would last three months, and was trying to turn it into a sermon that would be useful to her parishioners in a much more important context than good old-fashioned empty-nest syndrome.

"Take John Pollock," she said.

"Who?"

"One of the church trustees. His wife, Theresa, died this summer."

"Oh, yeah. Right." Dear Mrs. Pollock, the French hater.

"He's still grieving. Still trying to adjust to being a widower and living all alone. It's hard."

"I never heard what she died of."

Reverend B smiled. "I'm tempted to say a bad attitude, but that wouldn't be very charitable, would it?" The smile faded. "She wasn't the nicest person I've ever met in my life, but everyone deserves to be treated with dignity and Christian love. To answer your question, though, I believe it was natural causes. Old age. Heart failure. She was seventy-six."

"I was surprised she was buried next door. I didn't think the church was using that graveyard any more. Isn't there a new one down at the Corners, next to the new church?"

"Yes, but John bought a double plot for himself and Theresa in the old one a long time ago, back in the sixties. When his time comes, he'll be buried next to her. As far as I know, that'll be the last interment in that cemetery."

I watched the woods pass by on my side of the highway. Mrs. Pollock had been a nasty old bat when she was alive, but I was fairly sure she wasn't to blame for the bad feelings saturating the parsonage and the appearances of the dead woman who was, I reluctantly had to admit, trying to reach out to me.

Someone else—*something* else—was behind it all.

Something much, much more evil.

Reverend B sighed. "Sometimes death can bring about positive change. For the bereaved, I mean."

"It's traumatic," I said, speaking from experience.

"Yes, I know." She glanced over at me. "You went through three deaths in only seven years. First your mom, then your dad, then your grandmother. Incredibly difficult for a young person to handle. I'm constantly amazed that you've been able to deal with it and stay as strong as you are."

"Quinn helps."

She nodded. After a moment, she said, "My father passed away when I was at Wilfrid Laurier. He was a truck mechanic. One of the quietest, kindest souls you'd ever want to meet. He was overweight and had a heart attack on the job while carrying a heavy piece of machinery to his work bench."

"I'm very sorry to hear that."

She smiled. "Thank you, Maddie. I mention it because it brought about a positive change in my life. My parents were religious minded, and we went to church every Sunday when I was a child. After his funeral I decided that I'd enter the ministry when I finished my B.A. If his death hadn't happened at that point, and hadn't hit me so hard, I never would have thought about changing the direction I was heading in. I wasn't sure what I was going to do with an English degree—nobody is, really—but I thought I'd probably get into teaching at some level. His death was a wakeup call for me. A call to service."

"I see what you mean."

"I'd like to be able to convey that spirit of hope, that possibility that we can all change something terrible into something good, so that people like John Pollock, and, well, maybe someone like yourself, Maddie, can make sense of personal loss."

"'Nothing of him that doth fade, but doth suffer a sea-change into something rich and strange.'"

"Yes. That's good, Maddie. Shakespeare expressed it very well."

Personally, I thought it sounded more like a thinly veiled allusion to the death and resurrection of Christ and how she'd like her congregation (and maybe me, hint hint) to view their losses as a chance to renew their faith in a living Jesus, but I didn't say anything. I liked Reverend B, and I didn't have it in me to debate the thing with her. I'd experienced life after death in a way she couldn't possibly imagine, I'd seen things that were totally beyond her faith, but I didn't think it was my place to correct her perception of reality.

Besides, she wouldn't believe me. She'd think I was nuts. She'd pity me, maybe suggest I get counselling or therapy or something. Even worse, she'd probably pray for me.

It would be much better if she had no idea what my life was *really* like.

# 12

When Reverend B dropped me off, it was a few minutes before three thirty. Quinn wasn't due home on the bus until around four, so I took a look in the freezer and pulled out a big frozen mac and cheese dinner I could warm up in the oven for supper. I added a package of garlic toast and declared myself ready to get us through another meal.

The photo albums and the shoebox were still sitting on the kitchen table where I'd left them. I went to gather them up, thinking I'd put them in my bedroom closet for future reference, but instead I sat down, pulled the photo album closer, and turned the page.

Front and centre was a photograph of a man in a plaid shirt and khaki trousers, his sleeves rolled up above his elbows, his arms crossed as he leaned against the fender of an old truck. Black hair, a hooked Gallic nose, and a tiny smile at the corners of his mouth. My great-grandfather, Gilles Hamelin.

For most of his adult life he ran the general store in a little place in Quebec called Ste-Justine-de-Newton, a crossroads south of Rigaud that was less than a kilometre from the Ontario border and about twenty kilometres north of the Trans-Canada highway. He looked after the little post office substation at the back of the store while my great-grandmother, Lisette Fournier, was in charge of stocking the shelves and running the cash register at the front.

I looked at her picture next. It had been taken outdoors, in a garden. She held a wicker basket filled with cut flowers and wore a white floppy hat and a dress that was almost completely obscured by a greyish apron. It was hard to tell what colour it had been, as the photo was in black and white, like all the rest of them.

Her mouth was a strong, straight line, her cheekbones were high and pronounced, and her eyes were serious, almost sad. Having read her letters to my mother, letters written by a grandmother to a young, like-minded granddaughter, I could almost hear her voice in my head as I stared at the picture. French; wistful; gentle.

And oh, yes, I could see the family resemblance. Indeed I could. Every morning when I looked in the bathroom mirror I stared at the exact same eyes, the same prominent cheekbones, the same unsmiling mouth.

Parenthetically, to avoid confusion, I should explain at this point that I refer to my female ancestors using their birth surname rather than their married names. In Quebec, women retain their birth name after marriage, while their children receive the surname of their father. This traditional practice became law in Quebec in 1981, and frequently carries over into Franco-Ontarian practice as well. Hence Gabrielle Proulx, wife of Jean-Louis Fournier; Lisette Fournier, wife of Gilles Hamelin; Marie-Claire Hamelin, wife of Claude Desormeaux; Joelle Desormeaux, wife of Mark Hubbard. It's possible for children to have both parents' names, hyphenated or not, which you see quite often in Quebec these days, but this practice wasn't followed in my family.

Yay. I don't think I'd like to go around with a handle as bulky as Madeleine Veronica Desormeaux-Hubbard. Maddie Hubbard does me just fine, thank you.

Interesting, I'm sure. But I digress.

My great-grandparents Lisette and Gilles had three boys, all of whom grew up to become farmers in the area, before Marie-Claire was born in 1944. There were a few pictures of their sons in the album, all slender and Gallic-looking like their dad. One, Jean-Jacques, was photographed in his barnyard, sitting on his tractor, an old Massey Harris, while another, Gilbert, posed with his wife and three daughters in a studio somewhere.

I never knew any of these people, but they seemed as though they were probably very nice. Gilbert's oldest daughter, though, had a look on her face that I recognized. Her name wasn't written down in the album and I'd never heard it mentioned, so I didn't know exactly who she was. At some point I guess I should do some genealogical research and see what I can find out.

To see if she was another knot in the genetic skein reaching down from the distant past. If so, I might have to expand my genetic theory a little to accommodate the possibility that the ability gene could be passed through males to their daughters, as well as in a straight line from mother to daughter. Anyway. Something to think about on a rainy day when there's nothing else to do.

I never met Lisette in person, of course. She died when my mother was eight years old. But now, sitting at the kitchen table, I felt as though I'd begun to know her fairly well through her letters to the little girl who grew up to become my mother.

Kind, patient, with a wry sense of humour a little girl

like Joelle might not always pick up on. And apparently she had a talent for finding lost objects and was unbeatable at cards.

For her part, her daughter Marie-Claire was a typical rural Quebec girl. She liked going to school, she got along well with her teachers and the other kids, she loved her parents and her three big brothers, and she generally stayed out of trouble.

On the next page of the photo album was a picture taken when Marie-Claire was about six years old. It had been snapped in the store when she was helping her mother stock the shelves. She held a can of soup in her hand and stared rather seriously at the camera.

It's occurred to me to wonder several times lately if I'm the last of our line of females with special abilities, the last link in a chain running down through the generations. Or did Gilbert's daughter, a cousin of Joelle, also inherit a special ability which she later passed on to her own female child, a second cousin of mine?

Browsing through the other pictures of Marie-Claire as a girl and an awkward teenager, I was struck all over again by the resemblance between her and Lisette, and her and Joelle, and the three of them and me, the one at the end of the line. It was weird to think about Gilbert's family and wonder if there might be a relative of mine who was like me. Talented, bright, and very unhappy about it all.

Sometimes in the middle of the night I lie awake and worry about whether or not I should have a family of my own some day and potentially pass this stuff on to another little girl. Would that be an irresponsible thing to do? Was it a genetic flaw, like Lou Gehrig's Disease or something, that shouldn't be transmitted to future generations?

I don't know. I don't know I don't know I don't know.

I don't know.

Another decision for another day.

Anyway, as I looked at these images of Marie-Claire here in this photo album while sitting at what was at one time her kitchen table, I believed very strongly that she should be understood, as far as it was possible to do so.

Maybe I've made my grandmother seem taciturn, closed in on herself, inaccessible. That wasn't the case at all.

She was the best grandmother I could ever have asked for. She was very warm and loving. Quinn worshipped the ground she walked on. It was just that there were walls that she kept around certain things, and because she'd decided that was the way it was going to be and stuck with it for the rest of her life, I had to respect her silence on the subject.

Thankfully, Lisette had thought Joelle should know a few things about her mother, and she wrote about them in some detail. Mind you, she was addressing herself to a young girl, so she kept to a level that a child could understand. Just the same, it took very little effort for me to read between the lines.

One night when Marie-Claire was six years old, she woke up from a bad dream and couldn't stop crying. Lisette climbed into bed next to her and held her in her arms, trying to console her. Eventually Marie-Claire was able to control her sobbing long enough to describe her dream.

She was in an airplane. She'd never in her life seen the inside of a plane, of course—nor had she seen one on television, this being 1949 and years before the Hamelins owned a TV set—but she described the plane in great accuracy to her mother. They were about to fly over a very wide river when there was an explosion. The plane crashed into the middle of a forest. Passengers and luggage were thrown everywhere. She crawled around the wreckage, looking at the bloody and smashed faces of dead people before suddenly waking up, screaming.

Two days later Lisette was leafing through one of the newspapers dropped off at the general store when she saw a story that frightened her. About twelve hours after Marie-Claire had had her dream, a bomb had gone off on a Canadian Pacific Airlines DC-3 flying from Quebec City to Baie Comeau, killing twenty-three people. The plane came down in the woods near Cap Tourmente, close to the St. Lawrence River. Lisette stared at a grim black-and-white photograph of the wreckage among the trees. It matched exactly her daughter's frantic, tearful description of what she'd dreamed.

A week or so after that, a man came in to buy cigarettes. Lisette knew him slightly as a plumber who lived in nearby St-Polycarpe. Marie-Claire was sitting on a stool at the end of the counter, looking through a magazine. As soon as she caught sight of the man she let out a cry and ran off, down to the back of the store and up the stairs to their apartment. She stayed in bed for the rest of the day and all of that night. She refused to speak and wouldn't eat supper.

Lisette learned the next morning that the plumber had left the store and, just past St-Telesphore, collided with a gravel truck. He was killed instantly.

It was a long time before Marie-Claire would talk to her about it. She said she'd seen a dark cloud surrounding the man and that his face looked bloody and dead, like the people on the airplane.

There were other incidents after that, some minor and some that were quite upsetting. In 1954, when Marie-Claire was ten, she dreamed of a terrible storm that raged through a city. Once again, she saw a lot of dead people. The next day, Hurricane Hazel hit Toronto, killing eighty-one. Two years later, it was a dream about a dark place and men with blackened faces huddled together, frightened and suffocating. A few days later Lisette learned about the Springhill Mine disaster in Nova Scotia in which thirty-nine miners died and another eighty-eight were eventually rescued.

Having read these letters, I now understood that Marie-Claire had been a psychic dreamer, a Cassandra, an oracle of sorts who'd been able to predict disastrous events before they occurred. To me, she'd just been an ordinary grandmother. But I'd always understood there were things beneath the surface, things that connected her forward and backward in time on the inescapable thread of mitochondrial DNA, and I knew that her silence was self-imposed and driven by a number of different factors, fear being one of them.

I turned a page in the album to a picture of her with her husband, Claude Desormeaux. Standing in front of them, squinting up at the camera, was a very young Joelle. Faded colours and uncertain smiles. Marie-Claire held Robert in her arms, no more than a few months old, so the picture would have been taken in 1976. Joelle would have been three.

They stood in someone's back yard, perhaps their own in Smiths Falls, in front of a wooden fence. Claude was a house painter, not very intelligent, and a heavy drinker. Why had Marie-Claire married him? No one knew for sure.

I flipped through the shoebox and pulled out a letter Lisette had written not more than a year before her death, when Joelle was around thirteen. By this time Joelle had confided to Lisette that she was experiencing visions and a level of clairvoyance not normal for a girl her age, and in this response Lisette had done her best to reassure her that her ability might seem like a hardship and a trial, yes, but it must also be acknowledged as a gift she must try very hard to understand and be grateful for.

I unfolded the letter in my hand and began to reread it.

"Your mother never accepted her destiny as someone chosen to receive the dream visions," Lisette wrote. "Once she married and began to have you children, she rejected this heritage and suppressed it in her mind with a prayer that it would no longer torment her. I must tell you why."

Lisette went on to explain that Marie-Claire and her husband were living in Vaudreuil, just west of Montreal, when Claude became friends with a carpenter from Ontario. They were working on a housing project in Dorion, and the man convinced Claude to move to Smiths Falls with him to form a partnership in a home renovation business. Claude and Marie-Claire were living in a rundown tenement building at the time, and it sounded like an ideal opportunity.

A year after they moved, the guy dicked off and left Claude with a drawer full of unpaid bills and uncollected debts. It was a mess.

Around this time, Marie-Claire had another dream. It would be the last one she would ever speak about for the rest of her life.

In the dream, she saw Claude's brother, Richard, at work. He was the youngest in the family, only twenty-two, pampered and fussed over by his mother and sisters. In her dream, Richard was suddenly engulfed in fire. It consumed him. Killed him.

The next morning, upset, she told Claude what she'd seen. Busy with his morning toast and beer, he waved her off. Desperate, she launched into the whole story of her ability, the dreams that brought her visions of imminent disaster, the foretelling of other people's deaths.

She'd never shared any of this with him before. She'd always kept it to herself, and only Lisette had known about it. Until now.

He thought she'd gone nuts. At the time, she was pregnant with Joelle's little sister Nicolette, so maybe she was having some kind of hormonal crisis.

That morning at work, Claude spent all his time fending off creditors looking for their money. He came home for lunch, got into the rye and Coke, and didn't bother going back to his little office in the afternoon.

Late in the evening, the husband of his oldest sister called to tell them that the factory where Richard worked had been destroyed in an explosion. It was a plant owned by Canadian Industries Limited, CIL, located in McMaster, Quebec, just east of Montreal. They were making a new kind of explosives product called PowerMax 500, a substitute for nitroglycerin. Windows were blown out all over the town, and the fire could be seen for kilometres. Eight people were killed, including Richard.

It took Claude, who was pretty drunk, a few minutes to process the news. Then he began to babble about Marie-Claire and her dream. She'd known it was going to happen, he said. She'd *known*.

Why didn't you call? the brother-in-law wanted to know. Why didn't you warn us? We could have told Richard, convinced him to stay home today. We could have done *something*.

Claude was blubbering at this point, out of control, and the brother-in-law hung up on him.

The funeral was a nightmare for Marie-Claire. Claude's

sisters blamed her for everything, as illogical as it was on the face of it, and Claude, hung over and repentant, sided with his family. Somehow, in some bizarre way, the explosion and deaths were Marie-Claire's fault.

The Desormeauxs never spoke to her again.

As for Claude, he waited until a month after Nicolette was born to disappear. Apparently he ended up in Australia. He might still be there for all anyone knew. I never heard a word about him.

Who cared? Not me.

I looked up as the front door opened and Quinn bustled in, full of exuberance about something or other that I hoped would lift my spirits just a tiny little bit.

# 13

That night I was awakened from a deep sleep by a voice calling my name.

I rolled over and opened my eyes. Quinn was sitting on the side of the bed.

"What is it? What's wrong?"

"There's a problem, Maddie."

I looked at the clock and was surprised to see that it was only 10:46 in the evening. I did the arithmetic in my head and realized I'd only been asleep for little more than an hour. It felt as though it should be the middle of the night.

I sat up. "What kind of a problem?"

"I was travelling. I went to a plane I don't normally go to a lot. I talked to someone, and she showed me something pretty bad."

I saw that he was very upset. It was unusual for him to wake me up like this after one of his night-time experiences, and when he did it was always for something unpleasant.

I pushed back the covers and swung around onto the edge of the bed. "Tell me about it."

"There's this spirit lady, Penthea, who's always really nice to me. She shows me stuff. Galaxies and nebulas, and where comets come from. Cool stuff like that. But tonight she was different. Distressed. Her aura was dark and flaring, not pretty like it usually is. She showed me the parsonage."

"What? The parsonage?"

"Yeah Maddie, yeah! There's something wrong over there. Penthea showed me a place upstairs where somebody's stuck. They can't get out."

"Stuck? What are you talking about?"

"They're dead, Maddie, and they're stuck in that place. They can't get out. There's yelling and screaming and swearing."

I stood up and reached for my clothes. "What about Reverend B?"

"I saw her too, running around yelling for everything to stop. She's gone berserk."

"Okay, let me get dressed. Wait, I'll call first." I grabbed my cellphone from the bedside stand, found her number in my contacts list, and punched it.

No answer. It rang four times and went to voice mail.

I tried again, with the same result.

"Give me a minute to get dressed."

When he left the room, I changed out of my pyjamas into jeans and a sweater and hurried downstairs. He was pacing back and forth at the front door. I grabbed the car keys from the hall table and we ran outside. I figured it was quicker to drive over to the parsonage than run across the old church property in the dark. The ground was very uneven in spots, and I didn't feel like falling down and breaking my neck.

I drove into the parsonage driveway and pulled up behind Reverend B's Explorer just as she was running out the front door. I shut off the engine, and she waved frantically for me to get out of the way. I got out of the car and held up my hands.

"Wait! What's wrong? What's happening?"

"Get out of the way!" She dodged around me and fumbled at her car door handle.

"I saw it too!" Quinn exclaimed. "I heard it!"

She got the door opened but paused to stare at him. "You what?"

"The voices. The swearing and banging. I heard it too."

"You couldn't possibly have. That's absurd."

"Let's go back inside," I said. "Show us where it was coming from."

"Oh no, I'm not going back in there. I have to get out of here."

"Where were you going?"

"I don't know. Just out of here. I don't know."

"The new church?"

"I don't know. Maybe." She looked at me. "Yes."

I thought she might be coming out of her panic a bit, getting a little control over her breathing, starting to think.

"It may have stopped by now," I urged. "Let's go see."

She shook her head, but I could see her considering it. She was the adult here. If we weren't afraid, a couple of kids, why should she be?

"Is it possible it was just the noises you said you've heard before? 'Old bones that creak and groan'?"

She shut the car door. "Not unless the floorboards have learned how to swear like a longshoreman."

I touched her elbow. "Let's go back inside. Maybe we can help you figure it out."

"Oh, heavens." She closed her eyes for a moment and

her chin dropped. Maybe she was saying a silent prayer.

"All right."

We went inside and stood in the hallway, listening. Nothing.

"It's stopped," she said.

I looked at Quinn. "Show me."

He led the way to the bottom of the stairs.

"I don't understand," Reverend B said, trailing behind.

I glanced at her over my shoulder. "It's complicated."

Quinn started up the stairs. Despite the fact that they were carpeted, they creaked and groaned, but it was a sound I'd heard before. No big deal.

The second floor was divided into four rooms and the notorious bathroom where I'd seen the woman in the toilet. The two front rooms were bedrooms used by Reverend B and Stephen, the third was a study in which Stephen had done his homework and surfed the Internet on his laptop, and the fourth was Reverend B's office. I thought that maybe the sounds had been coming from one of these rooms, or maybe the accursed bathroom, but Quinn led the way to the staircase leading up to the third floor.

"Don't go up there," Reverend B said.

Quinn didn't answer, walking confidently up to the next landing. I followed, my hand on the banister. Reverend B hesitated before flicking a switch that turned on the light at the top of the stairs. I heard her footsteps behind me, but I was watching Quinn.

The third floor of the parsonage, as I mentioned before, was mostly used for storage. A lot of stuff left behind by previous pastors, according to what Stephen had told me. Old furniture, some covered with drop sheets and others stacked one piece on top of another, heavy with dust and cobwebs. A few old steamer trunks, cardboard boxes, and that sort of thing. The ceilings up here were sharply slanted, and there were several dormer windows covered with heavy, dusty curtains.

Quinn led the way through the clutter to the back wall. He moved aside an old typewriter on a rolling metal stand and put his hand on the cheap fake-wood panelling.

"Here."

I came up beside him. "Are you sure?"

He rolled his eyes at me.

"What are you talking about?" Reverend B demanded. "It's just the wall."

"No." Quinn turned around, his face half in shadows. "There's another room back here. A hidden room. That's where the trouble's coming from."

# 14

"I still don't understand how he knew this was here," Reverend B said the next morning.

I didn't answer, moving aside as John Pollock and his son clomped up the stairs to join us on the third floor. Pollock was short and stooped, white-haired and grim-faced, a perfect fit for the stereotype of a rural church trustee, but his son Matt, who was the church sexton, was his complete opposite, having inherited most of his genetic material from his late mother. He was tall, burly, square-jawed, and muscular.

Unlike either parent, he was also very good-natured.

"Got yourself an extra room, do you?" Matt maneuvered past his father and stood in front of the section of wall panelling we'd pried loose last night at Quinn's insistence. He grabbed the edge of the panel and pulled it back for a look.

"Yep. It's a door, all right. Did you know this was here, Pops?"

"I did not." Pollock moved aside the typewriter on the stand, which was in his way, and edged in to see for himself.

"Space accountability," he muttered. "Shoulda known,

I guess. Floor space up here not the same as the other two floors below. Wonder what's behind there."

"I'm afraid to find out," Reverend B said.

"Oh?" Pollock threw her a sharp look. "Why's that?"

"There might be an animal in there," I said quickly. "Reverend Northrop heard a lot of noise and moving around up here last night. We thought maybe a raccoon got in, or squirrels."

"We'll need the live trap then," Matt said.

"Let's not get ahead of ourselves." Pollock stepped back. "I don't hear a thing. If it's animals, they probably went out again."

Matt nodded and took a pair of work gloves from his back pocket. He slipped them on, gripped the edge of the panel, and gave it a yank. Nails groaned and popped out until the panel was halfway off. He rolled his shoulder muscles and pulled again. This time it came completely free along the top. He yanked down, then got inside it and pushed. Then pushed again. Then stepped back, grabbed the edge, and yanked down and back.

The panel came off. He threw it aside and clapped his hands together, raising a cloud of dust from his gloves.

"Nice door," he said. It was an old oak door with an ivory doorknob and brass fittings. The doorframe also looked like it was made of oak.

He tried the knob. "Locked."

Pollock stooped for a closer look. "Needs a skeleton key."

"I've got a bunch of old keys in the truck," Matt said. "Might be one that'll work."

He set off downstairs to get them. Pollock straightened slowly, his hands moving to the small of his back. "I can't imagine how it could be here all this time and I didn't know about it."

"It doesn't look like it's been opened for years," I said.

Pollock grunted.

Matt clumped back upstairs, keys jingling. "Got one right here I think will do the trick." He grinned at Reverend B. "Picked these up at an auction this spring and threw them behind the seat. Figured you never know when they might come in handy."

He knelt in front of the door, picked out a key from the ring, and tried it in the lock. It moved a few millimetres in a counter-clockwise direction and stopped.

"Stiff," he said. "Might need a shot of oil. Should have grabbed the can." He tried again. "No, wait. Here we go."

I could hear the lock click from where I was standing.

Matt lurched to his feet and tried the knob again.

"Careful," Pollock said, "in case they're still in there."

I glanced at Reverend B. Our invading animals cover story was definitely in play.

Matt slowly opened the door and looked inside. "I don't see anything."

"Nothing moving?" his father asked.

"Nope."

Matt went all the way inside. "It's a bedroom," he announced. "No window. Ceiling looks all right. No closet. Don't see how an animal would get in."

"Let's see." Pollock crowded in after him.

I looked at Reverend B again. She shook her head. Taking a deep breath, I went through the door.

I felt the cold right away, a bitter cold that cut right through my sweater to chill my bones.

"Must be no insulation up here," Matt said, his breath puffing a bit.

Against the far wall, in the middle, was a metal frame

bed. The mattress on it was old and discoloured. No bedding, and no pillow. Beside the bed was a night table with nothing on it. The floor was bare plank wood, badly stained and scuffed. In the corner was an old wardrobe that would have been used in the absence of a closet. The door hung open. It was empty.

"Stuff's not worth anything," Pollock remarked, perhaps disappointed they hadn't uncovered a cache of valuable antiques.

"Can't figure out why it'd be up here in the first place," Matt said. "Did any of the parsons take in boarders?"

Pollock shook his head. "Not that I can think of, off the top of my head."

"Well, anyway." He looked at me. "Weird, huh?"

I nodded, trying to keep my expression neutral. The room was saturated with bad energy. Everything I'd felt for the past four months when I came into the parsonage seemed to be concentrated here, in this room. An intense pressure of anguish, fear, and horror. It was almost incapacitating.

*There's somebody stuck in there*, Quinn had said. *They can't get out.*

I had to leave.

Now.

I had to get away from here.

"Excuse me." I pushed past Matt, aware of his puzzled expression, and hurried from the room. I almost ran down the stairs to the second floor. I stumbled on the landing, caught myself, and went down the other flight of stairs and out the front door.

Reverend B followed, calling my name.

I let her catch up to me on the front lawn. I bent over, hands on my knees, and tried to get my breathing back under control.

She bent down beside me. "I felt it, too. I felt it, Maddie! Something terrible."

I nodded, unwilling to speak.

"What on earth is going on?"

"Evil," I managed, not daring to look at her. "Something very, very evil."

# 15

Reverend B put a sandwich and a can of soda water in front of me and sat down at Marie-Claire's kitchen table. I thanked her but didn't reach for it. I knew where this was all going to go, and I just didn't have an appetite for food right at the moment.

She sipped her tea. "You need to explain to me what's going on."

Matt had taken his father home and returned with a hasp and a big metal padlock. Reverend B had insisted that the door be secured and not opened again, so while he did his thing, whistling cheerfully, oblivious to our distress, we walked over here for lunch.

"You won't like it," I said.

"I already don't like it. Talk, Maddie."

"All right." I paused to collect my thoughts before asking, "Do you believe in the paranormal?"

Reverend B put down her teacup. "Oh dear. No, not really. Not in the popular sense."

"You don't believe in the supernatural?"

"Well, Maddie, I'm a Christian, so I believe there's an afterlife, that we have a soul that's separate from our material body, that the spirit of Christ rose and, as the

Bible says, death hath no more dominion over Him, and the trumpet will sound for all of us and the dead will be raised. I believe that."

"Well, okay." I touched the sandwich but didn't pick it up. "There's a lot more to it, though. Do you know anything about the astral planes of existence?"

She sighed. "If you're talking about the Hindu belief in astral journeys, out-of-body experiences and the stuff the Theosophists wrote about, then no. I don't. I've read about it, but not very thoroughly. It just doesn't ring true."

"But it is true." I hesitated, afraid of disappointing her. But after all, she'd asked for it, so here it was. "Quinn's a traveller."

"A what?"

"At night, when he's asleep, his spirit leaves his body and travels to other places. Astral realms you've probably read about. He's done it since he was little. For us, it's no big deal. Usually."

"Oh, Maddie. You can't be serious."

There it was. The disappointment.

"Last night, he left his body and travelled to an astral plane where he talked to a spirit named Penthea. He's met this . . . entity before, but he said this time her aura was dark and she was upset about something. She showed him an image, well, I don't know exactly what it would have been, but anyway, she showed Quinn the room upstairs and told him someone was trapped there and couldn't get out. He heard the noise and he also saw you. He saw how upset you were."

"Oh dear."

"How else do you think he knew that room was there? Even Mr. Pollock didn't know about it, but Quinn led us right to it. A twelve-year-old boy. How'd he know? How did he know it was there? Because he saw it, Reverend. He *saw* it."

She said nothing, staring into her cup.

"Don't put that where I can see it."

When she frowned up at me, I nodded at her tea. "Haven't you noticed how I avoid open liquids? That I won't drink from a glass or cup?"

"Not really. Sorry, should I have?"

"Yes. Stephen was aware of it, but he didn't really take it very seriously. He was polite. He thought it was just a weird phobia I have. It's not."

"I'm afraid I just don't understand any of this."

"How well did you get to know Marie-Claire? My grandmother?"

She shrugged. "Not too well. She kept to herself, for the most part."

"You were here four years before she passed away last year, right?"

"Yes, I think so. I haven't kept track of time very well."

"What kind of person did you think she was?"

Reverend B smiled. "She was very nice. Sweet! Very French, and I guess very Catholic. She went to Mass regularly, didn't she?"

"Aunt Brigitte drove her. Until the last few months. After that, the priest would come around to see her, and he was here to give her the last rites when she died."

"I was very sorry to hear that she'd passed." Her smile had faded, but it remained at the corners of her eyes. "She had a dry wit. I liked that. She teased me about being a misguided Protestant."

"When she brought you flowers from her garden."

"Yes. Every Saturday morning in the summer. It was so sweet of her."

"She had premonitions. She foretold disasters before they happened. Like Cassandra, only she stopped telling people about them after a bad incident with her husband's family."

Reverend B sipped her tea.

"Joelle was a psychic. A clairvoyant. She actually worked as a consultant for the police quite a lot. She was in the news every now and again. One of the police detectives, Patrice Rogers, used to call her in from time to time to consult on investigations. Joelle found a missing child once, and solved a hit-and-run case. Then she—"

I couldn't finish.

Reverend B bit her lip, thinking it through. Finally, she frowned. "Your grandmother. Your mother. Even your brother. What about you, Maddie? What are you trying to tell me?"

"I was hoping we'd never have to talk about this. I don't want to lose you as a friend."

She ran a hand through her hair and grimaced. "I think you need to explain to me exactly what's going on here."

# 16

Slowly, reluctantly, I stood up and went into the pantry. I moved aside a carton of instant rice and reached for the wooden box that sat on the shelf behind it. Halfway there, my hand stopped. A low sound escaped from the back of my throat. I forced myself to pick up the box, blow away the dust that had settled on the top of it, and carry it out into the kitchen.

"What I do," I said, sitting down, "is called hydromancy. Using water to communicate with the dead. It's a form of scrying, which is a term usually connected to crystal ball gazing."

"Maddie. Really."

"You wanted to know, so here it is." I could hear the defensiveness in my voice, but I couldn't help it.

"Sorry." She absent-mindedly tugged at a handful of her hair. "Keep going."

The box was plain, without any decoration of any kind. It was made of oak, and at one time I'd kept it waxed and polished, using real beeswax and a silk cloth. That was a long time ago, of course, but sitting untouched in the pantry for several years had not affected its appearance in any way, except for the dust.

I picked out a small key on my key ring and unlocked the box. I raised the lid and took out a bowl that was about the size of what you'd have your morning cereal in.

"I use this when I want to deliberately contact someone." I made a face. "Instead of it happening accidentally, which is what's been going on at the parsonage. Over the years I taught myself how to control it, more or less. Joelle was going to help me with that, but she was killed before we could really get into it."

Reverend B raised her eyebrows.

"Anyway," I plowed on, "it's a bronze bowl, which doesn't mean anything as far as I'm concerned but apparently bronze was important to the ancient Greeks, who were into this type of scrying. Water was a big thing in their mythology. You can see the Greek-style decorations on the side."

I held it up and turned it around. She looked at it politely, her expression neutral.

I put it down on the table. "Hydromancers have different ways of doing this. Some people have a ring on a piece of string. They fill the bowl with water and shake it, then dip the ring into the water. The number of times the ring hits the side of the bowl is supposed to mean something.

"Sounded goofy to me, so I never tried it. Other people take olive oil and put a drop in the water, which is supposed to spread across the surface and create a portal of some kind. Then you're supposed to be able to talk to the dead through the portal. I tried it once, but nothing happened."

Inside the bowl was a wadded-up silk pocket scarf. Unwrapping it, I held up a small stone.

"I use this pebble. It's blue lace agate, which is generally thought to enhance communication and increase self-confidence. It's also supposed to have an energy that clears the chakra in the throat to help self-expression.

Reverend B frowned.

"I know," I blurted, "this is all stuff way out there on the edge. Just please be patient."

Through force of will, she relaxed the frown into a stare of benevolent concern.

I took out a thin leather loop with a silver leaf charm on it. "I wear this when I scry. It's supposed to protect me while I'm communicating with the dead. I'm not sure how. It's another Greek thing, connected to their version of the Egyptian god Set, who protected Ra when he battled the serpent of chaos. The Greeks insisted that the cord be made from the hide of an ass, which could be the butt of a few jokes, I know, but I'm just using a piece of cowhide lacing from an old baseball glove. Seems to work okay."

Putting the charm back into the box, I glanced at her. The frown was back and her mouth was tight, as though she were suppressing a response to what I was saying.

"I take the pebble," I plunged on, "and I drop it into the water. I watch the ripples, and when they start to settle down, a face sometimes appears. When it does, I can usually hear them talking to me."

"They're dead."

"Yeah, that's the whole idea, Reverend B. Not to be sarcastic, but this is what you wanted to know. This is what I do. Used to do." I took a breath. "I'd give you a demonstration, but I'm really not up to it right now."

She stood up. "I need to process this. I'm sorry."

I watched her walk out, knowing in my heart that it had been inevitable. There was no possible way that a mainstream Protestant pastor with her education and experience in conventional churches with normal con-gregations and basic, simple routines to follow day after day, week after week, year after year, would suddenly just swallow all this stuff about water scrying and Set and crystal balls without choking on it.

I'd expected too much of her.

Whatever I was soon going to be forced to do, it looked as though I'd have to do it myself, without her help.

# 17

We're a small group, the people who understand how paranormal phenomena work and what they can do to those of us who are blessed or cursed (yes, that ambivalence again) with abilities to perceive what lies beyond normal, everyday experience.

At some point I want to take a few minutes to explain how I was able to get some kind of control over this thing— for a while, at least—and how I was able to use it to search for specific people. And what happened when I reached out for Joelle after her murder, and why that horrible experience convinced me to stop altogether.

Right now, though, having described Reverend B's initial reaction to my revelation, or confession, if you will, that I had this weird and rather strange thing that I could do with water in a bowl and a pretty blue stone, I think you need to understand why I haven't talked about my friends and my social life and all that other stuff young women my age might be expected to go on and on about.

Other than Stephen, who did double duty as my next-door neighbour, I didn't have any friends. *Don't* have friends, to be specific.

In part I guess it's because of my winning personality.

I know what I can be like. Taciturn; a little withdrawn; no sense of humour; a poor conversationalist. Just ask Quinn. He'd be happy to explain it to you.

A lot of it, though, was out of my control.

One incident stands out in my mind. One of many, but it might give you an idea of what I'm talking about.

I may have mentioned earlier that I was fourteen when Mark was killed and Quinn and I moved from Ottawa to live with Marie-Claire on Twilight Road. Quinn, naturally, didn't have any problem fitting in at his new school, but for me it was pure torture.

At my old school I'd more or less found a comfort zone where people left me alone and I left them alone and everything was more or less tolerable. Hard to believe, isn't it? Well, it was true.

My grades were always the highest in my class but I wasn't insufferable about it and I tried my best not to act like a know-it-all, so kids knew who I was, they generally respected the fact that I was smart and introverted, and they didn't bother me very much.

I may have said something earlier about how difficult it was to leave our friends and move way out here. I should clarify that I was referring specifically to Quinn and his friends. I only had acquaintances I was leaving behind. Kids who'd talk to me and not treat me like a freak. Not friends, but tolerable human beings.

Anyway, transferring to a new high school in another city was a like a hard reboot right across the board. I had to contend with new teachers who didn't know me, a longer bus ride with an unfriendly driver who didn't care if I was out there on time or not, classrooms that were hard to find and uncomfortable to sit in, and, of course, other kids whose curiosity about the weird new girl might be idle and disinterested or active and malicious, depending on the situation.

Two girls in particular quickly became the bane of my existence. They rode on the same bus I did, and both of them were already there, side by side in their usual seat, three down on the left (my right, while walking down to the back), when the bus reached the end of Twilight Road to pick me up.

Because this was the autumn before Reverend B and Stephen moved into the parsonage next door, it was just little old me out there in the middle of nowhere, waiting to go to school. (Quinn's bus always arrived about ten minutes before mine, so I was left to stand out there all by myself.) It seemed to be the main reason why the driver formed an instant dislike to me, since she had to come all the way down to the end of the road just for one kid, and it gave the other kids something to pick up on and start chafing me about.

Sarah Garrett was a typical teenage princess, with golden hair and burgeoning womanhood and a personality to match. She was the alpha, so she got the window seat. Next to her, in the aisle, was Tiffany Stewart. She didn't have Sarah's looks or winning ways or haughty disregard for the proletariat, but she did have a mean streak and an insatiable desire to please her best pal Sarah.

It didn't take long for Tiffany to establish a morning routine in which she'd say something snide as I made my way down the aisle to the back of the bus. Something clever, like "now that Hillbilly Goth's here, can we *please* get to school?"

Haw haw.

Once or twice she put her foot out into the aisle so I'd trip over it on my way past. I'd stumble, lurch into someone sitting further back, and Tiffany would lead a chorus of derision and complaint about the clumsy weirdo from Twilightland.

Funny.

I soon learned to watch for it and to step high until I was past her. Something else for everyone to find hilariously ridiculous.

It got worse, though, and more malicious, when they somehow found out about Joelle.

I knew something was off, because Tiffany fell silent for a couple of days in a row. Evidently she was trying to process the news and find a really creative and twisted way to torment me about it. I sensed that her attitude had changed, that something serious had found its way into her warped thought processes, but I wasn't getting a clear picture at first of what it might be. Besides, I did my best to ignore her anyway, so I was mostly just grateful for the break and left it at that.

After the weekend had passed, as I got on the bus the next Monday morning and edged by Tiffany, she held up a forked stick and made a loud oooing sound like a cartoon ghost. The stick looked like a dousing rod, and she waved it at me and tipped it downward as I went by. Everyone roared, but I was just puzzled.

In the afternoon, though, as we boarded the bus for the long ride home, I got a second, more specific clue. Tiffany and Sarah were already in their seat, and as I made my way back along the aisle, she held up a spoon that had been nearly bent double.

"Mama, mama, you wrecked my spoon, mama. Why did you wreck my spoon?"

Uh oh.

It only stopped because of the intervention of our art

teacher, Mr. Berezna.

I took art as an optional course because I enjoyed it and wanted to learn how to draw and paint, but some students took it because they considered it a bird course and an easy credit. Mr. Berezna was well aware of the latter bunch, and he could get rather gruff when their attitude became more than he could take.

A few days after the bent spoon stunt, we were doing life drawing in Mr. Berezna's class, and unfortunately it was my turn to serve as model. It was all very harmless, of course. We kept our clothes on, we sat down on a chair in the middle of the room (the desks in his class being arranged in a large rectangle to facilitate this sort of thing), and we struck whatever pose he told us to take and tried to hold it for as long as we could without cramping up.

Mr. Berezna happened to like the dress I was wearing that day, ankle-length with puffy sleeves, and he spent some time pointing out to the class how the material draped and creased and fell into highlighted areas and shadows and so on before turning them loose. I kept my eyes down and tried to ignore the snickers from my two best buddies, who unfortunately were also present and accounted for.

The class fell silent, which was the way Mr. Berezna wanted it, and as he circulated around the room, looking over everyone's shoulders and whispering the odd comment, I tried to let my mind wander away to someplace safe and harmless.

Unfortunately, muffled laughter eventually began to issue from the peanut gallery. Mr. Berezna was on the other side of the classroom at the time. He looked up and hissed at them, but after a while Tiffany started up again and Sarah joined in, seemingly unable to help herself. As they laughed, the boy sitting on the other side of Tiffany looked over at her drawing and snorted.

Mr. Berezna wasted no time getting around to their side of the classroom. Fists on his hips, he took one look at Tiffany's sketch and cleared his throat.

"You. You think this is funny, do you?"

She burst into helpless laughter.

A few kids on that side got up to see what was going on. Some laughed, while others shook their heads and sat down again.

One boy whose name I didn't know said, "Not funny, Tiff. Not funny at all."

Mr. Berezna tore the page from her sketch pad and marched her down to the principal's office. After ten minutes or so, during which time I escaped the centre of the room and sat down at my desk, a student clerk came up to tell the rest of us that class was dismissed.

I had geography next period, but before it finished I was called down to the office. When I arrived, a secretary showed me in and I was told to sit on a wooden chair in front of a bookcase. The principal, whose name was Mr. Crawford, nodded at me.

"This is a very unpleasant business, Madeleine, but Mr. Berezna and I feel it's important that you should be here."

"All right." I looked around quickly before dropping my eyes. Tiffany was here, sitting in a chair across from Mr. Crawford, and next to her was a middle-aged woman I thought was probably her mother.

Mr. Berezna surged forward and unfurled the offending drawing on Mr. Crawford's desk. He spun it around so that Tiffany and her mother could see it.

"This is not art," he declared, addressing himself to her mother as he stabbed at the drawing with an angry index finger. "This is not funny. This is bullying. This is harassment. This is completely unacceptable behaviour."

I took a quick look at it. She'd made a quick sketch of me in the chair before adding the body of a dead woman on the floor at my feet, a bullet hole in her head and blood pooling out everywhere. Cartoon ghosts floated around my head, laughing at me.

I felt like I was going to be sick, but I sat there and said nothing.

"I came to this country as a boy with my parents," Mr. Berezna raged, "because the majority in my homeland thought it was smart politics to carry out a pogrom against our ethnic group. I saw much death, at an age no person should ever see it. This nation is supposed to be free of such insanity, and yet constantly I encounter children like yours, Mrs. Stewart, who have absolutely no idea how lucky they are to live here. No idea how to behave with decency and respect."

"I don't understand," Mrs. Stewart said, frowning at the drawing.

"This girl," Mr. Berezna declared, pointing at me, "lost her mother in a senseless murder not even two years ago. Brutally shot. Then her father dies last year, and she's an orphan. Her mother worked with the police as some kind of a consultant, I don't know what, a psychic or whatever it was, but that doesn't matter. What matters," he picked up the drawing, balled it up, and threw it into the corner, "is that your child behaves like an unruly little monster."

He turned on Tiffany, who wouldn't meet his eyes. "You think we teachers are stupid, we don't hear things? We don't know who are the bullies and who are the victims? This girl is different, and your kind doesn't like anyone who's different. So you bully and bully and bully. It makes me sick."

"You should apologize to Madeleine," Mr. Crawford said.

Tiffany, sullen and stubborn, said nothing.

"As of now," Mr. Crawford said to Mrs. Stewart, "Tiffany is under suspension for the rest of the week. The three of us will meet again here in this office on Friday afternoon to discuss the situation further."

He looked at me. "You may return to class now, Madeleine."

I left the room as quickly as I could.

I never saw Tiffany again. Apparently several nights later she made a half-hearted attempt at suicide that was prompted more by other troubles than by her treatment of me and her subsequent suspension. After being released from hospital her parents, who were well off, put her in a private school in Brockville. I don't know where she is now, and I don't care.

Sarah Garrett, the little blond goddess, immediately found herself another seatmate. It was the boy who'd snorted at Tiffany's drawing in class. It would seem that he and Sarah were old friends.

How nice.

I haven't gone through this sad little tale of adolescent trauma to make you feel sorry for me, the poor little victim of bullying, so don't fool yourself into thinking I'm looking for sympathy, because I'm not.

I'm making a point, the same one I started with.

We're a small group, the people who understand paranormal phenomena and what they do to those of us who are cursed with the ability to perceive beyond normal, everyday experience (not so ambivalent this time, now that I've relived that nice, dark little memory).

So I wasn't surprised that Reverend B got up and

walked out on me when I tried to explain what hydromancy was and how I used it to communicate with the dead. Not really. I figured that was how it would go. What Mr. Berezna said that day has always stuck in my head, that some people don't like others who are different. And so they either passively reject them, get up and walk away, or they actively attack them with ridicule and isolation.

How does that make me feel?

Embarrassed. Guilty, in a non-specific way, of having done something wrong. And really, really depressed.

# DEVLIN

# 18

On the third Saturday in March, Devlin drove into town to do the shopping. He and Beverley took turns handling this chore, and since it was Devlin's week he got an early start, hitting the grocery store only a few minutes after it opened.

It was a cold morning, one of those downward swings in the freeze-thaw cycle that was typical of the month. Accordingly, Devin wore his winter overcoat, a black woollen toque, and gloves, all of which he removed and threw into the shopping cart as soon as he was inside.

He had a list given to him by Beverley that he needed to follow, but since it was also his turn to cook dinner tonight he intended to take his time and browse the aisles, looking for inspiration and out-of-the-ordinary ingredients, condiments, and so on.

It was the sort of thing that sometimes stretched Beverley's patience to its limits, both the shopping for odd food items and the cooking of them for their Saturday evening meal, but it gave Devlin pleasure and a break from the stress and sadness of his work, so she always cut him some slack and kept the teasing to a token minimum.

When he finally made his way through the checkout

and pushed his heavy cart outside into the parking lot, he noticed a woman ahead of him walking to her car after having deposited her shopping cart in the corral. It took a moment for him to recognize her as Brigitte Desormeaux, Maddie's aunt.

He was parked about three spots farther down, so as he drew abreast of her back bumper he stopped his cart and leaned on the handle.

"Hello, Mrs. Desormeaux."

She got in the car, shut the door, and started the engine. Only then did she lower her window a crack and look out to see who had spoken to her.

"Oh, it's you, Dr. Devlin. I didn't see you there."

Devlin came up to her window. "How are you this morning?"

"Fine, thank you. You've been shopping too, I see."

Devlin smiled. "Spending more than I should."

"Can you believe the prices of things these days? Everything's through the roof." She adjusted the heater in her car to compensate for the open window. "How's Maddie doing, do you think?"

When Devlin hesitated, she nodded. "Oh yes, that's right, you can't talk about it without her permission. I'm sorry, I should have remembered."

"We have to protect her right to privacy," Devlin said.

"Yes. Well, I think she's improved quite a bit since she started seeing you."

"I hope so."

"I suppose," she said, looking up at him, "even though you can't talk to me about her, there's no reason why *I* can't talk to *you* about her. Maybe there's things I can throw a little light on."

"If you like, Mrs. Desormeaux." He smiled. "I *am* paid

to be a good listener."

She made a face. "I don't want to waste your time. I know you're a very busy man."

"It's my morning off. I don't have an appointment until one thirty this afternoon, so I'm as free as a bird."

"Why don't you come around and sit inside where it's warmer?"

"Tell you what. Could you give me a minute to put my groceries in the car, and then we can chat for a bit?"

"That would be fine. I'm not in any hurry this morning either."

Devlin wheeled his cart down to his car and stowed his purchases in the back hatch. It gave him a moment to think about Brigitte and what she might want to tell him. He was bursting with curiosity, but it wouldn't be appropriate for him to fire a bunch of questions at her left and right. He'd have to play it by ear; proceed carefully.

He locked his car and went back to sit in Brigitte's passenger seat. She'd raised the window and cranked up the heat, so he removed his toque and gloves and unzipped his overcoat so as not to suffocate right away.

"I'm so glad she's seeing you," Brigitte started in without preamble. "Our family doctor isn't qualified for this sort of thing, even though she's very good, and the psychiatrists were useless. Pill pushers with no idea what's actually going on in her head."

"I'm glad to be able to help."

"She's a sweet child. Always has been, ever since she was a baby. Robert and I were married for two years when she was born, and I'd already had my first boy." She gave her husband's name its French pronunciation: *Robe-AIR*.

"He'd moved down here from Ottawa to start his own business a year before we married. He's an electrician, but you probably already know that. So we didn't see Joelle and Mark all that much, just holidays and so on. But I always had the impression of Maddie as a sweet, quiet child."

Devlin nodded. He'd had no idea what Robert Desormeaux did for a living, and had actually met him in person only once, at Maddie's first session. After that, the man had stayed away and it was only Brigitte that he saw.

"Robert has always had very little to do with his family," she said, as though following his train of thought. "He's not a very emotional or sentimental man. He wasn't very pleased with Joelle's psychic business, or the rest of it with the women in that family."

Devlin nodded again, trying to keep his expression neutral.

"Anyway, you don't want to know about Robert. He's quite hands-off with Joelle's children, as he was with his mother before she passed away, God rest her soul, and that's all that can be said about it. But Maddie and Quinn are very dear to me. Maddie's quite bright. You've probably noticed that."

Devlin smiled.

"All through school she was always at the top of her class. It didn't matter which subject. Science, math, social studies, reading. A very, very bright child. Joelle was so proud of her."

A car horn tooted behind them, causing Devlin to jump half out of his skin.

"Oh, she's right there out front," Brigitte groused, "you don't need to honk at her. Some old geezers; they make you wonder why they're not confined to a hospital ward somewhere."

Devlin laughed despite himself.

"She was always a very serious child as well," Brigitte

went on. "Not one to joke around at all. And she had her strange side, just like her mother and grandmother. One time, I suppose it was a year or two before Joelle died, she showed me her bowl and tried to explain what she did with it. I guess she saw the expression on my face, because she stopped and put it away and never mentioned it again after that."

She shrugged, turning to look at Devlin. "I've never been a believer in that kind of thing, the medium business and talking to the dead and finding lost people and all that. Stuff you see on TV. Not that I thought Joelle was a fraud. Don't get me wrong. She was sincere in her beliefs, even if the Church didn't agree with them. I talked to the priest about it once, after Joelle was murdered. He said it might be possible for the living to talk to the dead, with God's permission, but if it happened it would most likely be because of an evil spirit of some kind. It wasn't something safe to be doing. What do you think, Dr. Devlin?"

"I don't know anything about it," Devlin replied cautiously. "It's not something I've ever given any serious thought to."

"Well, I have." She frowned at him. "All the time. I worry that Maddie's trying to take after her mother. She worshipped her, you know. They were like this." She held up two crossed fingers. "The psychic business got Joelle killed, and I'm very worried it may have almost killed Maddie too, last fall. I don't want anything else to happen to her, especially now that her grandmother's gone too and she's all alone out there with only her little brother for company. You can help her see that, can't you? That this medium stuff is too dangerous and has to be dropped for good?"

"I don't know," Devlin answered truthfully. "All I can

tell you is that I'll do everything in my power to try to help her return to a safe and stable state of mind. There are no guarantees, of course. It's entirely up to Maddie."

Brigitte sighed. "I guess that's as much as I can hope for, under the circumstances."

"You said that you've always found Maddie to be a sweet child, although quiet and serious."

She studied him for a moment out of the corner of her eye. "Yes. What are you thinking? That something terrible happened to her, that maybe someone abused her at some point?"

Devlin said nothing.

She shook her head emphatically. "I've never *ever* had any hint from her that something like that ever happened. Not at all. I'd be able to tell. A woman can sense these things. No, you're wrong if that's what you think."

Devlin nodded. After her session last Tuesday, he'd asked Maddie to stay behind for a few minutes to complete a few tests. When she asked whether or not Aunt Brigitte would have to pay for the extra time, Devlin laughed.

"No, not at all. Beverley will make her a cup of tea and keep her company. You can take as long as you need with the tests without worrying. They're actually quite simple and shouldn't take long."

Devlin wasn't a believer in administering a lot of tests at the beginning of his relationship with a client in a scattergun approach to see what might turn up. He'd started Maddie with the absolute basics and then waited to see what specific tools he might want to use later on, depending on what cropped up as they went along.

Maddie's stories of adolescent alienation and her feelings of isolation and rejection had prompted him to ask her to complete something referred to as the Test of Self-

Conscious Affect, in its third version (TOSCA-3), which provided a quantitative measure of guilt and shame felt by the subject. The fact that she'd specifically mentioned feelings of this type had been the deciding factor in his decision to administer the test.

The TOSCA-3 consisted of multiple-choice questions that presented different scenarios and asked the patient how they would respond to them. Without referring either to guilt or shame specifically, it was intended to capture affective, cognitive, and behavioural responses associated with shame, guilt, detachment, or unconcern, or other related emotions that might be experienced by the patient in the various situations presented in the questions.

He also asked her to complete the Guilt and Shame Proneness test (GASP), a newer approach to the TOSCA measure. This test consisted of pedestrian, embarrassing scenarios in which the subject was asked to imagine themselves. For example, the test suggested a situation where the patient received too much change back from a store clerk, who didn't notice the mistake. "How uncomfortable would you feel," the question asked, "about saying nothing and keeping the money?"

He followed the GASP with the Personal Feelings Questionnaire, which presented a list of emotions, such as "regret" or "feeling stupid," and asked the patient to indicate how often they experienced each one, using a five-point scale.

That evening he analyzed her responses and reviewed his notes from her previous sessions. The measures told him that while the level of guilt Maddie seemed to be feeling was more or less in the middle range of what one might expect from a twenty-year-old young woman who'd experienced the deaths of three close family members in only a few years, her proneness to shame was somewhat higher.

This discovery sent him back to his books in order to refresh his memory on the subject. While the popular understanding of the word "shame" linked it to disgrace or dishonour resulting from an improper act or moral failure, professionals in his line of work approached shame from a somewhat different angle. A form of negative self-evaluation, it often had a non-moral focus in which the person fastened on the discrepancies between their ideal vision of themselves and their actual self. And unlike guilt, which can lead to self-punishment or attempts to fix things, shame often resulted in withdrawal, depression, anxiety, and low self-esteem.

Given Maddie's history of—

"I should let you get going," Brigitte said, breaking into his thoughts.

"Yes." Devlin stirred, pulling his toque on and zipping up his overcoat.

"She never told me what happened in that old folks' home with that man last fall," Brigitte said, "but it wasn't molestation, that's for sure. I'm told he was comatose the whole time she was there. It had to do with this psychic paranormal stuff she believes in so much. She needs you, doctor. She needs your help to get away from it for good."

"I'll help her as best I can," Devlin replied, opening the car door, "but in the end it'll be Maddie's choice. She has to decide how to move on from whatever happened last fall."

"I know." Brigitte brushed away a tear. "She's a strong one, that girl. I just don't know if she's strong enough this time."

# 19

On the third Tuesday in March, Devlin went for a walk in the garden after breakfast. The morning air was fresh, and the sky was once more a cheerful blue. Beverley came with him, and as they strolled along the stone pathway behind the house, she chattered about the column she was currently writing.

She was the spirits critic for a popular food-and-drink-themed magazine, and she'd been researching a local distillery whose products had recently been made available to the public through the provincially-run liquor retail chain. She thought their vodka was particularly good but had taken a dislike to the owner, who came across to her as arrogant and overbearing. As a result, she was struggling to remain objective enough to write a piece that would be positive toward the vodka.

Since Devlin was a good listener, both in training and in disposition, he enjoyed the fact that she frequently used him as a sounding board for her ideas and opinions. They'd been married almost ten years now, and given that they'd decided not to have children and had mostly fallen out of contact with what was left of their families, they'd grown very close.

She was several centimetres taller than he was and filled with an unlimited supply of nervous energy. As they made their way along the winding path toward the little orchard at the back of their five-acre property on the island portion of Kilmarnock, a few kilometres east of Smiths Falls, she was forced several times to stop and wait for him to catch up so that he could hear what she was saying. Years ago she'd stopped trying to get him to keep up with her and had accepted the fact that he was a slow walker, and so her initial impatience had faded into amused tolerance of his ways.

"I was saying," she said, pretending to be irritated, "that I'd hate to trash his stuff and then run into him in the Walmart."

"That could be awkward," Devlin agreed.

"After all, the bottom line is whether or not the product's good enough for people to spend their money on."

"Do you think it is, Beverley? Is that your final verdict?"

She nodded over her shoulder at him, already a step ahead once again. "Price point's a bit high, but for a boutique outfit they're doing a really nice job. It mixes well, and it has some very good afternotes that the sipping crowd will like."

"Sounds like you've already written your column."

She laughed. "Yeah. Almost done." She pulled back her coat sleeve to check her watch. "Your client's due in about twenty minutes. We should probably go back inside."

"Yes." He stopped and turned, waiting for her to move alongside him again.

"She seems to be doing a lot better now," she said.

Devlin nodded. He never discussed his clients with her, again because of confidentiality restrictions, but as his receptionist and administrative assistant Beverley greeted everyone when they arrived for their appointments, she made small talk with them according to their mood and preference, and she was intelligent enough—more than intelligent enough!—to reach her own conclusions about whether or not they were making progress from session to session.

"She's a nice kid." Beverley opened the door and held it for him.

"I agree."

Back in his office, he glanced through his notes until Maddie arrived. Settled into their usual chairs in the consultation room, they exchanged small talk about the weather outside, but Devlin sensed immediately that she was chafing at the bit to get down to business.

"What would you like to talk about today, Maddie?"

"All week I thought about those tests you got me to do."

"Did they upset you?"

She nodded. "At first I didn't take them seriously. I mean, some of the situations they posited were pretty trivial. 'While playing with a friend you throw a ball and it hits her in the face.' Seriously? But after a while, I saw they were trying to figure out whether I felt guilty about what happened, or ashamed that maybe I'd messed up and wasn't the right person to do what needed to be done, and it made me a little mad, I guess. I don't think it's fair to make those kinds of assumptions based on a bunch of silly scenarios."

"And you'd like to set the record straight?"

She gave him a look. "Yes, Dr. Devlin. I'd like to set the record straight."

He spread his hands. "That's what we're here for,

Maddie."

"All right. Fine. That's fine with me. Then I need to get right to the things that happened at the church, and in the graveyard, that led to all this . . . turmoil. And I need to talk about Reverend B. More specifically."

Devlin crossed his legs. "Ready when you are."

# MADDIE

# 20

The day after Reverend B walked out on me while I was trying to explain hydromancy and what I did, I went into town to buy groceries. It was a Friday and a little busy in town. I had a list with me, and I stopped at several stores to hunt around for the things I was looking for. I was trying to improve my cooking a bit so that Quinn and I would have some healthy variations in our diet besides the usual cardboard and grease I normally threw together. I'd saved a few recipes from the Internet that looked both tasty and easy to make, so I had to drive around to several stores, chasing down all the ingredients I needed.

It was a nice fall day, so on the way home I took my time, driving up and down the back roads that would eventually take me to Bennett's Corners. It never ceased to amaze me that you couldn't drive in a straight line around here, either east-west or north-south, to get from point A to point B. It was like following the zigzag stitching on a seam finish. When the nineteenth-century brain trust first surveyed the land around here, they moved inland in a direction that was perpendicular to the shore of the St. Lawrence River, which of course ran diagonally from Lake Ontario to the Atlantic Ocean, southwest to northeast, instead of orienting themselves in a north-south direction which, I don't know, might have made sense to some of us coming along two centuries later.

Whatever, right? Drive thirty kilometres to get to somewhere twenty kilometres away. It helps pass the time, I guess, despite chewing up more expensive gasoline than necessary.

As I drove through the Corners and went by the new church, I thought about Reverend B. I still felt bad about what had happened, and I regretted showing her the bowl and explaining what I did and what my ability was, but I didn't feel as though I'd had a choice. She'd asked, after all.

The afternoon sun flickered through the trees as I drove, reminding me of the day I'd taken Stephen to his doctor's appointment. And, of course, the woman I'd seen in the water bowl in his kitchen afterward, the same one I'd seen later in the bathroom. She hadn't appeared to me since, but I knew she was somehow connected to the hidden bedroom on the third floor of the parsonage. Had she died up there? Was her ghost somehow trapped in the house, desperate to be released so she could cross over to the other side?

As I approached the parsonage, I saw that the little red flag was raised on the Northrop mailbox. Canada Post had already made their run down Twilight Road, dropping off something for Reverend B. I couldn't see if the flag was up on our mailbox. Not that I was expecting anything.

The door of the parsonage suddenly flew open and Reverend B ran outside with something in her hands. I hit the brakes. She ran across her front lawn to the church, carrying a fire extinguisher.

I turned into the little gravel space in front of the

church. Killing the engine, I jumped out.

"Reverend B! What is it?"

"Fire!" she shouted over her shoulder, running up the front steps.

I ran up and took the fire extinguisher from her as she fumbled with her keys. The front door was secured with a padlock and chain, put there by Matt Pollock when the church had been judged to be unsafe to enter. She tried a key in the lock and it was the wrong one. Groaning, she frantically sorted through the others on the ring.

*Goddamn you! Goddamn you to hell, you worthless, faithless bastard!*

I was shocked. It was a man's voice, deep and echoing, coming from inside the church. "Did you hear that?"

"Yes! And I saw flames in the window from my kitchen. It's burning down!"

Just as she'd feared, I thought, watching her find the right key. Now the trustees could make their insurance claim and be rid of this albatross for good.

She removed the padlock and stripped off the chain.

"Stay back," she said, reaching for the fire extinguisher.

"Be careful. It's dangerous."

She threw open the heavy double doors and stepped across the threshold.

Pigeons startled from the floor and flew up into the rafters.

Late afternoon sunlight streamed diagonally from the west-facing windows, tinted with colours from the stained glass, crossing the floor and highlighting the holes where several boards had broken through. A rodent of some kind stirred in the shadows deep in the back corner.

The pews, altar, and other fittings had been removed

long ago, refurbished and installed in the new church at the Corners, so the interior was empty from one wall to the other.

Silence.

Reverend B lowered the fire extinguisher, her jaw slack.

No fire.

"It looks okay," I said.

"I saw it. I looked out the window at the church and I saw the flames. I heard the screaming, and I heard the man's voice cursing like an insane person. I did!"

I was going to say that she may have seen sunlight glowing in the windows and thought it was fire, but the windows she would have been looking at were east-facing, on the opposite side of the building from the sun.

And nothing rational could explain the voice, which I'd also just heard.

She shouldered past me and stood on the little porch outside, at the top of the stairs. She let out a scream and threw the fire extinguisher as far as she could pitch it. It bounced on the lawn and rolled away. Then she sat down on the top step and began to cry.

I sat down next to her. I wasn't sure what to say, so I just kept my mouth shut until her crying became sobbing and her sobs became deep breathing.

"I'm sorry," she finally said.

"You don't have anything to be sorry for."

"Yes, I do. I've treated you horribly."

"No you haven't."

"Yes, I have." She ran a hand through her dishevelled hair. "I'm exhausted. I haven't slept properly since we found that room. When I do fall asleep, I have horrible dreams. Obscene dreams. I couldn't describe them to you.

They're too vulgar and awful and repulsive."

"That's terrible," I said.

"I can't read," she went on. "I can't work, I can't think. John Pollock called last night to tell me he'd heard from church administration in Toronto that they may close the new church down and sell off all the assets. I don't know what to do. Should I be glad? Should I just get out of here? With Stephen overseas and planning to find an apartment in Ottawa when he comes home, I have nothing here to hold me if they disband this congregation and send everyone into town. I don't know what to do."

"Quinn and I would hate to see you leave."

"I know." She wiped her eyes with the back of her hand. "I think I'm going insane."

"No," I said.

She turned to look at me. "How would you explain this, then? You with your water-mancy and flying through the astral planes and somehow discovering mysterious hidden bedrooms? How would *you* explain it?"

"I don't know. There's something wrong."

"Oh, *that's* an understatement." She went silent for a moment before sighing. "I'm sorry. I'm taking this out on you. I shouldn't." She looked at me again. "I'm sorry."

"It's all right. I don't mind. I understand."

"I saw fire. Flames inside the church. It was burning. It wasn't my imagination or a weird reflection in the windows. It was fire."

"I believe you," I said.

She stood up and shoved her hands into the pockets of her jeans. "There *is* something wrong. Something terribly wrong here. Something connected to this woman you say you keep seeing."

"I think so," I said, not wanting to venture into anything

more than that right now. She was still upset, and I didn't want to provoke her into lashing out at me again. It was hurtful. I looked up to her, really valued her opinion of me, and I felt like it was all being put at risk.

"You could use that bowl of yours to find out what's going on."

"Maybe," I said.

She nodded and started down the stairs. "We'll see. But let's try it my way first."

# 21

John Pollock lived in a large stone house on Buttermilk Road that had been built by the same Irish stonemasons who'd worked on the construction of the Rideau Canal in the 1820s. The back summer kitchen had been renovated years ago into a comfortable living space, and it was here that Pollock showed us into a sitting room with a fire burning in a fireplace, big comfortable chairs, and a wide-screen television tuned to the CBC news channel.

He muted the volume and, after we'd gotten settled and Reverend B had been served coffee and biscuits (nothing for me, thanks), Reverend B got right down to business.

"We've been doing a little research on the early history of the church," she said. "Maddie's doing a paper on it and I'm helping her with some of the background material."

"I see." He looked at me. "A paper, you say."

"For a Canadian history course," I fibbed. Rural churches in eastern Ontario. I figured, since I live right next door to one, it'd be a natural."

Pollock grunted, unimpressed.

"We went online this afternoon," Reverend B said, "looking up tax records for the property and all that. From what I could find, the land originally belonged to a man named David Bennett. An Irish Catholic from County Armagh. He emigrated in the 1880s and converted to Protestantism when he married his wife, Emily Porter, in 1894."

Pollock nodded, sipping his coffee. I couldn't tell if he actually knew any of this stuff or was just pretending he did.

"The big stone house down at the Corners is where they lived," she continued, "but he owned all the land right up to the end of Twilight Road on the north side. In 1900 he donated the lot the church was built on and paid for the construction of the church itself in 1901, entirely out of his own pocket."

"Is that so. You read all that on the Internet?"

"Yes." Reverend B gave him her sweetest smile. "It's amazing what you can find online these days."

"It's all garbage. Pornography and hate."

"Well, yes, there is a lot of that, but if you avoid those sites and use the safe search settings, you're generally okay. Stephen has had a lot of good use from it while researching his homework and school projects. And that's what we've been doing, Maddie and I."

He eyed me. "Not sure then how I can help you. I don't use a computer."

While Reverend B had been talking, I'd been looking around the room. There was a large photograph of Mrs. Pollock above the fireplace that seemed particularly disturbing. I could feel her eyes drilling into me and her scratchy old lady's voice intoning, *"Mene, mene, tekel upharsin"* or some similar disgusted condemnation of my worthless self.

I dragged my attention back to him and tried to match Reverend B's smile. Taking my notebook and a pen from my bag, I opened it on my knee and tried to look intelligent.

"I'd like to be able to include short sketches of the various parsons who were installed at the church during its history," I said. "I think the first one was, uh," I glanced down at my notes, "Ephraim Hope. He was personally recruited by David Bennett in 1908, as I understand it."

"Before my time."

Well, duh.

"He passed away in 1919," I went on, "the same year as Bennett, both in the Spanish flu pandemic, I guess it was. They're buried in the churchyard next door to the parsonage."

"That would be correct. Their monuments are prominent features of the cemetery."

"Reverend Hope's replacement was a man named John Prince. He was the pastor for fourteen years, until 1934. He's not buried in the churchyard though, is he?"

Pollock shook his head. "He went back to Nova Scotia, where he was from, and died there a few years later. My parents were married by him a few months before he left. My father always spoke highly of him."

"What kind of person was he, Mr. Pollock?"

He shrugged. "Can't say, having never known him myself. Father described him as a quiet, intellectual type. He wrote articles for a magazine published by the church."

"Is that right?" I made a note. "I'll look it up."

Pollock grunted.

"After the Depression, during World War Two, it was Warren Joiner."

"Baptized me."

"Do you remember him at all?"

"No. I was seven when he died. Two years after the end

of the war. He's out in the old cemetery close by Reverend Hope. His wife's buried there, too. Nice folks, so I'm told. Their kids went off somewhere when they grew up. England, I think it was. To help with the rebuilding."

I jotted it down. So far I wasn't getting anything useful from him, but I would want to find a picture of Mrs. Joiner to make sure she wasn't the woman I'd seen.

"Then there was Richard Wallerson during the fifties," I said, "and Donald Dryson during the sixties."

"Dryson married me and Theresa. An old fart, a widower. Made model ships in his spare time."

I suppressed a smile at his description of the pastor as an old fart. It took one to know one, as far as I was concerned. "And Reverend Wallerson?"

"Nice fellow. Great sense of humour. Popular with everyone in the congregation. Got himself hit by a delivery truck while he was on vacation in Toronto. Snapped his neck and killed him instantly. Everyone was pretty upset."

"I'm sorry to hear it. After that, it was Seymour Blackburn, wasn't it?"

Pollock's face went blank, as though steel shutters had dropped into place. "Rather not talk about him."

Reverend B leaned forward. "Why's that, Mr. Pollock?"

"Trouble hung around him like a black cloud. Him and that sexton he brought in. Tulk."

"I see. Why is that?"

Looking at her, I couldn't read anything into Reverend B's expression, but I could tell she was picking up a thread she thought might be worth following. I eased back, letting her take the lead.

"Rather not say. I wasn't a trustee at the time." He stared at her. "Matter of fact, that's what decided me to step up and take on the burden of responsibility after they were gone. Needed to clean up the mess left behind by that pair."

"What can you tell us about him? Reverend Blackburn?"

Pollock drained his coffee cup and set it down. He stared at his wife's portrait for a long moment before nodding to himself. His lips barely moved as he whispered, "All right."

I couldn't imagine why the memory of this particular pastor upset him when none of the others had, but I had a premonition that we were about to find out.

Not a figurative premonition, okay? A real one. What the dictionary would define as a presentiment of the future.

What I would call, in more personal terms, a feeling of certainty, based on no specific fact or reasoning, that Pollock was about to take me down a road I couldn't pretend later that I'd never walked. And along with that sense of certainty was a layer of dread.

I didn't want to travel down this path. I knew it without understanding why.

# 22

"He came to us from out west," Pollock said. "Saskatchewan. Originally from Weyburn, I believe it was, where he first entered the ministry in the mid-sixties. Then he moved to a church in North Battleford in, ah, I think it was 1970. He left after five years and was living in Regina when he saw our ad in the church newsletter. I made a few calls out there when we were considering his application, and I thought at the time the trustees I talked to were a little tight-lipped, but we were in a bit of a spot and needed a pastor after Reverend Dryson passed away and, well, there he was. No one else had applied for the job, so we were glad he was interested."

"What was he like?" Reverend B asked.

"Young. About thirty-five or so when he came to us. Single. Handsome and dashing, with wavy black hair and those bushy sideburns—mutton chops, they called them back then—and a bare upper lip. Very popular with the ladies. A little odd, though."

"Oh? How so?"

Pollock thought about it for a moment. "Secretive. Used rough language on occasion, which surprised all of us and shocked the older ones. Not particularly careful with his personal grooming or hygiene. Things like that."

He saw the look on my face. "You need to understand, young lady, that this was the late seventies, and while the psychedelic revolution was still going on, to be sure, a rural church congregation is a pretty conservative enclave at any time, let alone back then when most of the parishioners were elderly or getting close to it."

He shrugged. "I was only thirty-five when he settled in, and *I* thought he was beyond the pale."

I figured Pollock had probably been *born* a crotchety old man, but I kept my thoughts to myself.

"You mentioned something about his sexton," Reverend B prompted.

"Name of Tulk. Jack Tulk. Belinda, you've never seen the like. The trustees at the time were tied in knots by the guy. Six months after Blackburn convinced them to hire him on as sexton, they voted to dismiss him. Blackburn turned around and took him on as a personal assistant, so we were all stuck with the man. Took him into the parsonage to live with him. Didn't remember that right away, when Matt asked about boarders. I was thinking more about someone from town, which was frowned on. So that upstairs bedroom we found might have been his."

"I don't understand. Why was this Tulk seen as such a problem?"

Pollock shook his head. "Bad business. Don't like to talk about it. Blackburn found him down in Kingston, fresh out of the pen after serving what's known today as sexual assault but back then was rape, pure and simple. Blackburn insisted he was a reclamation project, a chance for us to participate in the rehabilitation of a repentant ex-con who only needed a fresh start in life. Some of the trustees swallowed it whole, but I couldn't see it, myself."

"What—"

"I'm sorry Belinda," he interrupted. "It took me years to get the stink of that pair out of my daily thoughts, and I really don't want to have to go back over it again, if you don't mind."

"Of course. My apologies. Just one more question, though. Reverend Blackburn died in 1993, didn't he? I've seen his headstone in the old cemetery."

Pollock nodded. "Strange and horrible, the whole thing."

"In what way?"

He made an unpleasant face. "Wood chipper. We had one on the property at the time, to clear away brush behind the graveyard and the parsonage that was creeping in and making a mess. Our sexton, the one we hired to replace Tulk, cut down a lot of the trees and shrubs, but Tulk chased him off before he could clean it all up. Apparently Reverend Blackburn decided to work the chipper himself and had an accident. A long branch pulled him in and, before he could let go, it mangled up his head pretty bad. Didn't see it myself, but they said it was gruesome. You couldn't hardly tell it was him."

"What happened to Tulk?"

"Took off. Blackburn lay there for two days before his body was found. That's what the police said. Tulk was never seen or heard from again. Might be dead by now. Only God knows for sure. That's all, if you don't mind. I'm tired, and it's time I took my evening sleep medication."

Reverend B stood up. I put my notebook and pen away and followed her to the door.

Pollock opened it and blocked my way with his arm. "None of that stuff is for your essay, understand?"

Reverend B turned around. "We understand, Mr.

Pollock."

He looked at me.

"Of course," I said. "I completely understand."

Outside, as we got in the car, I glanced back and saw that Pollock was still watching us through the curtain, a dark silhouette in a window half-obscured by the yellow reflection of the porch light.

# 23

The next morning, a Saturday, was the first day of October. I woke up tired, not having slept very well the night before. I drank my first cup of coffee before I was really aware of it going down the hatch. I made a second one, put on a sweater coat that had belonged to Marie-Claire, and went outside.

It was a cool morning. The air had a bit of snap to it, and I could see patches of light frost on the grass that would disappear once the sun cleared the treeline and got to work. I went around the side of the house, looking at the perennials that would have to be cut down and mulched for winter. I wasn't a big gardening nut, but if I saved it for the right time it could be relaxing and, well, therapeutic.

Quinn was sleeping in. Later in the morning, a friend was coming around with his parents to pick him up and take him to a movie in town. It must be nice to have friends. He's that way, though, easy going and popular with his classmates. Not sullen and withdrawn like his big sister.

Approaching the back corner of the house, I glanced over at the churchyard and was surprised to see Reverend B out there, walking among the tombstones. Curious, I set off across the lawn to see what she was up to.

Looking down at a clipboard in her hand, she was completely engrossed in what she was reading.

"Good morning!" I called out.

She startled, her head jerking up and her hand fumbling the clipboard. "Oh, my! Oh! It's you, Maddie."

"Good morning, Reverend B. Sorry, I didn't mean to scare the crap out of you."

"That's all right." She wiped at her brow with the back of her hand. "Lost in thought, I guess."

"Something I can help you with?"

"No. Actually, yes. Why not?" She passed the clipboard to me. "I'm locating all the plots and making a list of headstones that are missing or damaged and need repair. It's a task I've put off for several years."

"Isn't that something Matt Pollock should do? I mean, he's the sexton."

She smiled that sad little smile of hers. "I know, but I told him a long time ago it was something I'd take care of. I wouldn't feel right giving it back to him when it's something I'm perfectly capable of doing myself if I stop procrastinating."

I nodded. Vandals had hit the graveyard a few years before Quinn and I moved in with Marie-Claire, and while a few of the broken headstones had been dragged to the back of the cemetery out of the way, others still lay on the ground where they'd been toppled. Matt had simply been cutting the grass around them every summer, waiting for Reverend B to do her thing.

"Okay," I said. "Where are you at?"

"Well, this next plot is missing a marker." She pointed at a patch of ground with only a cement stub on it. "I was just trying to figure out whose grave it is when you . . ."

"Scared the crap out of you. Sorry. Let's see." After

studying the plot map for a moment, I looked around to orient myself among the names on nearby headstones.

Aha! I stabbed my finger at the page. "Here. Carson Bennett."

She took a look for herself and then nodded.

"All right. David Bennett's son, I believe. Let's see if it's here." She led the way through the graveyard. Years after Reverend Blackburn's untimely demise, shrubs and saplings had once again begun to encroach at the back, and dead leaves and weeds covered most of the stones and fragments that had been left there. We got down on our hands and knees, hunting for Carson Bennett's marker.

Most of the ones I found were fragments, with only part of a name or an inscription. I'm not a cemetery freak by any means, but I felt myself getting upset by the senseless damage and disrespect to the dead that the anonymous vandals had shown. They were probably grown up by now, married with young kids, maybe moved away to somewhere else, never regretting their blatant stupidity or even giving it the slightest thought.

Morons.

"Here it is." Reverend B dragged a chunk of flat stone out from under a bush and wiped the detritus from its surface.

I went over and crouched down beside her. The inscription identified it as the headstone of Carson Bennett, 1903–. The stone was broken diagonally, and the rest was missing.

"The other half's here," Reverend B said, forcing her fingers under the corner of another slab. Grunting, she got both hands under it and pulled. It budged a few centimetres and stopped.

I scrambled around and found the top edge. Working

my fingers under it, I managed to lift it a tiny bit. "Pull."

She pulled. It left its groove in the soil and came out. "Yes, this is the rest of it. The bigger half. It weighs a ton."

"What do you want to do with it?"

She sat back on her haunches. "I want to move all of them back onto the proper plots. Then I'll have Matt call the monuments service in town and get them to come out. There's money that's been sitting in the budget for a while now to have them repaired and put back in place." She winked at me. "So that's what I'll do. Spend that money!"

I went back for Marie-Claire's old wheelbarrow, and together we wrestled the larger piece into it. I pushed while Reverend B navigated with the clipboard, and once we were back at Carson Bennett's plot, we eased it out onto the ground and made the return trip for the other chunk.

Next on Reverend B's list was the headstone for Clarissa Porter, 1879-1963. It was a smaller stone, still intact, so once we found her plot on the chart we were able to bring up the marker with much less effort.

As we gently lowered it to the ground, Reverend B said, "I think this is the sister of Emily Porter, the wife of David Bennett." She pointed to the portion of the inscription that identified Clarissa as the daughter of James Porter and Lucinda Johnson.

I wandered over to David Bennett's monument, which dominated the graveyard as Mr. Pollock had said. On one side, marking the grave of his wife, the inscription referred to the same parents.

"You're right," I said, coming back to take command of the wheelbarrow for another trip. "Emily Porter's sister. Two years younger."

"There's a lot of history in cemeteries like these," she said, following me toward the back. "Especially the little rural ones. They document the settlement of the township, the family alliances and intermarriages, the hopes and dreams of immigrants in a new world."

"That's very poetic," I said over my shoulder.

"I suppose so." She caught up to me. "Let's do one more and then take a break. I'm getting a little tired."

The next candidate was a stone for Lily Tennant, 1918-1980, daughter of Robert Tennant and Jane Robinson, wife of Charles Peabody. It was a small marker, just large enough to accommodate the inscription, and I was able to pick it up and put it in the wheelbarrow without needing Reverend B's help.

While I was doing that, she knelt down to pick up a hunk of stone that looked like a corner piece. "I think I know where this is from."

She followed me to the plot we'd identified from the chart as belonging to Lily Tennant. I hefted the stone and gently laid it down on the grass.

In the distance, thunder rumbled.

"Storm's coming," I said.

"Funny," she replied, "I checked the forecast this morning and it's supposed to be clear and sunny all day. Oh well. That's Environment Canada for you." She started off across the cemetery.

I followed her to the headstone for Reverend Blackburn.

"See?" She held up the chunk. The engraved border, with its decorative knot in the corner and top portion of the capital letter N, matched a missing piece on the corner of Blackburn's headstone. I hadn't even noticed the damage before, but Reverend B had obviously seen it and remembered.

She checked the fit. It matched.

"I'll add it to the list of repairs." She turned away as thunder rumbled again across the sky, much louder this time. "I think—"

The ground began to shake.

For the first few seconds it was a distinct tremor, enough to make us both stagger. Then it was a violent shaking that threw me sideways, off my feet. I hit the ground and lay stunned for a moment, the wind knocked out of me.

Reverend B was shouting. I couldn't tell what she was saying.

I rolled onto my side, gasping. The parsonage was visibly shaking. I saw the satellite dish on the roof jump up out of its mooring and tumble down onto the ground. A window shattered.

After a few moments the waves began to ebb. I was able to get to my hands and knees, my breath thankfully coming back.

Reverend B was sitting on the ground, one leg tucked under her and the other extended straight out. Her mouth was open in shock, and she stared at me with wide, horrified eyes.

"It just missed me! It nearly killed me!"

"Are you all right?" I got up and staggered over to her.

She pointed.

I saw the chunk from Blackburn's headstone lying on the ground four or five metres away.

"It flew right off! I mean it didn't fall because of the shaking. It flew right off! Right at my head! Like a missile! It nearly killed me!"

I said nothing. She clearly believed this was what had happened.

Maybe Reverend B was starting to understand the world in which I lived, every single day of my life.

# 24

That evening after supper there was a knock at the front door. I let Reverend B in and led the way into the living room, where Quinn was stretched out on the couch, scribbling away in his sketchbook with his pastels.

"According to Environment Canada," she said, sitting down in a rocker in front of the bay window, "there was no earthquake today. Not in our area, not in eastern Ontario, not anywhere. Nothing."

I nodded, having already checked it out myself online.

"Matt came around and boarded up the broken window. He was his usual diplomatic self. They won't be able to replace the satellite dish for almost a week, though."

She bared her teeth. "So what the hell was that, anyway?"

"I don't know." I was surprised, a little shocked, that she had allowed herself to use harsh language. It was out of character for her, and a measure of how upset she really was.

"I don't understand what's happening. I know I keep saying that, but it's true." She wrung her hands, staring at me. "I know I said we'd try it my way. We did the research, looked into the background of the church and its pastors, all of that. We could look through the stuff in the attic for photographs of women, to see if you recognized any of them as the one you've seen in your visions or whatever, but that would mean acknowledging that you have this," she waved her hand around, "ability that's non-rational, that's paranormal. Extra-sensory. However you'd describe it. Is that where we are now?"

I looked at Quinn. His eyes were on his sketch book and his pastel was moving steadily as he drew his picture, but he was clearly listening. I was about to make a decision in which he had a stake, I knew, but I was going to make it regardless of what he might say, because I knew it had to be done.

"Yes, Reverend B. That's where we are."

"I see." She turned to Quinn. "You apparently fly around at night, young man. Your sister described it, but I'd like to hear about it from you yourself."

Quinn kept his eyes down, but his hand stopped moving. "Not much to tell. It's hard to explain."

"Maddie says you travel around on astral planes or other dimensions or some sort of thing like that."

"Yes."

"And that's how you knew the hidden room was there? You somehow learned about it while travelling around in the mystic beyond?"

"Yeah. Basically."

"Okay." She leaned forward, clasped her hands between her knees, and drew a deep breath. "Let's say I'm willing to . . . consider that there might be some truth to all this. Can you do your astral travelling thing and see what's going on right now? Find an explanation for the things I've been experiencing over there and all the things your sister says she's seeing?"

"No, Reverend. It doesn't work that way."

"Then how does it work?"

The sharpness in her voice brought his eyes up. He swung around on the couch and put down his sketchbook and pastel. "I don't have any control over it. Not right now. I need to find a yogi who can teach me what to do, but that's not going to happen around here, is it? In Smiths Falls? And it's not something you can just learn on the Internet."

He clasped his hands together. "We have five different bodies, all layered together in what they call sheaths. There's our physical sheath on the outside, and there's the energy sheath that runs all through it, what they call the *pranamaya kosha*. That's where all our vital energy is, what they call *prana*. There's also the mental sheath where our regular thoughts and knowledge and stuff are kept. Then there's the *anadamaya kosha*, what they call the bliss body, but I don't really understand exactly what that is. Where we reach a state of complete peace, or something. I don't know. I'm not explaining this very well."

"You said five bodies."

"Yeah. The other one is a sheath they often call the astral body. It's like a layer of transitory energy, I guess. That's how they describe it in everything I read. They say it's a combination of being smart and having a lot of intuition. I don't understand that, either. I just know this is the part of myself that's supposed to separate from the other sheaths when I travel."

"I see."

"It happens sometimes when I fall asleep. Instead of dreaming, I feel myself lifting up and I see myself in bed, asleep, and I go through the ceiling and the roof up into the sky like I'm flying through clouds. When I begin to travel to the astral planes, it's like I'm passing through skies of different colours. I think the colours mean different spheres. I can see different things, depending on where I am. Some spheres I only feel things, like someone is hugging me and telling me they love me, people I can't see properly but I think I know. Not Maman, though. Maybe Mémère is one of them. Anyway, on other levels I see . . . people, I guess you'd say. Not people I know, just different people."

He held up the sketchbook so that she could see what he'd been drawing. "She told me her name's Benedicta. I see her when I travel to the cyan sphere. At least, that's what I call it. Because it's all bluish-green."

"Blessed one," Reverend B murmured, looking at the sketch.

"Pardon?"

"Benedicta. It's a Latin name, Quinn. It means 'blessed one.' A benediction is a blessing."

"Okay. I wondered if she was an angel." Quinn put the sketchbook down, biting his lower lip. "I'm not sure, though."

"Well, I believe there are angels. If that makes you feel any better."

Quinn tried to smile and almost made it.

"Has she told you what's going on here, Quinn? Has she explained it?"

He shook his head. "She mostly asks questions. Like she wanted to know a lot about Maddie. And last night," he hesitated, "she asked about you."

Reverend's B's jaw dropped. "What? Why?"

He shrugged. "Just if I liked you, if you were nice to Maddie and me, that sort of stuff."

"Good heavens." Reverend B sat back. "But this . . . Benedicta hasn't told you what this is all about?"

"No. Nobody ever explains anything to me. Not yet, anyway. I guess it's because I'm just a kid. Same treatment as I get around here in my waking life."

I rolled my eyes at him.

Reverend B crossed her arms. "So you don't have any idea why there's a hidden room in the parsonage that makes me feel so horrible when I go near it? Why I saw a fire in the church when there was none? Why there was an earthquake that didn't actually happen, even though it caused real damage, and why a piece of stone almost took my damned head off? You don't know anything about any of this?"

Quinn stopped chewing on his lip long enough to shake his head.

She looked at me. "But you do, don't you, Maddie?"

# 25

I'd already tried once to explain to Reverend B what my ability was and how it worked, and I expect you remember how that went. I didn't see her for a couple of days afterward, during which time she was no doubt working through a deep funk about the wacko next door and trying to make up her mind whether or not just to ignore me for the rest of her life.

But now that she'd had several upsetting paranormal experiences of her own, incidents she couldn't explain away—or pray away, I guess—she was frustrated and frightened enough to try one more time to get some kind of rational explanation from dear little Maddie as to what was going on. Since I seemed to know more about it than she did.

And wasn't running around in circles yelling and screaming like some fool blonde in a low-budget horror movie.

So, fine. I'd take another shot.

There was no way, though, that I was going to go through the history of the iron pot with her. Trying to explain who I was through a crash course in genealogy with a little genetics thrown in on the side wasn't going to penetrate the wall she'd built up around herself.

Besides, I wasn't interested in another round of disapproving body language from her. Despite what test scores may say now about my proneness to shame, blah blah, I was never, ever ashamed of my ability to communicate with the dead.

Never!

Scared to death of it, yeah.

But never ashamed of what I could do.

As I think I mentioned before, the visions of dead people only began to come to me with the onset of puberty. I have no idea what the connection might be between these two lovely and delightful phenomena, and I don't really care very much right now. I'll think about that some other time.

They began as glimpses of unfamiliar faces in mud puddles and cereal bowls. I'd be walking down the sidewalk in the rain, and just as I was about to stroll through a puddle in my rubber boots I'd see someone looking up at me. Scared the living bejesus out of me.

It began to get serious at our cottage in the Gatineaus. I couldn't go near the water without hearing voices and seeing faces in the waves. Their eyes would sparkle with reflected sunlight. I felt like I was in some kind of incredibly strange production of *The Tempest*, with all these dead people undergoing a sea change right before my eyes. I began to insist that they let me stay at home instead of going up there with them until Joelle sat me down and got me to spill the beans.

There was something, though, that happened, that I still feel upset about when I think back on it, but it led to Joelle trying to help me get control over what was going on.

I'd been asking her questions about her consultation work with the police. A magazine article had recently appeared featuring her as a psychic medium who'd built up an impressive record of successful interventions in missing person cases, and after reading it I wanted her to tell me all about it.

At first she was reluctant to get into it with me, I guess because it was reflexive for her to protect her family from unwanted and often negative attention, but I continued to prod her and she eventually relented.

She told me about a case she was currently working on with Detective Constable Patrice Rogers of the Ontario Provincial Police. A child, a young boy of four, had gone missing from his home on Norway Lake, just north of Calabogie, which was about one hundred kilometres west of Ottawa. Patrice had interviewed his parents, who were both low-income seasonal workers, and they told the same story. The boy had disappeared from his bedroom on a Sunday morning, never to be seen again.

A search was conducted of the surrounding back pastures and woods, and the lake had been dragged, but there was no sign of him. There were several outbuildings on the property, holdovers from a time when a previous owner had raised beef cattle, but he wasn't found in any of them. He'd been adopted as an infant because the father, whose name I won't mention, was sterile, so there were no brothers or sisters to provide helpful suggestions about where he might have gone.

After several days, Patrice became increasingly worried that the boy would be suffering from hunger and exposure, so she asked Joelle if she'd be willing to help. Once she heard the particulars of the case, she reluctantly agreed.

She went to the house on Norway Lake, which was little

more than a shack, and talked to the parents. She patted their dog, an enormous German shepherd that normally was unfriendly with strangers, she watched the feral cats run back and forth around the stacks of firewood, and she stood in the boy's bedroom for a long time, trying to get a sense of who he was.

Later on I can talk a little bit more about how Joelle worked if it's relevant to what I need to say here, but for now I'll just explain that she didn't use props of any kind, like crystals or stuff belonging to the missing person or whatever. She didn't use a dowsing rod (sorry, Tiffany) or a pendulum or any other such device. She merely relaxed, concentrated, and waited for an image of the missing person to appear in her mind. That was how she described it to me, at least.

She went twice to Norway Lake without success.

When she described the situation to me, I said, "Maybe the little boy's dead."

"It could be, dear. I have much better luck sensing the living."

"Maybe I could try."

She rejected the idea out of hand. We still didn't know what it was exactly that I was doing, but we'd figured out at least that it was some sort of necromancy, communication with the dead. Just the same, there was no way she was going to involve me in police business. No way.

The case dragged on. I asked her several times about it. Finally, she was waiting to be picked up by Patrice for yet another trip out to Norway Lake when I came out and stood next to her at the end of the driveway. She said nothing. When Patrice arrived, Joelle opened the back door for me and I got in. Joelle looked at Patrice, and neither of them said anything.

At the ramshackle house on Norway Lake, I walked around as Joelle went from room to room with no result. I patted the dog, which seemed to like me as much as he liked Joelle, I watched the cats scurry back and forth outside, and I generally stayed away from the parents, who were angry at Joelle for wasting their time with a bunch of nonsense.

As they yelled and carried on, I wandered down to the water and went out onto the dock. Stepping over gaps where planks were missing, I walked past an old tied-up rowboat on my way down to the end. I sat down. Cross-legged, I rested my chin in my hands and looked at the water.

Before long, he came to me. A pale glow in darkness. Hair messy and covered with stuff. Bits of hay? His cheeks were scraped and stained with dried blood.

*I fell*, he said. *Dark. Cold.*

*Where are you? We're trying to find you.*

*I was bad. Didn't want to go to church. He yelled. I ran outside and hid.*

I closed my eyes and started to cry. After a few moments I got control of myself and opened my eyes again. He was gone.

I got up and walked back to the house. The parents were taking a break from their screamfest, so I was able to catch Joelle's attention.

"I saw him. He said he fell."

Joelle's shoulder's slumped. "Oh no."

She'd been hoping against hope that he was still alive. If I'd seen him, it meant that he was dead.

Patrice came up to see what we were talking about.

"His face was covered with pieces of hay or something."

Patrice frowned. "Hay?"

"He said it's dark and cold where he is."

"An old well?" Joelle said.

I shook my head. "He said he'd gone somewhere to hide."

"One of the outbuildings." Patrice pulled out her phone and walked off.

I looked at Joelle.

"The parents admitted they'd had a fight with him the Sunday morning he disappeared," she said. "Everyone thought he'd wandered off and was lost in the woods or had drowned in the lake."

I shook my head.

She frowned at me. "You saw him in the lake?"

"Yeah."

"He's not there, is he? At the bottom?"

I shook my head again. "He was telling me he went inside somewhere to hide."

A team of police searchers and forensics officers arrived a short while later in response to Patrice's calls. The outbuildings, which consisted of two large old barns and several sheds of various sizes in various stages of decay, had been searched before, but this time they went over every square inch with a fine-toothed comb.

They found him in a small, dug-out cold cellar beneath one of the barns. He'd climbed up into the hay loft, fell through, and landed on an old trap door that accessed the cellar, which was lined with stones and had apparently been used at one time to keep potatoes and other stuff in the winter. The trap door collapsed when he hit it, and he went down, bashing his head against the stones. They said later that he'd probably taken several hours to die.

No one found him because when the loft collapsed, it

dropped bales of hay down after him that landed on top of the trap door, covering it from view.

Previous searchers had noticed the loft had collapsed, but given the general condition of the barn they'd assumed it had happened quite a while ago. The parents had no idea the cold cellar existed, as they'd never used any of the outbuildings at all.

I didn't talk to Joelle for a week afterward. I couldn't. It was one thing to see disembodied faces in mud puddles and hear ethereal voices in my head but quite another to communicate with the ghost of a boy whose battered body was waiting to be found right there, only a few dozen metres away.

# 26

We sat at the table in Marie-Claire's kitchen, Reverend B on my right and Quinn directly across from me.

Quinn had filled a sippy cup with water from the tap. Putting the pendant around my neck, I rubbed the silver leaf between my thumb and index finger. To evoke its protective powers, I suppose. Then I slowly poured water into the bowl.

"I'm not sure if I explained before," I said, looking at Reverend B instead of the bowl, "the last time I did this I was trying to contact my mother. It didn't go well."

"You mentioned it, but you didn't explain."

"After she died, I really missed her." I glanced at Quinn. "We both did, terribly. It was so awful, what happened. She was helping the police track down a serial killer. She located him and went to the place herself before Detective Constable Rogers could get there. She was slashed to death with a knife. We just wanted to know if she had made it through to the other side all right. If she was okay now. At peace."

"I see."

I felt the water touch the tip of my finger, which I'd kept inside the rim of the bowl to be able to judge when it was full, the way a blind person would. I stopped pouring.

"I tried to contact her several times, and it didn't work. Then one night I got through. I really wish I hadn't."

"What was wrong?"

"She was in agony. Extreme torment. Surrounded by chaos. I tried to talk to her, to ask her what was going on. It invaded my mind, the chaos. I thought I was going insane. Somehow I got out, and I've never gone back in."

"Until now," Quinn said.

I didn't say anything. Technically he was right, that twice in the past several days I'd made contact with the other side, both times in the parsonage, but I didn't care to split hairs with him. He was also correct that this would be the first time I'd *deliberately* gone back in since then, and the first time using hydromancy.

I had no idea what I'd encounter under these terms, in a voluntary attempt at scrying. I picked up the bowl. Turning in my seat so that Reverend B could see what I was doing, I settled it into my lap.

"This has some kind of female symbolism, I guess. Anyway. I don't pay a lot of attention to that sort of thing. I just follow this ritual if I want to try to control what happens. It works when I do it this way, usually."

"You don't seem too sure of yourself."

"I guess not. Joelle was supposed to help me figure it out, but she was murdered only a few weeks later. Whatever I know I've learned on my own." I forced a smile. "An autodidactic necromancer."

"I didn't mean to sound disparaging, Maddie."

Whatever.

I dropped the pebble into the bowl. As the surface of the water rippled, I mumbled an incantation in Greek that I won't repeat now. For security reasons, right? Even though you can learn from the Internet how to make a dirty bomb or a handgun with a 3-D printer or that sort of thing, there's no way I'm going to explain here exactly how to summon the dead through hydromancy.

Sorry.

Roughly translated though, it was an appeal for any dead person nearby to reach out and communicate with me.

I watched the water. Nothing happened.

I was about to pick up the pebble to try again when I saw her.

# 27

*Maddie! My darling!* A voice that only I could hear spoke in my head.

"Marie-Claire!"

*Enfin! I thought you'd forgotten me.*

"Never!"

"Mémère?" Quinn yelped. "Is it her?"

*Tell him I miss my boy very much, but I know he's been good. They tell me about his visits.*

I repeated this to Quinn, and his eyes filled with tears.

"I don't see anything," Reverend B said, staring at the bowl. "Do you see someone?"

"Marie-Claire."

"Oh my God."

*She's undergoing a great test of faith,* Marie-Claire observed. *She should have been born Catholic.*

Smiling, I passed this message on to Reverend B, who wasn't sure how to take it. Was I stringing her along, after all? Mocking her in some sly post-adolescent manner?

*You have the ability to make her see and hear,* Marie-Claire said.

"No, I don't."

*Yes, you do.*

"I don't know how."

*You'll learn. Not from me. From . . .*

She faded.

"Marie-Claire!"

"What about Maman?" Quinn yelled. "Ask about Maman!"

*—here. Tell my boy Joelle is still somewhere else. I'm not sure where.*

"Is she all right?"

*—pas certain. In great difficulty. The last time . . . she said you were in danger. You and Quinn. Be—*

She was gone.

"Marie-Claire!" I fumbled for the pebble and dropped it in again. "Marie-Claire!"

*—je t'aime . . .*

"Marie-Claire!" I dropped the pebble over and over again, but that was all. It was done.

She was gone.

I pushed the bowl up onto the table and started to cry.

DEVLIN

# 28

"You don't believe a word I'm saying, do you?"

Devlin kept his expression neutral as he leaned back and crossed his legs.

"Maddie, most people lie to their therapist or counsellor during a session. It's a given, really. They lie by minimizing the distress they're feeling, they pretend things are fine when they're not, they dodge questions about subjects like suicide or anger or substance abuse, and they even say that their sessions are helping them when in fact they feel the opposite. As a professional I'm supposed to be really good at detecting lies and evasions and so on, but I'm only human. I miss things. And even when I catch them, should I confront the person and demand the truth, or should I continue to listen and try to learn what's behind the lie?"

"That's, like, the longest speech you've given so far, Dr. Devlin. What do they call that, deflection? Avoiding a question by talking about something else?"

Devlin sighed. "Yes, Maddie. It's deflection."

"And so the answer is—?"

"You asked me when we began to keep an open mind. That's what I'm doing, to the best of my ability. Look, I don't believe in the paranormal and I'm an agnostic when it comes to the afterlife. I don't have any personal experience in that area, obviously, and I haven't really studied it at all."

"Until now."

"Until now." He smiled wanly. "It's important for me to be honest with you, otherwise there's no basis for trust, is there?"

"True."

"So, proceed accordingly. I'll listen to absolutely everything you want to say, and give it a great deal of thought." He chuckled. "A *great* deal. Trust me on that one. But you must understand that right now, what I believe to be true is far less important than what you believe. You can see that, can't you?"

"Sure." She folded her hands on her knee. "Well, as Coleridge said, we must suspend disbelief in order to appreciate the truth of something that appears to us from the shadows, or words to that effect. I'm gambling that you're the man who can do that. That you'll hear me out."

"I'll hear you out, Maddie."

"Then let me explain how this works. For me. Speaking to the dead. I'll go into detail. If you think it's all a very elaborate delusion, well, fine. There's nothing I can do about it. But at least I'll have given it my best shot."

Devlin exhaled. "All right, Maddie. Try me."

"Okay. You asked for it."

MADDIE

# 29

I realize that I haven't talked much about my father to this point, and I wouldn't want to leave the impression that he was like Uncle Robert, distant and unsympathetic, because he wasn't.

Far from it.

Mark was a criminal defence attorney, as I may have already mentioned, and a partner in his law firm. He was a barrister, which meant that his quality time, professionally speaking, was spent in the courtroom. He represented a broad range of people charged with criminal offences, and from what I've heard he was a very good lawyer. He worked long hours, was detail oriented, and never gave up on a client's right to fair treatment in the judicial system. I never read anything negative about him in the news, ever, and people who talked to me about him were always very respectful and complimentary.

He had one hard and fast rule, and that was never, ever to take the case of anyone arrested as a result of Joelle's involvement in an investigation. The last thing he wanted to do was defend someone who'd been arrested and charged because of his wife. He refused to be put in a position where disparaging or discrediting the use of a psychic investigator might result in his client's acquittal. Other lawyers with other law firms might, and did, attack Joelle's credibility, in court and in the press, but Mark wasn't going to go there. Ever.

That was Mark the lawyer, but the person I always saw was Mark the dad and Mark the husband. His time at home was always limited because of the demands of his job, but when he was with us, he gave us his complete attention.

That is, when he wasn't reading a book or watching the news on TV or talking on the phone to his best friend, a forensic accountant who lived somewhere out west. The point I'm trying to make is that Mark made sure there was a sharp division between his work and his home life.

It took us both a while to deal with Joelle's murder. Quinn was only four when it happened, remember, and while he was an exceptionally bright kid he was a little more emotionally resilient than I was, I guess, because he adjusted fairly rapidly to the idea that his mother would no longer be with us. Mark was extra patient with him that summer, but at the end of the day I guess I was the one who needed more tender loving care.

I know I still haven't talked about her death in any detail. I know it's what the professionals call avoidance coping, talking around a stressor instead of dealing with it head on. Frankly, I think it's a miracle I can even refer to it at all, never mind pore over the horrible details. I'll get there. All right? One step at a time here.

It was the middle of July when I noticed an ad in the paper for a psychic fair taking place at the Nepean Sportsplex that Saturday. Normally I would have ignored such a thing, following Joelle's example of dismissing it as crass commercialism and outright chicanery. But something about it stuck in my head and wouldn't let go.

A premonition, yeah.

For the past few months, I'd been messing around with various methods and materials, I suppose you could say, trying to figure out how to concentrate all my efforts into a "controlled hydromantic experience." I tried cereal bowls and soup bowls from the cupboard, mixing bowls, even an old dog food bowl I found at a yard sale down the street. Nothing seemed to be working very well.

As I say, I was trying to learn how to control the whole thing. I was trying to shut down the involuntary visions, the ones that happened when I looked at mud puddles and so on, and figure out how to channel my ability into voluntary, concentrated sessions that I could manage consciously. I read whatever I could get my hands on, which wasn't a lot, really, and confirmed what I'd read read about before, that the ancients used hydromancy to summon gods or spirits of the dead in order to compel them to foretell the future.

I certainly didn't want to get into that sort of thing, so I skipped most of the methods described in the literature to be used if you wanted to shoot the breeze with Osiris or Serapis or whomever, which needed rainwater or seawater in a bronze bowl, and tried bottled spring water from the store instead. The book I was relying on, a translation of old Greek scrolls, recommended the olive oil method I'd mentioned to Reverend B in my ill-fated attempt to explain myself to her the first time around.

A drop or two of oil into the water. Mutter a few sentences in Greek. Stare intently.

Nothing happened.

After experimenting with this and that, I figured I probably needed an actual bronze bowl in order for it to work properly. So where the heck would I get one? Bed, Bath and Beyond?

When I saw the ad for the psychic fair, as I say, it got me thinking. Despite being a money trap for the gullible and naïve, the show might actually be worth checking out. The next question, of course, was how would I get there?

Since I was still only a week from turning thirteen, my options were limited. I could take the bus, but I didn't feel particularly comfortable going there by myself.

Which I'd have to do, since I didn't have any friends. There was no one I could call up and say, "Hey, want to go to the psychic fair with me on Saturday?"

There was only Mark.

Poor Mark.

It should be understood that, although I loved him dearly, I'd always been much closer to Joelle, and it was usually to her that I'd go when I wanted something. I understood that Mark was always busy and had to be judicious (pun intended) with his use of family time, and so I normally wouldn't pester him with something like this.

Now, however, I had no choice.

On the Saturday morning in question, I left the folded-up newspaper next to his coffee cup with the ad for the fair prominently in view. When he poured himself a cup and sat down, I watched him from the corner of my eye.

He sipped, looked at the ad, grunted, and turned the paper over to see if there was something more interesting on the other side.

After waiting an eternity in vain for him to get a clue, I said, "I was wondering if you could take me there."

"Sorry, Mads. Busy day today."

"Oh. Okay."

I ate the rest of my toast, kicking myself for not having figured out a backup plan.

He turned the page, flopped and folded it, and read some more.

Sipped his coffee.

"Got your heart set on it?"

Yay!

"Kind of."

"Your mom's probably rolling over in her grave, Mads. A psychic fair, for crying out loud."

"No she wouldn't. She'd understand."

"You realize they already know if you're going to be there or not."

I rolled my eyes.

He drained his coffee cup, put the newspaper aside, and stood up. "Give me a minute to make a couple of calls."

He left the room and came back a few minutes later. "Okay, we're all set. Perry's going to handle the meetings for me at the detention centre, and Mrs. Olafssen will come over and stay with Quinn. Sound good?"

"Sounds good. Thanks!"

Having never gone to a psychic fair before, I wasn't sure what to expect. The parking lot was extremely busy, but Mark explained that there were several other events going on at the Sportsplex at the same time, plus public swimming in the pools (yuck).

The fair was being held in one of the rinks, the ice surface covered with plywood and carpeting. Mark paid our entrance fees, looked around, and spotted a seating area in the back corner with what looked like a canteen.

"As you've heard me say before," he grinned, "I'm like Jack Reacher. I have an infinite capacity for coffee." He patted the pocket of his sports jacket, where he'd brought along a paperback novel to help pass the time. "Are you okay?"

"Sure," I chirped, relieved that he didn't feel obligated to stick to me like a burr on a dog's tail.

He took out his wallet and handed me a wad of bills. "You know where to find me when you're done. Have fun."

He disappeared into the crowd.

I moved off to the side and unslung my knapsack. I took out my wallet, put Mark's money in (along with the sixty bucks I'd brought with me), and buttoned the wallet into a patch pocket on the front left leg of my cargo pants. Tossing the knapsack over my shoulder, I dried my damp palms on the front of my brand-new *Conjuring* T-shirt, one that featured a photo of Patrick Wilson and Vera Farmiga as the Warrens, and set out in search of illumination.

A lot of the vendors had set up stalls with curtains and shrouds in order to offer readings with a semblance of privacy. You could choose tea leaves, Tarot cards (there must have been a dozen card readers at least), a crystal ball, or even chicken bones. I bypassed all of these and spent time with several book sellers, skipping the racks of speculative fiction and horror novels and poking around instead in their non-fiction sections related to magic and the paranormal.

By the time I was finally tired of looking at books, I had a nice little haul stuffed into my knapsack. I bought two books on Greek and Roman necromancy, one by Daniel Ogden and the other by Georg Luck; an interesting-looking one by Richard Kieckhefer called *Forbidden Rites: A Necromancer's Manual of the Fifteenth Century*, and a neat little 1932 hardcover by Armand Delatte, *La Catoptromancie Grecque et ses dérivés* (remember, I can read French as easily as I can English).

This last book was kind of an impulse purchase, I have

to admit. It cost twenty-five bucks, which I thought was outrageous, but I didn't want to leave the place without it. I'd never heard of catoptromancy before, but when I showed the book to another vendor she explained that it was an ancient form of necromancy which used mirrors and other reflective surfaces. She'd heard of the Delatte book, but had never seen a copy. She was impressed that I'd found it.

There were also quite a few vendors selling crystals, jewelry, and other assorted trinkets and minerals. I'd never really paid much attention to this kind of stuff before, since Joelle was never interested in it herself, but the displays were very eye-catching and it didn't take me long to become mesmerized.

One vendor in particular, a middle-aged woman who reminded me of my sixth-grade teacher (a nice lady who treated me very kindly), chatted me up and asked me questions about which stones I liked and what sort of healing properties I was interested in finding.

I ended up spending sixty bucks at her booth, and came away with a really cool-looking amethyst geode, several cabochons made of lapis lazuli, topaz, and turquoise, and the blue lace agate stone that I've mentioned before.

My last purchases came at a booth selling DVDs, VHS tapes, games, and other media. The vendor complimented me on my T-shirt and said she'd really liked the movie, which had just come out the previous year. She knew a bit about the Warrens, and we chatted for a while about their bona fides, the cases they'd been involved in, and how much we both really liked Patrick Wilson. (Poor Vera; in retrospect, the more I've watched her work, the more I've come to admire her acting, even above his. Those sad, sad eyes!)

I bought a copy of *Resident Evil* on DVD, which I'd never seen before but had heard was pretty good (Milla Jovovich looked pretty cool on the cover), and while she was getting my change I looked at a bowl of wrapped mint chocolates sitting on her table. There was only one left.

"Is it okay if I have this?"

She handed me the money and the little bag with my movie. "Sure. I've got more. I just haven't had time to refill the bowl."

I took the chocolate and slipped it in my pocket. Something about the bowl caught my eye. "This is nice."

"Yeah. It was my grandmother's. It's bronze. See the pictures on the side?"

I looked at representations of Greek-looking men and women, animals, and birds. "Bronze?"

"Yeah. You like it? You can buy it. Everything's for sale around here."

I couldn't believe it. I'd spent so much time looking at other stuff I'd forgotten I'd come here primarily to look for a bowl, and now here was one that looked exactly like what I wanted, sitting innocuously in front of me as though it had been waiting all this time for me to notice it.

Well, maybe it had been.

"How much?"

"Thirty bucks."

I don't ever haggle, because it makes me feel uncomfortable and awkward, but something made me snap out, "Twenty."

She grinned. "Sold. Want a bag?"

# 30

Two days after I'd contacted Marie-Claire with Reverend B and Quinn watching, the sun had risen on a grey and clammy Monday morning. Rain was in the forecast for the afternoon, and after I finished auditing an online lecture on Edgar Allan Poe, I didn't feel like doing anything else, so I poured another cup of coffee and stepped out onto the porch.

The lecturer had focused on Poe's dissolute lifestyle and demeaning death, rather than on his poetry or stories, and it was an hour that had left me depressed and not really sure of what to do with myself. Starvation, illness, anxiety, and alcoholism. The destruction of an incredible imagination housed inside a personality completely unable to manage itself in a normal, stable life.

It was very sad.

I pulled my sweater close against my neck and stepped off the verandah. Noises next door drew me around the side of the house, and I saw several figures in the cemetery.

Reverend B stood off to one side, arms folded, watching Matt Pollock and another man working away at one of the plots where we'd left a broken stone. Pulled up in front of the church was a dark blue van with lettering on the side:

Thackeray Monuments.

I wandered over. I should probably explain, in case it's not yet perfectly clear, that although I may be sullen sometimes, a little taciturn, yes, and not the kind of person who goes out of her way to look for friends and go to parties and blah blah blah, I'm not at all shy. I don't mind inviting myself over to the graveyard next door to see what's going on if it crosses my mind to do so.

"Good morning," I said to everyone.

"Hey Maddie," Matt said, not looking up.

Reverend B nodded. She wore a purple and gold Wilfrid Laurier University windbreaker that was zipped up tight under her chin. Her expression was grim.

Gord Thackeray ignored me, not having been introduced. I knew who he was, though, because he had his first name stitched on the front of his coveralls and his last name painted on his van.

He was putting the finishing touches on cement that had been poured from a wheelbarrow (not Marie-Claire's, which was back home where it belonged) into a freshly built wooden foundation frame dug into the ground for the headstone in question, which belonged to Clarissa Porter, the late sister-in-law of David Bennett. Matt knelt next to him, ready to drop the stone into place as soon as Thackeray gave him the thumbs up.

Sipping my coffee, I looked around. The bottom half of Carson Bennett's headstone had already been returned to its proper place, and the upper half waited on the ground next to it. Probably until the cement had a chance to set, I figured, not knowing anything about stone masonry or the affiliated arts but was willing to guess.

My eyes strayed to Lily Tennant's plot. Her headstone still lay untouched, where I'd put it on Saturday. Ditto for the chunk of Blackburn's marker that had shot past Reverend B's ear as though fired from a cannon (according to her) and which she was studiously ignoring for the time being.

"How was church yesterday?" I asked, trying to make conversation.

"Fine." Reverend B shot me a quick glance. "I was a little distracted."

"I can imagine."

We watched Matt pick up Clarissa's headstone and slowly lower it into its resting place. He handled the thing as though it were made of Styrofoam. Although it wasn't a large stone, it had taken both Reverend B and me to get it in and out of the wheelbarrow, and I thought it must be very nice to have the kind of physical strength Matt took for granted.

Thackeray fussed around the base, double-checking with his measuring tape to make sure the soil wouldn't cover any engraving when replaced. He used a level to verify that it wasn't leaning or tipped over. Fuss fuss fuss. Finally, he pronounced himself satisfied with the result and stood up.

"Once it sets," he told Matt, "you can fill it in."

"Okey doke."

"What's next?"

Matt looked around and, after a moment pointed with his chin at Lily Tennant's headstone. "That one, I guess."

"I'm going in," Reverend B announced. She turned on her heel and started off for the parsonage. "Come on, Maddie."

Once we were inside, we settled down on stools around the kitchen island. She topped up my coffee, which had gotten cold outside, and poured one for herself.

"I think I'm losing my mind." She pulled off her windbreaker and draped it over the corner of the island.

"I know it's hard."

She gave me a look, started to say something, then shook her head. "No."

I wasn't sure what she was referring to, so I just kept quiet.

"Tom Harpur," she said, "is a man whose work I respect, if not necessarily agree with on many points, because he doesn't believe that Christianity is a living, breathing miracle but only a composite mythology drawn from other, earlier religions. Like many other contemporary scholars, I'm afraid. Nevertheless, he wrote a whole chapter in his book *Life After Death* on mediums, channellers, and all those various other people who claim to perform astounding acts of necromancy. Although normally quite diplomatic, he came right out and said that after researching the subject, he was forced to conclude that he'd never encountered such a mish-mash of weird speculation and downright nonsense in his life."

*He never met me,* I thought.

"Until now," she went on, "I had agreed with him wholeheartedly." She took a slug of coffee, as though to brace herself. "Until now."

We heard a faint yelp from the graveyard.

Alarmed, Reverend B hurried out of the kitchen. I heard her in the parlour, no doubt looking out the window to see what had happened.

After a few moments she came back in and sat down again. "Looks like Matt dropped Lily's stone on his foot. He's limping around like an old sailor with a peg leg."

I rolled my eyes. "I thought he was wearing safety boots."

"So did I." She picked up her coffee cup and put it down again. "Okay. All right. Maddie, I have to ask you to do something for me."

"What?"

"Afterward, I'm going to call a good friend of mine who's a psychoanalyst and get some serious therapy. And maybe some appropriate medications. Right now, though, I need to do this. *We* need to do this."

I knew what she was going to come out with, but I wasn't going to say it for her. No way. I steeled myself for it.

"I want you to contact her. This woman. I want you to tell her to go away, to leave us alone. Is it Lily Tennant? Is that who it is? I searched the files and couldn't find a picture of her, and the satellite dish is kaput so I can't look her up online. Maybe it's her. Maybe it's someone else. I don't know. I want you to find out."

"I don't—"

"You have to! This can't go on. There's something wrong here, terribly wrong, and we have to do something about it. You're the only one, apparently, who has the ability to do that. Conduct one of your séances, or whatever you call it, and get rid of her."

"It doesn't work that way."

"Of course it works that way. It works exactly that way, doesn't it? You contact her; you find out what she wants; you do *that* thing, whatever it is she wants; and then she goes away. Passes over to the light, or whatever it is these . . . ghost-things do."

*It's not that simple,* I wanted to say, but I knew she didn't entirely appreciate the gravity of the situation and wouldn't understand my reluctance. It wasn't just fear that held me back, but what we might set in motion, a chain reaction of events that might pull us into a situation we definitely didn't want to find ourselves in.

"Maddie." She brought her hands together. "I'm begging you. Do something."

"All right," I said, regretting the words as soon as they passed through my lips. "Tonight."

"Thank you." She raised her coffee cup and lowered it again. "That spell, or incantation, or whatever you call it, that you recite when you're summoning these spirits. What does it mean? Or should I not ask?"

"It's ancient Greek." I shrugged, unwilling to give away my secrets even now. "It basically calls to any ghosts or spirits that might be nearby, within earshot, figuratively speaking, and invites them to appear before me. In the water."

"And if they hear this spell they have no choice? They have to make themselves visible?"

"Not with the incantation I use. There are versions where you name a god or demon specifically and they're forced to show themselves and obey your commands, but I've never tried that sort of thing and I don't intend to."

"Just as well. Not that I believe in any of this."

"The incantation I use," I went on, ignoring her editorial comment, "just asks anyone nearby to speak to me. I can name someone specific, but I haven't had much luck with that so far. I don't know why. So I just use an open invitation, kind of, and see if anyone shows up. It's not very precise and orderly, but maybe some day I'll figure out what I'm doing wrong and get better."

"Why you?" She stared at me, her expression much less pleasant than I'd ever seen before. "What is it about you that seems to draw them out?"

"I don't know."

"I mean, if I tried it, with the bowl and the stone and

the spell thing, would it work for me? Would I see them?"

"Probably not. No."

"Why not? What is it about you that makes you so special?"

Again, the way she said that last word made it sound like something repulsive and not something good. I was feeling worse by the minute.

"I don't know," I repeated. "I guess it's something genetic." I forced a laugh. "Like I'm a mutant or something. Maddie-X."

She shook her head, sighing in exasperation. "I have some work to do this afternoon," she said. "Can you come over this evening? So we can try this out and maybe get rid of whatever this thing is?"

"If you want."

"I *don't* want, Maddie. Definitely not. But I'm desperate. You get that, don't you?"

"Yeah" She didn't need to hit me over the head with a sledge hammer to get her point across.

# 31

I put my foot down and made Quinn stay at home. He still had homework to do, so I used that as an excuse to keep him away from the parsonage. I didn't have a good feeling about how this was going to go, and I wanted him to be safe.

Well, relatively safe.

And out from underfoot.

Reverend B let me stand outside on the step for a few moments before deciding to let me in. She was wearing a burgundy wrap-around sweater, blue jeans, and moccasins, trying to look casual and comfortable, but the creases at the corners of her eyes and the tightness of her mouth gave her away.

"Would you like a cup of tea or something first?"

"No, thanks." I followed her to the bottom of the stairs. "Are you sure you want to do this?"

She put her hand on the banister and turned, barely suppressing an eye roll. "Yes, I'm sure, Maddie. Let's get this over with, shall we?"

Up the stairs to the second floor. Down the hallway to the staircase leading up to the attic. As she turned on the light, I hesitated.

My head was starting to pound. My breathing was getting short, almost like the panting of a frightened animal. Which I was. A frightened animal.

Up the stairs to the attic.

I felt an oppressive pressure in my mind. I was a little confused, because it was clearly some kind of psychic pressure, the same thing I'd felt before in the parsonage, but now that I was face to face with it and committed to finding out what was going on, it struck me that what I was sensing was different than what I normally felt during my bowl-and-water ritual. It was almost like the sort of thing Joelle had described to me once—a sudden light-headedness followed by a sensation of falling, then a weakness in the knees, and then—

But that was Joelle, who experienced psychic visions connected to people who were still alive.

I didn't have that ability. I could only communicate with the dead.

It was *very* confusing.

I fought for breath, clenching my teeth. Reverend B stood to one side, arms folded, staring at the oak door with its padlock and forbidding dark panels. She was completely unaware of what I was going through, because she was totally absorbed in what was happening inside her own head right now.

*You have the ability to make her see and hear,* Marie-Claire had said.

Was it true? Was I affecting her with my own distress? Transmitting my fear and dread to her?

I stripped off my knapsack and put it down on the floor, rejecting the idea. Once again, I didn't have that kind of ability. It didn't make sense.

Pulling a small side table and two chairs into the

middle of the attic space, I motioned for Reverend B to sit down. Reluctantly, as though walking to her execution, she lowered herself onto the edge of one of the chairs. I took the one across from her and began to unpack my knapsack.

Sippy cup full of tap water from Marie-Claire's house, fed by the sweet underground spring that ran below Twilight Road.

Oak box. Keys.

I unlocked the box and, as Reverend B stared like a paralyzed bird, I lifted the bowl from its silk wrapping and put it on the table in front of me.

"Are you okay?" I whispered, picking up the silver leaf pendant and rubbing it between my thumb and index finger.

Reverend B nodded. Shuddering, she produced a small spiral notebook and a stub of pencil from the hip pocket of her jeans and set them on the table in front of her. Apparently she'd decided to take notes.

I put the pendant around my neck and poured water from the sippy cup into the bowl, averting my eyes as always and waiting for the wetness to touch the tip of my finger inside the rim.

There.

I took out the blue agate pebble and rolled it in my palm.

"Go ahead," she rasped. "Nothing's going to happen, right? It's just a crazy fantasy I've built up in my head, right? I'm going to feel like an idiot afterward, but it'll be just fine and completely all right. Right?"

I didn't answer, assuming her questions were rhetorical.

Moving the bowl to my lap, I murmured the incantation

and dropped the pebble into the water.

Immediately I saw a face.

Not the same woman.

She was younger. Asian. Her hair was long and black. She opened her mouth, staring at me.

*Where is he? Is he gone? Oh please, is he gone?*

"Is who gone?" I asked. "What's your name?"

"What is it?" Reverend B, her voice high and stressed. "What do you see?"

The Asian woman disappeared as the ripples on the surface of the water subsided. I gave Reverend B a hasty description of who I'd seen. She scribbled in the notebook. I figured it was a good idea because it gave her something to do, something to focus on besides her fear.

I was surprised that someone had appeared to me so quickly. Usually it took a couple of tries, when it worked at all. Given the pain and the pressure in my head, though, it was like the place was psychically supercharged right now.

Great. Wonderful.

I took a moment to calm my breathing (from the diaphragm, Maddie, and not from the top of the lungs like a panting, frightened dog), and then I dropped the pebble into the bowl again.

Another woman appeared, this one middle-aged, with red hair turning grey. She cried out and quickly vanished, replaced by a young blonde who couldn't stop crying.

"Who are you?" I asked. "What's wrong?"

The blonde disappeared. I described them to Reverend B, who scribbled.

"I don't know who these people would be," she muttered. "Where are they coming from?"

"From here," I said. "From this house."

"Not possible."

"Should I stop?"

She bit her lip. She closed her eyes for a moment, waggling the pencil stub between her fingers. She opened her eyes and frowned at the notes she'd written.

"Maybe try one more time."

My head pounded. The pain was so intense it made my teeth ache. If I could have, I would have gotten up and left the parsonage without looking back. Never to return.

But I knew I didn't have a choice.

I repeated the incantation, although it wasn't necessary, strictly speaking. Any spirit close enough to appear would likely have been close enough to hear it the first time. I dropped the pebble into the water.

An older woman with nicely styled grey hair. A young brunette. A girl with short ginger hair and bruises on her face. A middle-aged woman who might have been Indigenous. They passed in quick succession across the surface of the rippling water, so quickly I barely had time to register them in my mind. They babbled at me, but I couldn't understand what they were saying. It was too much all at once. I did my best to describe them to Reverend B, who wrote it all down.

I'd never experienced anything like this before.

It was horrifying.

They were all dead. All trapped here. All desperate, frightened, pleading.

"There may be more," Reverend B muttered. "Do it again."

I groaned.

"Maddie, we have to."

"No."

"Please. Something's *really* wrong with this place. We

*have* to know."

"All right. Give me a minute."

Breathe. Slowly and calmly. With grace and dignity.

Okay.

I dropped the pebble.

And looked at the face of an older woman, maybe in her early sixties, her hair curled as though she'd had a perm just before her death, or had been given one by a hairdresser summoned by the undertaker.

She stared up at me. And didn't vanish, like the others.

*He defiled me.*

"What's your name?" I asked.

*He refused to let me rest. He defiled my body and then gave it to the other evil bastard so he could defile me too.*

"I don't understand. Who are you talking about? What did they do?"

*How can I ever rest when they've done this horrible, unspeakable thing to me?*

"What's your name?"

*Mary Elliott. Taggart. No rest for me, no rest until he's dead. Dead. Dead.*

"Until who's dead, Mrs. Taggart?"

She was gone. The water was still. Clear.

I sat back, exhausted.

That was it for me. I was done.

"Mrs. Taggart?" Reverend B asked.

I nodded. "I guess her maiden name was Mary Elliott. That's what she said."

"It was as though I could see her myself, like a glowing image coming from the bowl." She wrote in her notebook. "I recognize the name. Mary Elliott. She's buried out there in the cemetery."

"What was she was talking about?"

Reverend B said nothing, writing in her notebook.

I looked down at the bowl in my lap, plucked out the pebble, and put it on the table.

"I can feel it," Reverend B said, putting down her pencil. "The same sense of oppression I felt when Matt opened the door. Despair and horror."

"Yeah."

She got up and took a few steps toward the door. "What happened in there? What horrible things?"

I said nothing. I wasn't a kid, naive and innocent. I'd learned a long time ago that the world could be a grim and ugly place, and I was starting to get an idea of what had occurred here.

She came back from the door and stood next to me, looking down at the bowl. "I don't understand. It's just water. I know it has an extensive symbolic significance, water does, throughout multiple cultures over several thousand years, but to actually be able to communicate with the dead like this? It's completely fantastic."

She picked up the pebble and looked at it. "It's just a stone. Just a stone, making ripples in water."

Before I could say anything, she dropped the pebble into the bowl.

A woman's tortured face swam up at us.

*Maddie! No! Nooooo!*

"Joelle!" I shouted.

Reverend B screamed and swiped at the bowl, upending it from my lap and knocking it onto the floor.

Water soaked my skirt and ran across the floorboards.

It was dark and red. Like blood.

# 32

The next morning, which was Tuesday, rain was falling in a steady light mist. From the bathroom window, which faced east, I saw that Reverend B was once again walking through the graveyard, head down, clipboard in hand.

I still had a bad headache, but it was more like a combination hangover from last night's madness and a weather migraine. I went downstairs and fixed myself a cup of coffee, which I used to take my medication. Hopefully it would lower the hammering in my temples to the level of a dull roar.

As I guess I mentioned before, I got migraine headaches from time to time and I was more or less used to them, but the agony I'd experienced recently next door was a new and different little treat. The pain was worse than usual, more sharp and engulfing and miserable, and it was starting to worry me.

The parsonage and old church were rapidly becoming a source of new and very unpleasant experiences. For the first time, for example, I was hearing disembodied voices, as I had with Reverend B at the church, that were unconnected to my scrying. And I'd never experienced the intense pressure and searing pain that I was currently enduring while undergoing water visions, either voluntary or involuntary. Something very weird and unsettling was going on.

On top of the pain, I was still trying to deal with having seen Joelle last night. I slept only a few hours and spent most of the time staring at the ceiling, trying to think of something, *anything* other than her. But it was no good. My mother was in serious trouble on the other side, and she needed help. But there was nothing I could do.

Nothing!

It's important to bear in mind that I only *communicated* with the dead in what was essentially a passive activity. I didn't travel over there, I didn't intervene, I didn't perform exorcisms or any other sort of esoteric rituals that could change things on either side. I knew zip about that sort of stuff anyway, and I didn't know anyone who *did* know about it. Oh, Quinn could travel to other spheres and communicate with spirits, but his adventures were also passive. He drifted around, made friends with talking lions and glowing ladies, and behaved more like a sightseeing tourist than anything else.

Whatever sphere or dimension or netherworld currently held Joelle captive had never been on his itinerary, and I prayed it never would be.

Joelle was in major trouble, and there was nothing we could do about it.

It was extremely upsetting.

I grabbed a baseball cap from the hall closet, tugged it on, and headed out.

Reverend B had stuck the clipboard inside a plastic bag to keep the pages dry. The hood of her windbreaker was pulled up over her head in an attempt to keep her hair dry. Her face, when she nodded at me, was damp.

She reached under the bag to flip the page. "I'm looking for the women you said you saw last night."

I noticed the "said" part but didn't react. Your alleged communications with the dead. Your fantastical hallucinations. I was feeling tired and sore, as I said before, not to mention depressed, defensive, and impatient for the migraine medication to start working.

Plus, I wasn't the one walking around in the rain with a cemetery plot diagram trying to locate the graves of said hallucinations, thank you very much.

*Now* who's taking this seriously?

She waved the clipboard behind her. "I've already found Mary Elliott, the wife of John Taggart. Over there. Born 1926, died 1989, age sixty-three." She fumbled under the bag, pulled out a five-by-seven photo card, and handed it to me. "Printed this out. Scanned it from a church bulletin in the filing cabinet."

It was the woman I'd seen last night in the parsonage attic. "Yep."

"Mmm." She took it back from me. "Matches the description you gave me, anyway."

Oh, so very cautious. Come on, Reverend B. Work with me here, would you?

"What about the others?"

Reverend B handed me another photo. It was the young blonde, the woman who couldn't stop crying.

"She didn't give a name," I said.

"Bethany Green. Died in 1984 at the age of twenty. She was in another bulletin. Her father was a trustee. I cropped her out of a family picture. I was looking for her plot just now."

I stepped aside, reading inscriptions on the nearby headstones. I couldn't spot her name anywhere.

"There she is." Reverend B set off in a straight line, then cut between the graves to a marker three rows back.

I joined her to stare down at the stone, which apparently belonged to the young woman I'd seen last night.

"These were the only two I could find. I went through the entire damned filing cabinet. I made notes on eight different women that you described to me, including Mary Taggart, the Asian woman, and the Indigenous woman, and these are the only two I could find in the parish records. Only two!"

"So who are the others?"

"I have absolutely no idea. That's the question, isn't it? Who are they? Who *were* they?"

I thought for a moment. "They could be anyone. They could have died at any time. Maybe they somehow got left off your chart. Maybe their headstones are lost, at the back under dirt and leaves, covered up."

"Did I really see a face in that bowl? At the end?"

I wasn't sure how to answer.

"Who was it, Maddie? She looked a lot like you."

God, she *had* seen her. "Joelle. My mother."

"Good lord."

Reverend B said nothing for a moment, thinking it over. Finally, she pulled out another photo. She studied it for a moment before handing it to me. "What do you see here?"

It was a photograph of the graveyard during a burial ceremony. It looked as though it had been taken on an angle from just behind the church. There was a large mound of soil four or five rows back, a group of people in suits and black dresses, and a pastor reading from the Bible. He had his back to the camera, so his face wasn't visible.

"Whose funeral?" I asked.

"A man named Richard Knapp. A trustee who died in

1990. By all accounts a sober, honest man much loved by his widow and adult children. Given the date, the pastor must have been Seymour Blackburn, although you can't tell from this. Whatever. Look closer."

I wiped dampness from my face and studied the photo. It was in black and white and had been shot by someone with a steady hand using a good quality camera, probably a 35-millimetre SLR. You could see the shrubs and bushes at the back in some detail. They didn't seem to be encroaching quite as much as they were now.

"I'm not sure what I'm supposed to be seeing."

"Here." Reverend B reached over my shoulder and tapped the photo. "This space at the back."

Between the last row of headstones and the fringe of shrubbery was a stretch of empty grass. On the left, near a birch sapling, there was a patch that was bare soil. No grass. I caught my breath.

"An unmarked grave," Reverend B said.

"What? Are you sure?"

"No, of course I'm not sure. May I?" She took the photo back and walked through the graves until she stood in front of the tombstone of Richard Knapp, 1915-1990. She looked behind her at the church, trying to gauge where the photographer had stood to take the picture, based on the angle. I did the same. Then she turned around, took two steps to her left, checked the picture, swivelled to face her ten o'clock, and started walking through the rows. I followed.

She stopped at the last row of monuments. "I'd say about four metres back from here. What do you think?"

I looked over her shoulder at the picture, which was now beaded with moisture. "I guess so."

She paced it off, wading into tall grass and weeds gone

to seed, and stopped. "Right around here."

Crouching, we searched the ground. There was nothing: no flat marker, no corner stones, no indication whatsoever of a grave, marked or unmarked.

We stood up.

"I'm not going to dig," she said, "and neither are you."

"Nope."

"I'm really going to need that psychotherapy when this is all done."

I thought of something. "When my mother worked with the police, they would bring out cadaver dogs and ground-penetrating radar to search the places where they thought someone was buried. I don't mean someone she saw, because she only saw the living. I mean if they thought someone had been murdered and buried somewhere."

She laughed without humour. "I can picture myself calling the police. 'Hello, I think there are bodies buried at the back of my cemetery.' 'Well duh, lady. Where else would they be buried?' They'll think I've gone out of my mind."

We both turned at the sound of a vehicle pulling into the parking space in front of the church. It was Matt Pollock. We walked up through the graveyard to meet him.

"Just checking on the headstone repairs," he said, showing us his usual shaggy-dog grin. "What are you two ladies doing out here on such a messy day?"

"You wouldn't believe me if I told you," Reverend B said.

I stepped forward, feeling irritated, frustrated, and generally pissed off by the entire situation that had us spinning our wheels and going nowhere fast.

"Matt," I said, "could I ask you kind of an off-the-wall question?"

# 33

"You said what, again? GPR?"

I nodded, folding my arms. "Yeah. Is there any place around here that would have one of those things?"

He shrugged, a puzzled expression on his face. "Sure. What do you want it for?"

"Well," I said, thinking fast, "we think there might be something buried at the back of the cemetery. Left there by one of the other parsons. Reverend B saw something in the records, and we think this guy hid something back there. Years ago. A lock box of some kind, maybe, or a wooden trunk with old stuff that might be valuable."

"A treasure hunt?" He gave me a look of disbelief.

"Yeah."

"Well, how about a metal detector? I got one of those at home. A good one."

"We could try it," I said, "but if it's a wooden box it might not find it."

I glanced at Reverend B. She was staring off into space, wishing she were somewhere else. Anywhere else.

"I don't know. Maybe not. I can bring it over, though, and give it a shot."

"Where would we get hold of a ground-penetrating

radar device though, Matt?"

"You can rent them. People do it all the time to find underground cables and stuff when they have to excavate. There's a guy in town who has one."

"Could you do that for us? Right now? Rent it and bring it over so we can try it out?"

"Right now? In the rain?"

"What about tomorrow?" I pressed. "It's supposed to be nice."

He glanced at Reverend B. "Sure. I could do that, I guess. I was going to put the new glass in your window, Belinda, but if you want I can do this first."

"This first, if you don't mind," she said. "I'll pay for it out of my personal budget."

"Well, okay."

I patted him on the shoulder. "I really appreciate it, Matt."

He laughed. "You two are into some pretty weird stuff these days, eh? Hidden rooms and buried treasure? What's next, UFOs?"

"You never know." I tried to look mysterious. "We're not alone, you know."

He laughed again, shook his head, and shuffled off to check out the repaired headstones.

# 34

The following afternoon gave lie to the dirty rumour that Environment Canada couldn't forecast the weather to save their lives. The sky was clear, the ground had dried up from yesterday's unending drizzle, and the breeze was crisp and fresh.

Matt arrived in his pickup truck and unloaded a contraption that looked like a black-and-yellow lawn mower. He slung a metal detector on a strap over his shoulder and wheeled the GPR device to the back of the cemetery where Reverend B and I were waiting for him.

"We'll try the metal detector first," he said, swinging it off his shoulder with a grunt. "Any place in particular, or do you want me just to make a few passes back and forth along here?"

"We were thinking somewhere around here," Reverend B said, pointing to the spot where we thought the unmarked grave might be.

I was relieved that she was finally buying into the process and taking the lead. I'd brought over Marie-Claire's gas-powered weed trimmer this morning to clear away the wild grass and overgrowth as best I could, and when she'd heard the racket I was making she'd come out and pitched in. Her embarrassment from yesterday had morphed into something close to grim determination to see the wretched thing through. Which sort of matched my own attitude.

"Nothing," Matt said, lifting the metal detector and brushing off a few strands of whacked weeds. "I thought maybe an old button or some coins, but zipperoo."

"What about the GPR?" I asked.

"Aye aye, captain," he grinned at me.

I shrugged and tried to grin back.

As he strode away, I glanced at Reverend B and saw she was wiping her cheek with the back of her hand.

"I'm sorry," I said, as though this entire thing were my fault.

"This is horrible."

Her misery was palpable. It rolled over me in waves, shocking me. I felt it as though it were my own, except it was tinged with Christian *agape* mixed with Christian guilt mixed with Christian fear of an angry and vengeful God. It was flowing from her and entering my mind like a flood. It wasn't empathy. It was like a radio broadcast, loud and clear, in surround-sound stereo.

"Stop." I put my hands to my head and walked away.

She stared at me, saying nothing.

I looked over at the house. "Marie-Claire, for godsakes, what's happening to me? Mémère! Help me, please. "

Wind puffed in my ears.

The misery receded as she got a grip on herself.

I wiped away a few tears of my own.

After an eternity, Matt came back with the GPR device. I watched him flick a few switches, fiddle with the controls on a small display panel attached to the handlebar, and then he started moving in a straight line along the grass.

"If there's a buried treasure chest back here," he declared, "this baby'll find it."

I risked a glance at Reverend B. Her eyes were down, her arms were folded defensively, and her face was carved from stone. The tears were gone.

He trundled back and forth, watching the display panel. "Nothing so far."

"Keep looking," I piped up, trying to sound chirpy. "I'm sure there's something there."

"So, do I get a cut? Say, a third of the proceeds? I know a guy who can auction off the valuable stuff for you, if you want."

"We'll see." I tried to sound cagey, but it came off as awkward and rehearsed.

"I sometimes think they should combine one of these things with a riding lawnmower," he said. "Then you could multi-task, right? Of course, if I brought it over here to cut the grass, all I'd see is—Jesus."

He stopped dead, staring at the display.

He frowned. "What the fuck."

He moved the device back, and then forward again.

"Christ. What the hell."

Reverend B snapped out of her paralysis and stepped forward. "What is it, Matt?"

"Look for yourself. Bones. Is there supposed to be a grave here?"

She swallowed. Licked her lips. "Not according to the plot map."

"Shit." He moved the detector forward. "Okay. Nothing now." He pushed it several metres forward. "What the—"

"Matt?"

"More bones. A different—. What the hell. Jesus. What the hell's going on, Belinda?"

"I think," she said, "we'd better call 911."

# DEVLIN

# 35

On the evening of the fourth Sunday in March, Devlin poured himself a stiff drink, bourbon neat, and drank it down in one gulp at the sideboard in the living room. He poured another one and took it into his office, where he sat down at his desk, picked up the portable phone, and punched in a number.

"Hello?"

"Hello, David. It's Dennis."

"My goodness, so it is. How's my boy?"

"I'm well, thanks. And yourself?"

"Oh, the damned diabetes. They finally had to switch me over to insulin. I just love jabbing myself every day. Goddamned pain in the—well, you know."

Devlin smiled. Dr. David McGarrigle had been retired for nearly a decade now, and had even given up his emeritus title in order to enjoy a life free from all academic cares and responsibilities, but he never seemed to lose his edge.

"How's the island?" Devlin asked. "Still covered in snow?"

"Christ, no. Haven't you ever heard of global warming? It's clean as a whistle around here. You miss the place, don't you?"

It was true, although he'd never admit it. Born and raised in the town of North Rustico, Prince Edward Island, Devlin had studied exclusively at UPEI in order to remain close to his mother. His father, a fisherman who'd built a successful local business as a fishmonger and distributor, died when Devlin was fourteen. While his mother kept busy as a family physician with a thriving practice in the local clinic, she was very lonely and missed her husband. Since Devlin's older sister, Connie, had married and moved to Saint John, he'd felt he could keep his mother company while still getting an education at UPEI.

It was an idea that soon took on the appearance of sheer inspiration once he met David McGarrigle. As a first-year undergraduate student, he'd been uncertain about his major until he attended a lecture given by McGarrigle in the introductory psych course he'd signed up for out of boredom more than anything else. Speaking on the psychology of curiosity and its role in critical and creative learning, McGarrigle had immediately struck a chord with Devlin. Who would have thought that a subject as dry and fuzzy as psychology could suddenly become so fascinating?

After that, Devlin enrolled in every course taught by McGarrigle, and by the time he was ready to begin his pre-doctoral internship, he'd grown very close to the older man, who'd become his mentor and supervisor. They'd remained in touch over the years, although not as much as Devlin would have liked.

"I miss the place, yeah." Devlin hesitated. "Have I caught you at a bad time?"

"No, of course not. Still two hours before I turn in. Night owl, remember?"

Devlin remembered. "There's something I want to

run by you. Something we've never actually talked about before, believe it or not."

McGarrigle laughed. "Must be something pretty off the wall if we haven't covered it already, Dennis."

"It is. Kind of."

"Well, fire away. My tea's still warm and I've got my feet up on the corner of my desk. I'm all yours."

"Okay." Devlin had spent the day rehearsing this, and now that he'd finally worked up the nerve to make the call, his mind was a frustrating blank. "Um."

"Broad strokes first, son."

"Uh, all right. Um. This will sound weird, David. I'm sorry. Do you, have you had any experience with the paranormal? Practical experience?"

There was silence at the other end for a long moment. Finally, McGarrigle cleared his throat. "You did say it was off the wall."

"Yeah."

"When you say paranormal, what are you referring to?"

"I was wondering if you'd ever treated a patient, or perhaps observed a patient, experiencing delusions or hallucinations associated with clairvoyance, necromancy, or that sort of thing."

"Hmm. May I ask if your interest is merely academic, or does it have a more practical impetus?"

"The latter, actually."

"Well, now. I may need another cup of tea after all. Just a moment." McGarrigle put him on hold, no doubt to ask his wife if she'd be so kind as to bring him a refill of his beloved Earl Grey.

Devlin could see the room in his mind's eye, the walls filled with bookshelves, the cluttered desk with barely enough room for McGarrigle's feet. His long white hair, his wire-framed glasses, and his relaxed, smiling mouth.

Yes, Devlin would freely admit that David McGarrigle served as a father figure, a substitute for the parent he'd lost as a teenager. So what? Everyone needed someone to look up to. Everyone needed to feel that there was still someone hovering at their shoulder, ready to answer the questions that confounded them, ready to help make the decisions they hesitated over, to be the court of last resort in times of trouble.

No one wanted to be the last one standing at the end of the line. No one behind them to turn to, no one to pass the burden to when it became too heavy.

In a flash of insight, he realized that this was exactly how Maddie Hubbard felt. The last one, standing at the end of the line, with no one else to turn to.

"Sorry," McGarrigle said, coming back on the line. "Christa was about to make a fresh pot, so I'm in luck. Plus, it gave me a moment to think. An old ploy, but a good one. Something I picked up from McGee, who was long before your time. He liked to tap out his pipe, fill it with fresh tobacco, and fire it up before tackling a difficult question. It was a ritual that drove us all absolutely bonkers."

"Sorry to bother you like this," Devlin said.

"Don't be ridiculous. As a matter of fact, I can answer your question in the affirmative."

"Oh?" Devlin was surprised.

"Indeed. Rather unexpected, eh? Not what you thought you'd get from the old duff. But before I go on, what are you able to tell me from your end?"

"I have a client, a twenty-year-old female, who suffered a severely traumatic event of some kind last October. I've been seeing her since February and she's now showing marked improvement, although she hasn't yet explained the exact nature of the event that set her back so drastically. To the point, though: she claims that she's some sort of a medium. A necromancer. A hydromancer, specifically, using water in a bowl to communicate with the dead."

"Oh my, my, my. Now that's interesting. Is it all entirely subjective and anecdotal, or have you observed or noted anything objective to lend credence to her reports?"

"Well, no, not really. I've been able to verify that this sort of thing seems to run in the family, though. On the female side, predominantly. Her mother was a well-known psychic in Ottawa who consulted with various police departments at one time. I've read several articles online describing her, ah, accomplishments."

"And now you're wondering whether your client's delusional, or perhaps just trying to imitate mother, or maybe there's actually more to this than meets the eye."

Devlin sighed. "She's very intelligent. And apart from this . . . aberration, I believe she's emotionally stable. Or certainly getting back there." He drank some of his bourbon and cleared his throat. "I just don't know what to think."

"And you're looking for a little advice and guidance from the old dude."

Devlin forced a laugh.

"Despite the eternal debate," McGarrigle said, "as to whether our field is a science or a soft social science or whatever, you and I have been educated and trained to value objective data whenever and wherever possible."

"Yeah."

"However, there are times when one must wade out over one's head and start to swim."

"I'm not sure I can do that, David."

"All right. Fair enough. I understand. You asked if

I've ever observed someone encountering this kind of experience in the past, and I said that I have. So, to make your call worthwhile, I should tell you about it."

"Thank you."

"This is something I've never actually shared with anyone before. Not even Christa. At first, I'd thought it might be good for an article of some sort, but I soon changed my mind. You'll see why, if I can stop deflecting and start telling you about it."

"I appreciate it, David."

"Very well, then. This goes back quite a ways, to when I was a young dog wanting to stick my nose into anything and everything. You may not remember this, but at one time, in the early eighties I think, there was a small outfit of paranormal investigators working the island out of Charlottetown. Ghost hunters. I forget what they called themselves. Something funky, no doubt, but for a while they were getting some interesting press. Eventually I couldn't resist, so I made arrangements to accompany them on a couple of their so-called psychic interventions. Almost like a police ride-along, I suppose you could say."

"I had no idea." Devlin became conscious that his stress level was slowly dropping as McGarrigle talked. He'd built up a dreadful fear that his mentor would somehow be upset and disappointed with him for raising the subject, but it appeared he'd made the right decision to call him after all.

"A lot of it was the usual stuff you see on television. Going into a supposedly haunted house at night, waving around a lot of electronic devices and asking foolish questions of the darkness, hoping for some kind of clatter or groan in reply."

Devlin heard the study door open on the other end of

the line as Mrs. McGarrigle brought in his fresh cup of tea.

"Thank you, dear. It's Dennis."

"Hello, Dennis," she called out to him.

"Hello, Christa," Devlin called back.

The door closed, McGarrigle slurped, and then he chuckled. "What a lark it was. They made a pretence of debunking sensory phenomena that clearly had a rational explanation, like air bubbles in old water pipes, expanding or contracting floorboards, and the like. But my God, how they were longing for something supernatural. It was almost sad, really. They were desperate for something to prove their belief in the paranormal."

"Did they record any sensory data at all?"

"Some, but I thought it was a stretch to interpret any of it as otherworldly. They filmed a lot of dust motes floating around, for example, and theorized they were mysterious orbs embodying the spirits of the dead. Pfftht. Come on. They were airborne dust particles, period."

"I see. So are you saying it was all delusional?"

"Pretty much, yes." McGarrigle hesitated. "Up until the final one. The last one I went out on with them."

Devlin waited.

"It was an old farmhouse near Hunter River. An elderly woman had lived in it for years all by herself, and when she passed away there were no relatives to inherit, and she'd died intestate, so the place was put up for sale to pay for back taxes, expenses, and so on. The real estate agent contacted this paranormal group, I wish I could remember what they called themselves, and said she was afraid to go into the house. So they arranged to go out and spend the night there, and of course I trooped along with them.

"This stuff was all a great adventure, you understand. It

was complete nonsense, but incredibly entertaining. One of the team, an older woman, was a medium. She claimed to be able to sense the proximity of disembodied souls, ghosts trapped in this world and unable to pass over, and all that claptrap. She'd direct the rest of them to a specific room where they could set up their hardware and go to work. It was she that I was particularly interested in, because while the others were trying very hard to be scientific with their gauges and electromagnetic meters and microphones and all that stuff, she was the one most likely to be emotionally disturbed. So I followed her around more than the rest."

He paused to lubricate his vocal chords with Earl Grey.

"And?"

"*And*," he continued, "it was around two o'clock in the morning in this dusty old farmhouse and I was getting bored and very tired. While the others explored the second floor, I went back downstairs and wandered around, trying to decide whether or not I was just wasting my time. Maybe I should just go back home and get some sleep, eh?

"I went into the kitchen and tried the tap to see if there was still water. It ran, so I thought I'd look to see if there was a glass in the cupboard for a quick drink. I heard a noise in the back summer kitchen, a big room through an open door just past the oven, so I went over to see if it was one of the crew setting up cameras or some such thing. I took a few steps inside and there was this, well, this girl standing there. Maybe fourteen or fifteen. Skirt, blouse, sneakers, nothing too unusual. I had no idea who she was, so I said hello.

"She said, 'You shouldn't be here. You, of all people.' Then she wasn't there. Just. Wasn't. There."

"Good lord."

"Yeah! Cripes. I turned around, and there was that damned medium standing right behind me. She said, 'You saw her too, didn't you?'

"Well, let me tell you, I got out of there as fast as I could, and I never went back. Didn't answer their phone calls; didn't have anything else whatsoever to do with them; didn't write the article; didn't say a word about it to anyone. To this day, I don't know for sure if they pulled some kind of stunt on me, a practical joke of some kind that I was supposed to see through and laugh about, or if it was exactly the kind of phenomenon they'd been spending their entire lives looking for."

"Wow," Devlin said.

"So what do you think of old McGarrigle now, eh?"

"I don't know what to say."

"Damned old fool."

"No," Devlin protested, "not at all. Quite the opposite."

"The thing that gets me, the thing that really bugs the hell out of me, is why she would say *that* to me. 'You, of all people.' What the hell was wrong with me being there? I mean, I had absolutely no connection to the property or the house or any of the people that might have lived there, it was just some random place on the island as far as I was concerned, so what was the big deal with me being there?"

"As a psychologist, you—"

"Oh, bullshit. I don't know. Maybe it was McGarrigle the skeptic she was talking to, or McGarrigle the young fool, or McGarrigle the complete and total lunatic. To this day, I still don't know. But anyway. You asked, so I thought I'd share that little bit of personal hallucinatory experience with you."

"You've given me a lot to think about."

He laughed. "Oh, I'm sure of that, Dennis. I'm definitely sure of that. But here's one more thing to think about. I know, deep down inside me, that they didn't prank me that night. Nor did I experience a hallucination brought on by fatigue or post-hypnotic suggestion or whatever the hell else. I saw a ghost that night, and that's all there is to it."

# 36

On the morning of the fourth Tuesday in March, Devlin sat across from Maddie Hubbard in his consultation room and tried to maintain an aura of professional calm. It was his job today to pick up the threads from last week's conversation, merge them into her experiences over the past week, and see if she was willing to continue telling him her story. However, to say that he was growing more and more uncomfortable with where this whole thing was going was a definite understatement.

Taking her back to the moment when Matt Pollock called 911 after the discovery of the bodies, which is where they'd left off last Tuesday, he asked, "How did you feel about being interviewed by the police?"

"Not happy." Maddie kept her expression neutral, but she made eye contact with Devlin and held it. "I don't like lying, but we had to stick to that ridiculous story about a buried box because the alternative would have made us sound like a couple of complete wack jobs."

"You were afraid they wouldn't believe your statement that the discovery of the bodies happened through some kind of, ah, psychic insight?"

"Of course. People like simple, rational explanations.

Especially the police. They feel most comfortable with concrete, provable stuff, like Newton's third law. Logical. Familiar."

"Which one's that, again?"

"When two objects interact, they have an equal and opposite effect on each other. Something like that. The point is, Dr. Devlin, I learned at a very young age not to get into the kind of stuff people don't believe in unless it's really, really necessary."

"Like it is right now. Between you and me."

"Yeah. I guess."

Devlin leaned back in his chair, trying to appear casual. "I went back and read the media coverage of the discovery of the bodies at the old church. I remembered it, because it happened not too far from us here, but I didn't see you mentioned in the news stories except very peripherally. As one of the people present when the bodies were found. You weren't interviewed at all."

Maddie looked away, clearly uncomfortable with the subject. "Reverend B said she'd do the talking. To the reporters, I mean. I gave my statement to the police, but no one else."

"You weren't contacted for an interview?"

She rolled her eyes. "It was awful. They kept calling. One guy sat in his car on the side of the road for an entire day. On the other side of the police barrier. Waiting for me to come out. I finally had to complain to the police. At least it gave Uncle Robert a reason to have that stupid landline taken out once and for all. I got a new cellphone number. Not that very many people had it to begin with, but it was a good idea anyway."

"How did all this sudden attention make you feel?"

She shook her head. For a moment, Devlin thought

she wasn't going to answer the question, thinking it was too obvious to deserve a response. Then she looked off to the side, choosing her words, and said, "Claustrophobic. Suffocated."

"And yet that's what your mother's life was like for years," Devlin said. "Doing what she did for the police, the consulting work, it all had a very public face to it, didn't it? How did you feel about that? About the publicity she got, her picture in the paper, quotes, all of that sort of thing?"

"I don't know. She seemed okay with it. She didn't go looking for it, she wasn't that kind of person, but if a reporter wanted to ask her some questions, she tried to give them something. Depending on who they wrote for, of course. When someone showed up from one of the tabloids, she shut them down pretty fast."

"So she was reasonably comfortable with the attention."

"I'm not sure comfortable's the right word. She tolerated it. She wanted people to understand that there was more to existence than what they experienced in their normal, everyday lives. It was hard. A lot of people sneered at her or insulted her or just got really angry."

Devlin knew she'd avoided his earlier question about how she herself had felt about her mother's publicity, which led to how she felt about her own exposure to the public—what he really wanted to hear her talk about—so he worked his way back toward it now.

"You were a child at the time she was doing these cases. Did any of the journalists try to ask you questions?"

She shook her head. "Joelle wouldn't allow it. No possible way it was going to happen."

"How did that make you feel, being excluded from the limelight?"

She laughed without humour. "Relieved. Very. It was bad enough hearing it from the kids at school whenever they ran a story about her in the paper. They thought they were being funny, but it was just hurtful and dumb. At least that eventually went away at Barrhaven and they just left me alone. But yeah, to answer your question, I was glad I didn't have to sit there and try to think of stuff to say into some guy's microphone."

"What about now? You made a decision a few weeks ago to talk to me about what happened last fall and your feelings about it. So far, I have to say, you've been very forthcoming. You've confided in me, which I appreciate. I don't take that trust for granted. But why, if you felt so claustrophobic about any sort of attention over these matters, would you talk to me about them now? At such length, and in such detail?"

Moments passed as she considered her response. Suddenly she blurted, "I have to. I don't have a choice. It's survival, pure and simple."

"I'm not sure I understand."

"I'm all alone. Except for Quinn, and I know he tries, but he really has only a superficial idea of what happened to me. So here I am, no family to talk to who would understand. No friends. No one close to me at all. I almost went insane, Dr. Devlin. I think you know I was pretty far gone for a while. Even now, although I feel a lot better, my mind's still going around and around in circles like a rat in a cage. I can't stand it. I have to get it out. I *have* to talk about it, work through it out in the open instead of just inside my head. I trust you. You're not a brainless moron. I can talk to you. I have to get *all* the way through this. Do you understand?"

"I think I do," Devlin answered carefully. "At least, I'm

starting to."

"But you don't believe a single word I've been saying this entire time."

Devlin opened his mouth to reply and then closed it again. He smiled, a tiny little smile, unplanned and prompted by genuine affection. She'd won him over, at least a little bit.

"Let's just say I'm reserving judgment for the moment. That I have an open mind."

"What more could I ask for. I mean, really."

He blinked at her tone, but she softened it with a sigh.

"We're not there yet. You may think that finding the bodies was the big trauma that set me off into catatonic land, the terrible experience that nearly finished me, but it wasn't. I'll get to that little nugget of joy soon enough."

"All right," Devin said.

"We have to talk some more about the voices in my head."

Devlin tried not to react.

She raised an eyebrow. "I know, I know. Auditory hallucinations indicate an affective disorder of some kind or else plain old schizophrenia. I looked it up online."

Now he did react, rolling his eyes.

"I'm serious, though. I hear voices. Not my own inner voice—well, yeah, I hear that one, but I'm talking about other voices. Other people. Who are outside my head. Thinking this stuff. Which I overhear, figuratively speaking."

"I see. Well, then, tell me about them."

"I will. And to do that, I'm also going to have to talk to you about Aunt Nicolette."

# MADDIE

# 37

The week that followed the discovery of the unmarked graves at the back of the old cemetery was a very difficult time for me.

As I've said, I was able to hide behind Reverend B and her willingness to bear the brunt of public scrutiny, sparing me the necessity of submitting to cameras and microphones and pushy journalists sniffing around the edges of what was on its own a rather sensational story. Just the same, the trauma that followed Matt Pollock's 911 call and the stress that persisted for days afterward was, honestly, extremely difficult to take.

All in all, the police were not too hard to deal with. I'd been around uniformed officers and detectives and community services auxiliaries for most of my childhood, so I was used to their grim expressions and professional manner. I kept the tears to a minimum, stuck to my story, and got through it.

With one little blip on the radar, as I'll explain.

The two detectives who came around, a man and a woman, sent me home with a uniformed officer to wait until they had time to question us. I'm guessing that they started with Matt, got his explanation of what he was doing with a GPR device in the first place, and then sat down with Reverend B to hear her side of the story.

I knew she would show them the photograph of the Knapp funeral from her filing cabinet and point out the bare patch we'd both focused on. She'd mention the research she was helping me with for my history paper and tell them we thought there might be useful, perhaps even valuable, items that had been buried in that spot. Old photographs, maybe. Or papers. Who knows why they'd be buried, but it was worth taking a chance to look for them. Blah blah blah.

This was where it would get a little murky. Why did you think this Reverend Blackburn would have gone to all the trouble of burying a box of stuff at the back of the cemetery when he could just as easily have sent it off to the dump or left it in the donation bin of a thrift shop somewhere?

"I don't know," would be the only possible answer.

The uniformed officer sent Quinn upstairs to his room and sat with me in the living room until the detectives showed up. After a few preliminaries, the uniform left and the man, whose name was Sheckley, went upstairs to use the washroom while the woman, Detective Constable Swift, sat down with me.

"Tell me about this essay you're working on."

I explained that I was interested in writing about rural churches, and since I lived next door to one, I thought it might be a good place to start. Basically the same line I'd fed John Pollock. When she asked to see it, I told her I hadn't started it yet, but I found my notebook and let her flip through the few pages of notes I'd made at Mr. Pollock's house.

It suddenly reminded me of Reverend B's notebook and the stuff she'd written down about the women I'd seen while scrying. I fervently hoped she'd gotten rid of those pages before the police had arrived.

*Makes no sense. Unmarked graves. How old? One of these guys?*

I nearly jumped out of my skin. It was her voice, loud and clear, inside my head as I watched her page through my notes about the pastors who'd preceded Reverend B.

*Kid can't tell us anything.*

Her lips moved, I swear to God. I saw her shape the word *can't* as it echoed in my mind.

Sudden pain flared in my head, as bright as lightning.

Detective Constable Sheckley clomped downstairs, gave Swift a look, and went outside.

She closed the notebook and gave it to me. Standing up, she thanked me for my time and gave me a business card with a number I could call if I thought of anything else she should know.

I watched her follow her partner out the front door.

As soon as I heard their footsteps going down the stairs I bolted for the kitchen and grabbed my migraine medication from the cupboard. I downed a cap with a Coke from the fridge, sobbing from the pain.

My lip felt wet.

I wiped it with the back of my hand.

Blood.

I pulled tissues from the box on the counter and they came away from my nose and mouth with streaks of red.

After a few moments the bleeding stopped.

Quinn trailed into the kitchen, took one look at me, and came right over. "What's wrong, Mads?"

I started to cry.

He helped me over to a chair. I sat down. He took the bloody tissues from me, threw them in the waste basket, and shoved a clean wad into my hand. I dabbed, but the bleeding hadn't started again.

"What is it?" He sat down next to me. "What's wrong?"

I shook my head, sobbing.

"Why's your nose bleeding?"

"I don't know," I whispered. "My head's killing me."

"I'll get them to call an ambulance."

"No." I grabbed his arm. "No, Quinn. Nobody can know about this."

"Know about what? You're suddenly getting nosebleeds with your migraines?"

"I heard her, Quinn." I coughed and spat into the tissues. It was red from the blood that had leaked into my throat from my nose. "I heard her voice in my head."

"What? Who? Whose voice?"

"The detective. When she was questioning me. I heard what she was thinking."

He leaned back, staring at me. "Whoa. No way."

I sighed, a long and ragged exhalation that seemed to come all the way up from my toes.

"What did you hear? What was she thinking?"

"That I didn't know anything useful. That she didn't understand the connection between the former pastors and the unmarked graves."

"Yeah, well, that makes two of us. But never mind that, Mads. You were reading her mind?"

"I don't know. Maybe."

"Coool!"

"No, Quinn," I murmured. "It's not cool at all."

# 38

They worked in the cemetery for the next five days straight. According to the news, they found a total of six bodies in unmarked graves, all women, all buried for at least thirty to forty years. Some had arm fractures and dislocations, likely the result of violence inflicted on them perimortem, and some had broken finger bones and wrists consistent with defensive injuries. None was buried in a coffin, of course; they were all dumped into holes in the ground and covered over. Each one was ruled by the coroner as a homicide victim.

Once they had begun removing them from the ground, I called Aunt Brigitte and had a long talk with her. She knew what was going on, of course, because it was all over the news, and we'd spoken briefly before, but Uncle Robert had decreed that they were going to stay clear of the whole mess.

Our end of Twilight Road was blocked off while the police and coroner did their thing, and he used that as an excuse, but I could see through it without any effort at all. To him it looked like more trouble from the family he'd rather forget about, and that's all there was to it.

I knew Aunt Brigitte was much more sympathetic, so I

gave her my best sales pitch.

"Quinn needs to be out of this. The school bus can't come down here; I feel like I'm going through Checkpoint Charlie every day when I drive him in and then go to pick him up again to bring him home. The other thing is, he shouldn't be around this kind of thing. It's very upsetting for him. He's only a boy."

"You're quite right, Maddie."

"It would only be for a week or so."

"Of course, dear. I'll have the upstairs guest room ready for him this evening, if you like."

Predictably, Quinn was a lot harder to convince: "No way. Not a chance. What were you thinking?"

"Quinn, be reasonable. It's not good for you to be here while all this stuff is going on next door."

"That's ridiculous. It's really cool. I've been watching them from upstairs."

"With binoculars," I said, shaking my head.

"Well, duh. There was one skeleton, they had to—"

"I don't want to hear about it. No more discussion. Pack a week's worth of clothing. I'm taking you in tonight."

He made a face and punched the air. "No. No way."

"Yes way. Go get your stuff ready. Now. Get moving. And don't forget your tablet."

"Maddie. You know how he is."

"Yeah, I know."

"He thinks we're mental cases."

"I know, Quinn. But Aunt Brigitte's on our side."

"She doesn't understand, either. Not any more than he does."

"Maybe not, but she's really nice. She'll spoil you rotten."

He pouted, but I knew he was thinking about that aspect of it.

"Chocolate muffins."

I knew he was thinking about the icing she put on top of them. With sprinkles.

"Look," I added, "I'll make you a deal."

"What kind of a deal?"

"I've been thinking about this for a while. We've got all that money, right? I'll be able to access mine next summer after my birthday. Right?"

"Yeah. So what?"

As I mentioned before, we'd inherited the entirety of Mark's estate when he died, in two equal shares, and it had been quite a lot—several million dollars for each of us. Mark was a lawyer, remember. He knew how to manage money. Plus, he'd been careful to keep up his insurance policies. The money was sitting in trust for us, earning interest, until we turned twenty-one. Which I would, on the first day of June next year.

"I've been thinking about us taking a trip. That guy you always talk about, the guru, are you still in touch with him?"

"Yeah."

"He's in Mumbai, right?"

"Yeahhhh?"

"He offered to help you. Maybe we could go there next summer, after this is over. I'd really like to see you get some help with your travelling. Some coaching, you know, in person, from someone who knows what it's all about."

He shrugged. "Yeah. Maybe."

I could tell he was intrigued by the idea. He wasn't nearly as good at hiding his feelings as he thought he was.

I smiled. "You might come back a Hindu mystic, Quinn. How cool would that be? Freak out all your friends at school."

He snorted. "Yeah right. I could entertain them by walking through fire or lying on a bed of nails."

"It's just a thought."

"So what's the catch? I go stay with Aunt Brigitte and Uncle Venom, and you bribe me with a trip for next summer?"

"Yep."

"Deal."

Uncle Venom—uh, Robert—wasn't home when I drove Quinn there, thankfully. He was at some kind of meeting, the Rotary Club or Kinsmen or something, so Quinn felt okay about it when Aunt Brigitte let us in.

They lived in a nice, large house in one of the better neighbourhoods in town, on a quiet street with big trees, sidewalks, and pretty gardens filled with the kind of plants that bloom in the fall, like a consolation prize for losing the warm weather for another year.

Quinn had never been here before—that's how little we'd had to do with them—and he was impressed, although he tried not to show it. When Mark died and we left the Barrhaven mansion to live with Marie-Claire on Twilight Road, he was six. His memories of our former home were vague, and he'd grown used to Marie-Claire's little house in the country, so I guess the idea of four big bedrooms upstairs, Uncle Robert's finished rec room in the basement with a pool table and entertainment centre, and a two-car garage and workshop to putter around in on weekends was a bit dazzling.

On the other hand, I wasn't all that starry-eyed about the place. It was way too middle class and self-satisfied for my taste. Of course, I'd never criticize Aunt Brigitte for her values or lifestyle because she was a complete sweetheart.

Uncle Robert, on the other hand . . .

Aunt Brigitte had brownies and hot chocolate waiting for Quinn, along with a big hug and lots of motherly talk, so I was able to make a quick getaway.

The house was really quiet when I got home. I missed the little twerp already.

# 39

During all this time I hadn't spoken to Reverend B or heard from her at all. I'd decided to lie low, and if she wanted to come to me to talk about what had happened, then she could. I'd talk to her. But she didn't call, and she didn't come over, so I just let it ride.

Services that Sunday at the new church at Bennett's Corners were cancelled by the trustees, who recommended that the congregation worship in town for the next few weeks. I expect they were all quite upset, especially the older folks who were around when this was going on and had had no idea what was happening right under their noses. Nothing prepares people in a quiet little rural community for something like this. Nothing.

Sunday evening, I finally caved and went over to see how she was doing.

We sat on the front porch, listening to the frogs singing in the ditch along the side of the road. It was a clear night. Moonlight painted the front lawn and glittered off the windshield of Reverend B's car. It was mild enough that we only needed sweaters to stay warm.

"This is far from over," she said.

"I know." I'd chosen her old-fashioned wooden glider

to sit in, and I moved gently back and forth, knowing we had to talk about it but not really wanting to.

Besides dreading the subject of the evening conversation, I was also starting to get one of those damned headaches again. Sorry for the bad language, but they really were starting to get under my skin.

Reverend B shifted in her chair. "I've prayed for understanding. It hasn't helped. I always tell Stephen, 'When in doubt, pray, and God will throw light into your darkest shadows.' But it isn't helping. God's taking the Fifth on this one, apparently."

*God's on vacation in another galaxy,* I wanted to say. *Soaking up the cosmic rays in some distant place wherever supreme beings go when they want to be unreachable and unimpeachable.*

"When it comes to this paranormal business," she said, "the Bible doesn't offer much in the way of guidance. There's a ghost story in the Old Testament where Saul convinces a medium at Endor to raise the spirit of Samuel, but who's to say whether it actually happened or it's just allegory? Who can be sure? And in this kind of situation, in the here and now, you really, really need to be sure."

I had enough sense not to offer a comment. I knew this was becoming a crisis of faith for her, and I didn't want to upset her any more than she already was.

"Those poor women. Jack Tulk, the sexton, must have been a sexual predator. Blackburn must have known what was going on. Maybe he even . . . participated. The whole thing's completely repulsive. I'm not sure the congregation here can survive the scandal. The church executive may decide to close down the church for good. Then I'll be out of a job."

"I'd hate to see that."

"I'll have to start thinking about where I'll go if that's the way it turns out. I just don't know." She sighed. "I'm still trying to process the horror of what happened. In this house. Upstairs in that room. I'm seriously thinking of moving into town, regardless. I don't think I can stay here. I'm getting nightmares."

"As bad as before?"

"Worse. I'm afraid I'm having a nervous breakdown. I have to do something. I just don't know what."

I felt bad for her, but I didn't know what to say. This was completely out of my league.

"There's something called religious deferral," she said. "It's what people fall back on in a crisis situation when they say, 'There's nothing I can do. It's in God's hands. Whatever happens is God's will.' They choose inaction instead of action and tell themselves it'll be okay because God will look after them."

She listened to the frogs for a moment. "I've always tried to discourage that behaviour when I've come across it in my congregation. Doing nothing, trusting that fate will treat you well, is like throwing yourself in front of a cosmic dump truck and believing that it'll swerve around you at the last minute because it doesn't want you to be hurt. Reality is completely neutral. It never plays favourites. It crushes anyone who gets in its way. That's why I've always believed in free will. In doing what it takes to live a good life, to help others in their lives, and to make choices based on intelligent thinking and meditation, all while having faith that God values our good behaviour and will reward us when the time comes."

"Okay," I said.

"So the whole argument then, free will instead of fate, rests on the understanding, doesn't it, that there's always *something* we can do? Something that makes sense in the moment that will affect the outcome of a crisis situation? So okay, Maddie, what am I supposed to do right now, in the middle of this horror show, in the middle of a spiritual crisis I never thought *I'd* face, that will make a difference one way or the other? Tell me. What am I supposed to do?"

"I don't know."

*Of course she doesn't. She's just a kid.*

It was her voice, as clear as a bell, inside my head. I nearly fell through the floor.

"Of course you don't," she said. "You're just a kid. I should be talking to my archbishop, or a Tibetan monk, or an exorcist or something. This is completely insane. Completely out of control."

I squeezed my eyes shut against the pain. *Go away,* I thought desperately, *go away and leave me alone.*

Reverend B shook her head and frowned at me. "Are you all right?"

I nodded, rubbing my temples.

*She's exhausted. Like me.*

*Stop,* I thought. *I don't want to hear you.* I was hearing her thoughts. The way I'd started hearing other people's thoughts lately. Like I was a bloody psychic radio or something.

I didn't want it. Another accursed ability? Are you kidding me?

She leaned forward. "I feel like you're—"

At that moment my cellphone began to buzz with an incoming call.

I took it out and looked at the display.

It was Quinn.

# 40

"Are you at home right now?" he blurted, without saying hello first.

"I'm over at Reverend B's. Why? What's up?"

"You have to go home. Right now."

"Why? What's wrong?"

"I saw her again."

"Who, Benedicta?"

"Yeah, Maddie. Uncle Robert had some friends over, so I came upstairs after supper. I fell asleep early. Right away, I started to travel. It was like she was summoning me. I went right there to the sphere she's always on, the cyan one. She was waiting for me."

"Okay," I said. "Look, I'm sitting here with Reverend B. I'll put you on speaker."

"Are you sure?"

"Yeah, I'm sure." I tapped the screen. "All right, Quinn, we can both hear you. So what did Benedicta want?"

"Hi, Reverend B," he said.

Her eyes were narrowed and her arms were folded in a defensive posture. "Hi, Quinn. Are you okay?"

"Yeah, I'm fine. Maddie, Benedicta told me to give you a message."

"A message? What message? Why would she have a message for me? What's going on, Quinn?"

"She said to tell you that someone needs to talk to you."

I digested this for a moment, rubbing my aching forehead. "Did she say who?"

"No, sorry. That's all I got from her. I don't usually get anything at all, so it was something, at least."

"Couldn't this have waited until later, Quinn?"

"She said it was urgent. You have to contact whoever it is right now."

"Right now? Like, right *now*?"

"Yep."

"Why would it be urgent, Quinn? It's the afterlife. It's not like they're on a schedule over there."

"I don't know, Mads. Urgent for you, I guess. Something you need to know about right now. Look, why don't you just contact them and find out for yourself? Jeez."

"All right. Okay. Don't get stressed."

"I'm not stressed. I just don't get why you have to be so pricky sometimes."

"Quinn."

"Sorry. Sorry, Reverend B."

She didn't respond. Her eyes were averted, and she was gnawing on her lower lip. Thankfully, I couldn't hear what she was thinking at the moment.

"All right," I said, "I'll go home and see what it's all about. Who am I supposed to be looking for? Her? Benedicta?"

"I don't know. I don't think so. I think whoever it is will be waiting for you. It sounds like they're over there already, like, inside the house."

"It isn't Marie-Claire, is it?" I really wasn't up to seeing her again right now.

"I don't know Mads, I don't know. It could be anyone."

It suddenly occurred to me that he was hoping it was Joelle. I knew it wouldn't be, it couldn't be, and I didn't want him to get his hopes up and then be disappointed afterward. I dithered for a moment and finally said, quietly, "It's not her, Quinn."

"It might be. How do you know it isn't? Maybe she finally found a way to get through to you."

"It's not her. Marie-Claire . . . when I contacted her, she said Joelle was lost somewhere, in great difficulty. It's not her, Quinn. She's still in trouble somewhere."

"Then we've got to help her. That's all there is to it."

"I know. But what's going on right now, this stuff we have to deal with right now, is not about her. It's about something else."

He was silent for a long moment. I knew he was struggling with what must be happening to our mother. Finally, he sighed. "Yeah. I guess so."

"I know so. Look, I'll let you go. Are you going back to sleep?"

"No way. Not a chance."

"Okay, Quinn. I'll call you later. When I've . . . you know."

"Sure. Thanks, Mads."

I ended the call and stood up. "I have to go."

"I'll come with you."

"You don't need to. I'll be okay."

She got to her feet. "Yes, I most certainly do need to."

"Are you sure?"

"Yes. I'm sure."

"If you're not up to it. . ."

"This is probably what I was talking about," she said, shoving her hands into the pockets of her jeans and hunching her shoulders. "The importance of doing something? Making a choice of my own free will and trying to help someone achieve a positive outcome in a crisis situation? This is probably it. So there you go. 'Lay on, Macduff; and damned be him that first cries Hold, enough!'"

# 41

I got my stuff from the pantry, and we took our places at the kitchen table. Reverend B had brought along her notebook again and was ready to write down whatever I said I was seeing and hearing. Thankfully, now that I was safely away from the parsonage and back in Marie-Claire's house, the pain in my head had subsided and I couldn't hear what Reverend B was thinking.

A double relief.

And now, on to the next stressful event of the evening.

I settled the bowl in my lap, filled it with water from the sippy cup, and dropped in the stone.

After a few tries and muttered incantations, a woman's face appeared in the ripples. At first I thought it was my own reflection, but when she smiled, my heart jumped and I caught my breath.

*Salut bien, Madeleine. How are you feeling, my dearest?*

It wasn't Joelle. It was someone younger . . .

*You don't know who I am?*

"I'm trying . . ."

Light laughter. Amusement. *The last time we were in the same room together, you were only a few months old. And it was only for a minute or two. I wasn't very well then, darling, and I couldn't hold it together for any longer than that.*

"Oh my God," I said.

She smiled. *Oui!*

"Aunt Nicolette!"

*Mais oui!*

I told Reverend B who it was that I'd contacted. She dutifully wrote it down.

"Are you . . ."

Again, laughter. *Insane? No, darling, the madness is gone, and my spirit is well. Enfin. But this method of communicating is very haphazard at best. We have little time, unfortunately, and none of it to talk about me.*

The resemblance to Joelle was striking. Actually, the resemblance to me was even more of a shock: the narrow face; the long, straight black hair; the slightly hooded blue eyes. Her lips were fuller, more sensual, and her nose was less pointed and, well, less woodpeckerish than mine. But—she was an incredibly more beautiful version of, well, me.

I'd never seen a photograph of her as an adult. People tend not to take fun snapshots of people after they've been institutionalized in psychiatric hospitals. Marie-Claire's albums contained two or three pictures of her as a small girl, but nothing after she'd reached school age. To see her, then, as an adult woman was startling.

I took a few breaths to calm myself. "Quinn said someone needed to talk to me."

*Yes. I do. Two things. First, something dear to the boy's heart. Your mother's been trying to contact you. In vain, I'm afraid.*

"I had a glimpse of her. A week ago. By accident. It was

. . . awful."

*She's in a place I can't reach, a place of great disorder and difficulty, and so we haven't actually communicated, but I became aware of a very strong feeling that I knew was coming from her to me. A feeling of danger, something connected to a threat to you and the boy. And a sense of urgency. Terrible urgency.*

"I don't understand."

*Nor I. It's not my place to know the greater workings of this . . . I don't know what it is. I'm . . . not quite sure where I am. I was able to reach you because we have a special bond, and someone has helped me. An ethereal being, I think. Through the boy, who is much loved over here by many spirits.*

"You said there were two things you needed to tell me."

*Yes. There's something you must do. You'll need to go into his mind to learn the way to be safe.*

"I don't understand. Whose mind? Quinn's?"

*No.*

"Joelle said you were a telepath, Aunt Nicolette. She said that's what drove you, well—"

*Mad.*

"I don't want to go there. I'm scared to death of what's happening to me. This is bad enough." I waved my hand at the bowl.

*Have courage. You were born to do this. To succeed where I failed.*

"I don't understand why this is suddenly happening to me."

*Not sudden at all. Dearest. When I talked about the last time we were in a room together, I didn't mean it was the last time until now that we'd talked to each other.*

"I don't understand," I said again.

*You were a little girl, five years old, when I took my life and ended the insanity. Sometimes, before then, we would talk. Like this, but you didn't need the water to see and hear me. We just talked.*

"I don't—"

*You told me about a boy, remember? Who took your toy car. You hit him with a hammer. Broke his wrist. When you told me about it, I said to you, 'Don't hit people in places other people will find out about later.'*

It took me a moment. I've always had a very good memory for things that happened in my early childhood. Hammer? Oh, of course! The boy who lived next door to us in Barrhaven. He was a few years older and mean as a snake. He'd wrecked one of my toys, smashed it to pieces, so I took a hammer from Mark's garage and went over to settle his hash. I'd gotten into a lot of trouble, which always happens when you're the retaliator and not the instigator. Ask any professional hockey player.

"Joelle must have mentioned it to you," I said.

*No, love. You did. And many other things. You told your mother I was your invisible friend. Joelle knew, though, who it was you were talking to. She loved me in spite of what I'd become when the voices finally drove me mad, and she knew I 'd never harm you.*

"I don't remember an invisible friend." Then, suddenly, I did. I'd called her . . .

Oh, shit. Lettie. I talked to her all the time, told her all my troubles. I remembered! Kind, sweet Lettie. She always called me Madeleine. Sometimes she wasn't there when I called out to her, but often she was. Then one day she stopped answering altogether. Eventually, as children often do, I turned my attention elsewhere and forgot all about her. Until now.

"Oh, my God. Lettie?"

*Yes, my precious love. You and I are so alike. We have the same ability. You just hid it away and never used it again. O God, how I wish I could have done the same thing. The voices in my head drove me insane because there were too many of them and they never fell silent, never went away. Even at night, they wouldn't stop. I couldn't sleep. I couldn't stand it. Sometimes the medications they gave me helped, but sometimes . . .*

"What's going on, Aunt Nicolette? What's happening?"

*Unfinished business in the place where you are. You need to be strong.*

"Aunt Nicolette! Please!"

*The door between the spheres is closing. We may not be able to talk to each other again. In my rare quiet moments, love, while I was living, I often thought of you. I still do. With such fondness.*

"Wait! I don't know what to do!"

*Reach into your mind. Bring out the strength you ran away from after I . . .*

"I can barely hear you. What's happening?"

*. . . stop running from yourself . . . je t'aime . . . be careful. . . .*

She was gone.

DEVLIN

# 42

"You were afraid," Devlin said, "that you'd end up like your aunt. Is that what you thought when you were hospitalized, Maddie? That you'd never get out again?"

She leaned over and helped herself to more tissues from the box on the table between them.

"I guess."

She wiped her cheeks and blew her nose. She wore no makeup, so it was only tears that needed attention, but Devlin felt his heart go out to her nonetheless. He hated to see people cry. Even while he knew that crying was an important release of pent-up feelings, a form of expression that often helped clear log-jammed emotions from the mind, it still pained his heart.

"I was pretty much out of it at first. I think I slept for a solid week. Plus the medications they put me on."

Devlin knew from her file that initially she'd been put on some heavy-duty anti-psychotic drugs until her advanced withdrawal had indicated a different approach. It was his opinion that the whole thing had been botched from the beginning, but there was the report from Reverend Northrop of delusions and extensive hallucinations that they'd been forced to take as their basis of treatment, so he wasn't surprised.

"But yeah," Maddie said, "when I was lucid, I was worried. Maybe this was it for me. Institutionalization, just like her."

"You said she was twenty-nine when she committed suicide."

"Yeah."

"That must have been very upsetting for your mother."

Maddie stared out the window at the bare branches of the apple tree.

"We don't have to talk about this right now if you don't want to."

After a moment, she shrugged. "I said I would. So I will."

Devlin waited. Outside, somewhere behind the house where an old oak and maple forest persevered against the ravages of man and nature, he heard the sound of crows cawing back and forth to one another. It was a sound he always equated with spring, the busy noise of crows, despite the fact that they stuck around all year. Exercising their tribal right to shout into the wind with great enthusiasm, trying to outdo one another in their vociferous joy at having survived another year.

"Everything I know about her," Maddie eventually said, "came from Joelle. The fact that she turned out to be Lettie was an incredible shock. But when she and I communicated back then, it was never about her. Only about me. I mean, I was just a little girl."

"Of course."

"Joelle said she noticed odd behaviour from Nicolette when she was small, after she started going to school. She'd say really weird stuff about people. So it wasn't really like me, because my scrying ability didn't start until I reached puberty. So we were different."

She frowned. "But if it's true that she was Lettie and we were actually talking to each other telepathically, then I guess I had this other thing when I was very small, too. I just suppressed it."

She dropped the wadded tissues into a plastic waste basket next to her chair and smoothed her skirt across her knees.

"Joelle said it all fell apart late one night. She was eighteen, and Nicolette was fourteen. She woke up to the sound of screaming coming from Nicolette's bedroom. She and Marie-Claire ran in and found her crouched in a corner, pulling out her hair and crying uncontrollably. Her mind had broken. She couldn't take the voices any more. She kept screaming, 'Stop! Shut up! I don't want it! Go away!' They couldn't calm her down. They had to call an ambulance."

Maddie took a deep breath. Her crying had stopped. "This was in Smiths Falls," she said, "in ninety-two. They admitted her to the hospital and put her in the psych wing. While she was there they ran a bunch of tests, Joelle told me, looking for physical causes."

"Yes," Devlin nodded. "They'd be running lab tests and brain scans for epilepsy, lesions, tumours, and that sort of thing. In many cases patients complain of a lack of voluntary control over the voices, as you've described. So they'd also be looking for something causing a functional disconnect between the pre-frontal cortex and posterior areas of the brain that would suggest the frontal portion is unable to control functions originating in the hindbrain." He hesitated. "They'd also test her for hallucinogenic drug consumption."

"Like me. All those tests and stuff. I went through that

too, right?"

"Yes, Maddie."

"And they found zip. Right?"

"Yes, Maddie."

"Which leaves us with the psycho diagnosis."

"Three out of four schizophrenics report auditory hallucinations," Devlin said. "As do almost half of those diagnosed with bipolar disorder, and so on. In the absence of a detectible physiological cause, it must be taken as a major indicator of psychosis, yes."

"And so off she went, to a psychiatric institution, on a steady diet of anti-psychotics and constant observation."

Devlin nodded, allowing her a moment to consider what she wanted to say next.

"Joelle told me about a number of times Aunt Nicolette talked to her about the voices. She could hear the thoughts of everyone in the house. She knew what went on in Marie-Claire's head, and she often described to Joelle what she herself had been thinking. Accurately, Joelle said. And it wasn't just them. It was neighbours, kids and teachers at school; everyone. She struggled to block them out. Sometimes she could, at least for a while, but other times she couldn't.

"There was a thing she'd do with Joelle. They'd be sitting on a bus together, and Nicolette would guess what someone was going to say an instant before they'd say it. It was freaky. Joelle never doubted that she was telepathic. At first, when they took her to the hospital, Joelle tried to explain. They shut her down right away, and Marie-Claire told her there was nothing they could do to help her. For a long time, Joelle blamed her mother for knowing the truth and doing nothing about it. It was so hard. But the hard reality was that they didn't know what to do to help her. It was uncontrollable. They had to let her go."

It was a long speech. Devlin understood how important to Maddie it was to get it out. She clearly identified with her aunt, perhaps even more so than with her mother, and was afraid she'd suffer a similar fate of indeterminate hospitalization.

"It was just as well I wasn't talking very much when I first went in," she added. "Reverend B must have said something, because they were trying to get me to talk about voices and all that, but I had already retreated into a shell and they didn't get there."

She gave him a look. "I'm talking to you about them now because A, you're a psychologist and won't automatically slap me back on anti-psychotics instead of what I'm on now, which is tolerable; and B, you've got that look on your face that's been there since I first started telling you all this stuff."

"Look?"

That amused set to her mouth; the almost-smile. "Yeah. The look of a guy who's trying to figure out if he just missed his bus stop or if it's still a few blocks up the street."

It took Devlin a second, and then he laughed. "Understood. I'm not there yet, so I shouldn't ring the bell and stand up."

"Not quite yet. I'm wiped, Dr. Devlin. That's it for today."

He looked through the doorway into his office, where he could see a big, old-fashioned IBM clock on the wall, the type that used to hang in school classrooms and was easily readable from five kilometres away. She still had ten minutes left, but he could hear the fatigue in her voice.

"All right, Maddie."

They stood up.

"Next week, I'm going to talk about Joelle. What happened to her. It's sort of the last thing I need to clear out of my frazzled brain before we get to last October."

"That would be fine, Maddie."

"I appreciate your patience, Dr. Devlin."

"Not at all."

She looked at him for a moment, as though weighing him in the balance, then she nodded and walked out.

MADDIE

# 43

This part, as you can well imagine, is difficult to talk about. But I have to get through it.

The morning after I contacted Aunt Nicolette, with Reverend B as my reluctant note-taker, it was a Monday. I tried to get some reading done—*The Sound and the Fury* by William Faulkner—but it was a struggle. I couldn't stop thinking about last night. I was still trying to deal with the shock that Lettie, my forgotten imaginary friend, had actually been Aunt Nicolette. That I'd been communicating with her all that time, up to her death.

*You and I are alike.*

I really didn't want to consider it as a possibility. I didn't *want* these abilities. I wanted to be normal. You know, with friends and stuff. Normal.

Good luck with that, Maddie.

After lunch I was about to go for a short walk to clear my head before tackling an essay on Alexander Pope (gakkkh) when there was a knock on the door.

"You must be Maddie."

She was middle-aged, tall and large-boned. Her straight hair, mouse-brown with streaks of grey, was gathered up in a long ponytail. She wore a tan jacket and knee-length skirt. She looked vaguely familiar, but I couldn't place her.

My eyes went to the badge hanging on a lanyard around her neck. "May I help you?"

"You don't remember me. I understand. It's been a while."

I didn't, and then suddenly I did. She looked older, her hair was different, and she wore makeup.

"Hi."

She smiled. "May I come in for a few minutes? Do you mind?"

"No, of course not. Please." I held the door open and stepped back.

We sat down in the living room. She paused for a moment, probably to allow me to offer tea or coffee or a cold drink, but since that was something I normally never did when someone came in, the moment passed in awkward silence.

"I should show you this," she said, leaning forward to hold out her warrant card in a leather wallet.

I looked at her picture, which was as unflattering as they all are on photo IDs, and read the plain, unadorned text that identified her as Sergeant Patrice Rogers, Ontario Provincial Police.

"Back then it was detective constable," she said, putting the wallet away, "but they kicked me upstairs a few years ago. I'm with the regional community response team these days."

"I see," I said, not really seeing at all. Why was she here?

"I saw your name in a report and I thought, 'I know who that is. My goodness, what a horrible thing for her to be caught up in.' So I had a word with the detective sergeant in charge of the crime unit and volunteered myself as a victim liaison officer for the case. Normally it would be a constable who'd get the assignment, but I thought since we knew each other, a bit anyway, it might help. I might be able to help."

"Victim liaison." I wasn't sure yet what she was talking about.

"We classify victims as primary or secondary, Maddie. A primary victim is someone directly affected by a crime, while a secondary victim is indirectly affected. The women in those graves were primary victims, while you fall into the latter category, a witness who was there when the graves were discovered. Which is extremely upsetting for anyone. Us included. Being a police officer doesn't make you immune from trauma any more than anyone else. But anyway, to make a long story short, the OPP has an obligation to offer you assistance in whatever way we can. Which is what brings me out here this afternoon."

"I don't really need any assistance."

Patrice nodded. "I can also fill you in on where the investigation is right now."

"Okay."

She crossed her legs and folded her hands on her knee. "Forensics is telling us the women were murdered thirty to forty-five years ago. So from about 1976 to 1992. Which is when Seymour Blackburn was the pastor and when he had the former sexton Jack Tulk living with him. The attic room you found has been gone over to a microscopic level for fingerprints, DNA residue, anything at all that might help put the victims and the two men in there. Tulk was an ex-con, so his prints are on file, but there's no guarantee that his latents would have lasted that long in the room. It'll take a while for the lab work to be done, but we're hopeful. If we can place the victims in that room and show that Blackburn or Tulk—or both—were responsible for the killings, the case will probably be closed if no other leads come up. And that'll be it."

I nodded. She was looking at me, studying me carefully. I felt a pressure coming from her, an expectation of something that she wanted me to say or do. It made me feel more and more uncomfortable.

She smiled. "The last time I saw you, I think you were eleven. No, twelve. Your mother was very upset with herself for allowing you to come with us that day to Norway Lake. I kept trying to tell her it was my fault, that I was the one who should have refused permission and didn't, but she wasn't going to listen to that."

"It wasn't anyone's fault. I went because I wanted to."

She shrugged. "Your mother was such an incredible person. She loved you very much. I'd drop her off at your house and leave without coming inside. But sometimes you'd be standing there when she opened the front door, and I'd catch a glimpse of you. She always gave you a big hug, didn't she?"

I nodded, remembering.

"And of course, she talked about you a lot."

"She did?"

"Oh, all the time. My goodness. We did a lot of driving, back and forth to crime scenes and the detachment office and your place, a lot of time on the road, and in a situation like that people get to know each other. I talked about my family, such as it was, and she talked about hers. She was intensely, intensely proud of you."

I nodded, not trusting myself to speak. After eight years, the pain had never gone away.

Patrice looked around. "This was her mother's place, is

that right? Marie-Claire?"

"Yes."

"Your mom didn't say much about her, but I gathered she also had some kind of special talent, I'm not sure how you'd describe it, that let her see things other people couldn't see."

I didn't say anything. I didn't like getting into this subject with people. Not even someone who'd known Joelle and what she could do. My experiences with Reverend B were brutal reminders that many things were better left unsaid.

"When your mother was killed," Patrice went on, "they put me on administrative leave right away, and it took almost a year for the investigation to finish. They cleared me of any wrongdoing, thankfully, and then sent me here, to regional headquarters, on a make-work assignment to keep me out of trouble. I heard that your father had died, and that you'd gone to live with your grandmother, but I didn't know until now that you were out here. I thought she was in Ottawa."

"No."

"Your mother was incredible, Maddie. She was so intelligent, she was soft-spoken and kind, and she was really good at what she did. I'd never believed in stuff like psychics and clairvoyance and all that until I started working with her, and I was blown away by what she could do.

"She never talked directly about your grandmother, but I could read between the lines. It's what I do for a living." She smiled faintly. "I figured out that Joelle likely inherited her talent, probably from her mother, who was also special in some way. Abilities passed down from mother to daughter. I saw at Norway Lake that it had also been passed down to you, too, Maddie."

I said nothing.

She stared at me. "Was it a complete coincidence, finding all those unmarked graves next door, or did you have something in particular to do with it? Using your special ability?"

There it was. The reason she'd come around to see me today.

"I don't want to talk about any of this."

Patrice held up a hand. "Just a minute. I understand completely but let me say something first. All right?"

"Sure."

"Your mother and I were quite a team, for a while. No one else wanted to bring in a psychic, for crying out loud, and I took a lot of flak for it, but her track record was so incredible even the loudmouths eventually shut up and left us alone. At one point, I thought it was actually helping my career. Five different missing persons cases closed, four happily and one not so much, plus two hit-and-runs, one resulting in a vehicular manslaughter conviction, and three different homicides. Before the last one, of course. The serial one."

She stopped for a moment and looked away, her throat working. In a flash of insight—yes, that kind of insight—I saw that she'd truly loved Joelle as a friend and colleague and was still grieving over her death, just as bitterly and wretchedly as I was.

"It's all right," I said.

She held up a hand. "I need to finish what I was saying. Afterward, after her murder, my career went into the tank, as I mentioned before. Now I've more or less found a good niche in community services and I'm happy with what I'm doing, and I'm perfectly content to finish out my career there. I don't need any more major crime involvement, thank you very much. So that's not why I'm here. Sniffing around for a way to get back on the glory trail."

"Okay."

"I saw your name. I sat down with Sheckley and Swift, the detectives who interviewed you. They walked me through the case when I said I was a former friend of the family. It made sense I might be able to help you get hrough what would no doubt be a very traumatic experience, so here I am.

"But right away, up here," she tapped her forehead, "a little voice kept telling me that if there was more to this than meets the eye, if Reverend Northrop's bullshit story about a treasure box was just that, bullshit, then maybe you could be into something more frightening than anyone would realize. Maybe it's connected to the fact that you're your mother's daughter and you have a talent of your own that brought all of this horror to light. Maybe you could use a little help from someone official who understands this sort of thing."

I looked at my hands.

"You're still so young, Maddie. Your mother was a very experienced and mature individual, and she could handle whatever I threw at her. She was amazing. Not to say you're not, but like I say, you're very young. I'm worried you might be over your head in something that could turn out to be very bad. And I'd like to help you, if I can."

I still didn't say anything.

"Will you let me? Help you?"

I closed my eyes. I could sense her presence, the intensity of her gaze, the worry that filled her mind, and the sincerity of her desire to prevent any harm from coming to me.

My head started to hurt, and I knew what was coming.
*Please forgive me.*
There it was. But could I?

# 44

It was a Saturday, and Quinn and I were both at home. Mark was in his study downstairs when the doorbell rang. I was upstairs, in my bedroom, reading. Curious as to who would be coming around on a quiet weekend afternoon, I put aside my book and went to my window, which looked out onto the street.

There were two cars. One of them I recognized, a black unmarked Crown Victoria that Patrice Rogers always drove when she picked up Joelle. The other I didn't know, a light-blue, four-door car. I moved the curtain so I could see who was standing on the front step.

A tall, thin man in a black suit and a dog collar; obviously a priest. A woman in a dark jacket and skirt. And Patrice, ringing the doorbell a second time.

Patrice, here on our doorstep in Barrhaven.

Without Joelle.

I knew.

I knew I knew I knew.

I slipped out of my room and down the hallway, pausing at Quinn's open door. He was sitting at his desk, headphones on, bobbing back and forth to music as he flipped through a comic book. He hadn't heard the doorbell.

I went to the top of the stairs and sat down as Mark opened the front door.

"Patrice. I didn't expect you. Is Joelle in the car?"

"Mark, may we come in?"

I listened to the shuffling and the closing of the door.

"What's going on?" Mark asked.

"May we sit down?" Patrice's voice was higher than I thought it would be, and it had a quaver in it. Stress.

"First you need to tell me what this is all about."

"I'm afraid we have bad news. It's Joelle."

"What about her? Is she hurt?"

"She's dead, Mark. I'm so sorry."

"No. What is this? You must be wrong."

"Please, we should sit down. This is Father Jackson Magill and Mrs. Jane Penhurst from community services."

"We're so very sorry for your loss," said a male voice, no doubt Father Magill.

So it went. They took Mark into the living room and got him into an armchair while Mrs. Penhurst went into the kitchen for coffee. I came halfway down the stairs so I could hear them.

"I should have been there," Patrice was saying. "It was a horrible miscommunication."

"I don't understand," Mark said, struggling to hold it together. "What the hell happened?"

Patrice sobbed. It was a strange, unnatural sound, especially coming from an experienced police detective. "I don't . . . did she talk to you at all about our cases?"

"Not really. We didn't discuss work."

"She was helping on the Navan investigation."

"What?"

China clattered as Mrs. Penhurst came into the room,

passed the coffee around, and sat down. Mark made a few low sounds. Mrs. Penhurst murmured something to him. They gave him a few minutes. I used the same time to suppress the wild shrieking in my own heart. Mark wouldn't want me to make a spectacle of myself right now.

"All right," he finally muttered. "Tell me what happened."

"There've been three murders," Patrice said. "Post-mortems confirmed the killer held them for several days. Joelle was getting something, and she felt she could find the next victim before . . . We were going to visit the home of a missing girl who fit the victim profile. I got a call from school that my son was taken to hospital this morning. I couldn't pick Joelle up. She said she'd meet me in Blackburn Hamlet. Where the victim lived."

"I don't understand," Mark said. "Your son?"

"Appendicitis. He's all right. Anyway."

I heard Mark get up and cross the room. "I need a drink. Anyone?"

"Thanks," said Father Magill.

Glasses clinking. Whisky being poured.

"Thank you," said Father Magill.

"Patrice? Mrs. Penhurst?"

Murmurs.

"I don't believe any of this," Mark said, "but you might as well tell me the rest."

"When I came out of the hospital I turned on my phone. Joelle had left a voicemail. She'd gone to Blackburn Hamlet, talked to the mother, and she knew where the girl was being held. She gave me an address, a farm just outside Navan. I'm so sorry, Mark. I'm so sorry."

"You're telling me she went there by herself? Joelle did?"

"I called back, but her phone went right to voicemail. I left a message. 'Stop wherever you are and wait for me to get there.' I went to the address she'd given. As fast as I could, believe me, Mark. I was too late."

"Unbelievable. How could you let her go like that? She's completely untrained to handle that kind of situation! Incredible."

"I know. I'm so very sorry."

I found out afterward from newspaper reports that Patrice arrived at the farm in time to catch the killer, a man named Marvin Albert Bell, just as he was trying to escape in a pickup truck with his latest kidnap victim tied up in the passenger seat. He'd already killed Joelle, who'd tried to stop him. She'd bled out from a gunshot wound in the abdomen.

Bell was convicted on four counts of murder, the fourth being my mother, in addition to kidnapping, forcible confinement, and every other charge they could lay against him.

He's still behind bars, serving consecutive life sentences.

Joelle, it would seem, is also in a prison, but in one that's infinitely worse than the one in which her killer will spend the rest of his life.

After that, who knows what further punishment awaits him.

I looked at Patrice now, sitting patiently across from me in Marie-Claire's living room, wanting to help me, wanting forgiveness.

Aunt Nicolette had said, *Stop running from yourself.*

This whole thing, right from the start, had been a series of decisions I hadn't wanted to make, and here was another one that was perhaps the most important of all.

If I confided in Patrice, I would renew that commitment to walking down the road I dreaded, right down to the end. I couldn't turn back on it. It was, as I've said before, a pathway into horror that I couldn't pretend later I'd never walked.

What would Joelle want me to do?

That was an easy question to answer. My mother had been a courageous woman who'd never turned away from her gift and had tried her very hardest to use it to help other people.

"We have a great responsibility," she'd once said to me, "and a great burden. We've all had to carry it, Maddie. Me, your grandmother, your great-grandmother, and who knows how many other women in our family going far back into the past. We can't turn away from it. Do you understand what I'm telling you?"

Oh, I understood, all right.

Two weeks after she'd said that to me, she was dead.

I looked at Patrice, who was quietly waiting, hands folded in her lap.

"All right," I whispered.

# 45

I told Patrice I had to attend an online lecture at eleven o'clock that I couldn't afford to miss. It was for a Classical Lit course I was taking because I needed the credit, and I was having a bit of trouble with it because I just wasn't very interested. This lecture was important, though, because the professor was going to summarize why Euripides was such a key figure in the history of tragedy, and since I didn't have the first clue as to why that would be, and this course had a final exam I would have to pass, I needed as much help as I could get.

Patrice said she'd come back with lunch for us, but she stuck around for a few minutes while I fired up the laptop and signed in. She said she thought distance learning was a great thing and had taken a few refresher courses that way herself through their headquarters training centre in Orillia. She wanted to see how the university managed it, but I think she also wanted to make sure I was telling her the truth about the lecture and not trying to get rid of her.

An hour on Euripides and his various plays was incredibly boring, as I knew it would be, but I took a lot of notes. Sometimes you do what you have to do.

Patrice came back a few minutes after twelve, and we

ate submarine sandwiches and drank iced tea from paper cups with the lids on. While we ate, I gave her a thumbnail sketch of the ability that had been passed down to me as the next female in line. She'd never heard of hydromancy before, but thankfully she didn't ask for a demonstration.

I didn't mention anything about clairvoyance or being able to read minds like Aunt Nicolette or any of that other stuff.

After lunch, she got down to business.

"I talked to Reverend Northrop this morning," she said, wiping her fingers with a napkin. "She repeated essentially the same story that was in her statement, that she was helping you with a paper and you both thought there might be some interesting stuff, I don't know what exactly, buried in a trunk or something."

I concentrated on my lunch.

"Sheckley and Swift are fine with that, as lame as it sounds. And as I said this morning, the general consensus is, if the lab can connect the dots between the victims, Blackburn, Tulk, and that attic room in the parsonage, then that's it. The file would be closed, and they could move on to other things. A horrible, terrible case with a conclusion that would put everything to rest once and for all."

I nodded, still not looking at her.

"I know there's more to it than just that," she said. "It's never quite that simple, is it? They went through the church with a microscope and didn't find anything important. No bodies under the floorboards, no physical evidence pointing a finger at the two men, nothing. But there's something in there, isn't that right?"

"Maybe." I screwed up my courage to look at her. "I don't know what, though."

"I asked the reverend to go over to the church with me.

It's still part of the crime scene, of course, and it'll stay that way until the coroner finishes her report, but I've been cleared by our forensics people to take a look inside if I need to. Reverend Northrop flat-out refused. No way she was going in there. The thought of having to do so really upset her."

"About a week ago," I said, "she thought it was on fire. She saw flames through the windows and went running over, but there was nothing."

"I see. Were you with her?"

I nodded. "She was mistaken."

"Let's go over there now." She looked at my plate, which was nearly empty. "Finish up and let's go take a look."

I didn't have any choice. I'd said I'd let her help me. She knew I wasn't telling her the whole story. On the other hand, I knew she wouldn't treat me like an idiot or a deluded person if I did actually tell her what I thought might be going on.

So I popped the last bit of sub bun into my mouth and nodded.

"Let's go."

# 46

Birds flew up into the rafters as we eased through the front doors of the church and edged along the inside wall, following a path that had been marked by the forensics team as being safe to walk along. Sunlight filled with drifting dust motes streamed diagonally from the windows.

It didn't look the same as the last time I'd been in here. The police had left behind a lot of caution tape, scaffolding, trash bags, and fingerprint powder. It was an even worse mess than before.

"Too bad they let it deteriorate like this," Patrice said.

I assumed she was referring to the church trustees and not her own colleagues. "Yeah."

"The way it would work with your mother, I'd just keep my mouth shut and let her walk around, you know, doing her thing, and wait until she had something to tell me. We can try that, if you like."

"Sure." I walked around a bit, but not with any specific purpose in mind. I had no idea what Joelle would have done in a situation like this, and it wasn't my thing, so I just kind of went through the motions.

I didn't like being in here. I didn't like old buildings, and I particularly didn't like old abandoned buildings.

They gave me the creeps, like the ceiling was about to fall down on my head and crush out my brains or something. It smelled stale and musty and generally unpleasant. The floor was filthy with dead leaves and bird droppings and stuff that squirrels and raccoons had left behind during their visits. It was beginning to give me a headache.

I grimaced, rubbing my temples.

Patrice stirred. "Something wrong?"

"No." I sighed. "Headache."

"I wonder if it's more than that."

I gave her a look. "What, don't tell me you're clairvoyant too."

"Ha ha. Not at all. But I'm very well trained in body language, Maddie, non-verbals, and yours are off the charts right now. Why don't you tell me what's going on? What are you upset about?"

"I hate this place. It's a . . . dump."

"Go on."

"I don't know." I started walking toward her. "I don't see any specific presence here, if that's what you're waiting for. There's nothing. No faces. Just . . . a lot of bad feelings."

"Okay." She opened her handbag and took out a photograph. "Take a look at this."

I stood next to her. It was a mug shot of a very unpleasant-looking man, cropped to remove the identifying information.

"Do you recognize him?"

I shook my head.

"How about him?" She pulled out another photograph and tapped the man in the middle of a group of people. The picture had been taken at some sort of an event. A wedding reception, judging by the way everyone was dressed.

"No."

"The Reverend Seymour Blackburn. In his heyday. Sort of a handsome devil."

"Whatever." I wasn't partial to mutton chops and dark, heavy eyebrows.

"This one," she waggled the first photo, "was Jack Tulk. Nasty piece of work, apparently. You haven't seen either of these guys in your visions?"

"No. Just women."

"And you only see them in water? Not in your head, just walking around like this, like your mom would have?"

"No, Patrice. Weighed in the balance and found wanting, I guess, eh?"

"Not at all." Her voice was crisp, business-like. "Do you get *anything* from in here? Anything?"

"No." I hesitated. "Just bad feelings."

"Describe these feelings to me."

I thought for a moment. She wasn't treating me like an idiot or a wack job. She seemed to be taking it all very seriously. So I made an effort. "Uh. My headache's getting worse, so give me a second."

"Is the headache connected to your water visions?"

"Not usually." I thought about the sudden headaches I'd been getting in the parsonage, and again wondered if the telepathic stirrings I'd been experiencing were responsible. I thought it best not to mention it to Patrice right now.

"There's also non-physical pain that I'm getting," I said, as a sort of a consolation prize. "If you know what I mean."

She'd produced a notebook and was furiously scribbling in it with a ballpoint pen. I thought of Reverend B's notes and hoped again that she'd destroyed them. This time, though, what Patrice wrote down would become part of an official record of some kind or other, since it was in her police notebook, so I knew I'd better choose my words carefully.

"Describe this non-physical pain."

"Loss. It's pain being felt by someone. I don't know who. Loss of faith. Loss of everything." I took a deep breath. "Anger. Hatred. Very pervasive. Anger at everyone and everything."

I closed my eyes against the throbbing in my temples.

"What else, Maddie? Keep trying."

I concentrated on my breathing for a few moments, trying to will the pain in my head to subside. "Confusion. That's all."

She was still writing in her notebook.

I sank to my knees and sat down with a thud, exhausted. I thought about my migraine medication at home in the kitchen cupboard, next to the refrigerator, but I wasn't sure I had the strength to get up and go back there right now to get it.

Putting away her notebook and pen, Patrice crouched down beside me. "Are you all right?"

"I guess so."

She took a tissue from her handbag and passed it to me. "Your nose is bleeding."

I took it and wiped. Sure enough: blood. I hadn't even been aware of it.

"I'm sorry, I couldn't see anyone. Or hear any voices."

"Have you heard voices in here before?"

I nodded, trying to stop my nose from bleeding. Joelle had always said, 'Don't tip your head back; the blood will flow backwards and choke you. Lean forward and let it bleed until it stops.' So I did. There wasn't a lot of blood, just a trickle, but I followed her advice just the same.

"What kind of voices had you heard, Maddie?"

"Just a man," I mumbled. "Very, very pissed off. Foul-mouthed. We heard him when Reverend B thought it was burning."

"We? You mean Reverend Northrop heard this voice as well?"

I nodded. Sorry, Reverend B. Busted.

"Any other voices?"

"No," I said, thinking that hearing people's thoughts in my head would qualify as a different kind of voice altogether from what she was asking me about. Not to split hairs or anything.

"Would you be willing, tomorrow maybe, to bring your bowl in here and try the hydromancy? If I'm here with you?"

"I guess," I said.

"Are you sure you'll feel up to it?"

"Yeah. Of course."

She took me gently under the arm and helped me to my feet.

"Let's get you back home," she said.

# 47

I couldn't sleep that night.

I had one of those clocks that projected the time onto the ceiling, for convenient reference when I woke up in the middle of the night and wanted to know how much sleep I'd gotten so far. Or how little, depending on what kind of a night it was. Usually I just glanced at it, rolled over, and eventually dozed off again. But not this time.

I watched it reach midnight and tried to clear my mind of all thought.

That worked for about ten seconds.

I tried deep breathing to lower my heart rate and ease my body into restfulness. I pictured oxygen flooding my brain cells and—

I stopped when my arms started to tingle and I felt dizzy. Was I hyperventilating?

I waited for the red numbers to change a few times and then did stretching exercises beneath the covers to try to relax my muscles and thereby induce sleepiness.

I had to stop when my right calf cramped up. Excruciating pain that eventually subsided after half an eternity.

I tried counting; not sheep, which is stupid, but just

visualizing the numbers in a large, sans serif font as they appeared in my mind's eye.

I gave up after eighty-three.

I watched the red numbers on the ceiling creep past twelve thirty, slip forward to twelve forty-five, and then I reluctantly crawled out of bed and got dressed.

It was one of those rare times I was glad I was alone in the house. I didn't have to worry about waking Quinn, who was a light sleeper when he wasn't travelling. I went downstairs to the kitchen and grabbed a large tetra pack of apple juice from the fridge. I drank half of it while trying to talk myself out of what I was about to do. Finally, I gave up and accepted the inevitable.

I shoved my scrying stuff into my knapsack, put on a jacket, grabbed a battery-operated lantern from the cellar head shelf, and went outside.

The air was nippy. I zipped the jacket tight around my neck as I crossed the lawn to the church, trying to remember where the dips and irregularities were so I wouldn't fall and break an ankle. I could have driven around, I guess, but this late at night it seemed a lot more effort than it was worth.

The sky was overcast, and no stars were visible. The moon wasn't up; the lantern was the only source of light available to me. I staggered once or twice before I finally made it to the bottom of the church stairs.

I really didn't want to do this, but I didn't have a choice. This situation, whatever it was, needed to be met head on, right now, and I was the only one who could do it.

Lucky me, eh?

I went up the stairs, opened the doors, and slipped inside.

I held the lantern up and saw a few small shapes hurry

into the deeper shadows. Great! My wilderness friends were present and accounted for. I edged forward a few paces and then slowly, reluctantly, sat down on the floor.

"I'm here."

My voice echoed around. I moved the lantern back and forth, saw nothing to be worried about as a potential threat—as far as teeth and claws were concerned, that is—so I set it down on the floor beside me and took off my knapsack.

The smell of the place was a bit worse than before because of the dampness coming in from the cool night air. Thankfully, though, whatever living creatures were in here with me had also settled down, no doubt to watch the upcoming show with beady eyes from the safety of the darkness.

The place became silent.

Slowly, reluctantly, I unpacked my knapsack.

Instead of my sippy cup filled with tap water, I'd brought a container of rainwater that Quinn had collected for me a while ago in case I needed it for, well, a rainy day. And here we were, then.

Slipping on my protective silver leaf charm, I poured the rainwater into the bowl. Screwing up my courage, I recited a different incantation than the one I normally used.

Translated from the ancient Greek, it was something along the lines of "Come hither to me, heavenly spirit, appear before me and do not frighten my eyes. Be attentive to me and answer my questions truthfully."

Words to that effect.

I took out a small container of olive oil and poured a small dollop on the water. As it spread toward the edges of the bowl, I repeated the chant, silently praying that I wouldn't summon some kind of nasty entity who'd make me sorry I was ever born.

I'd tried oil before, as I've mentioned, and it hadn't worked for me. I hadn't tried it with this particular incantation, though. This was something I'd dug out of my books earlier this evening, a spell intended to reach out and establish contact with someone other than a dead person. Someone with a little more power.

Part of me hoped that it would work, that I'd connect with a spirit from the other side who could help me understand what was going on. The other part of me hoped that nothing would happen so I could go back home and try again to get some sleep.

The lantern shone across the surface of the water in the bowl. The oil reached the sides and sat there.

Okay. What next?

Closing my eyes, I whispered the spell one more time.

Something began to glow through my eyelids. Warmth bathed my face. The bowl in my lap became uncomfortably hot. I put it down on the floor in front of me and looked.

*You called out, Madeleine, and I've answered.*

The light shining from the bowl was pale blue. The face was golden. Her hair was long, wavy and brown. "Who are you? What's your name?" I asked.

*I'm known to the boy as Benedicta. You may call me that.*

Knowing the name of a spirit or demon or whatever from the other side was supposed to give you some kind of power over it, so I realized that her answer was deliberately evasive. She was playing it cagey, giving me a name that might or might not be her real one. To retain control, I guess.

Whatever. I wasn't going to order her to rob a bank for me or kill my worst enemy (I didn't really have one) or pick the winning numbers in the next lottery draw, so it didn't matter.

"Quinn's told me about you," I said. "He thinks you're an angel."

*I've never been human. But I'm not an angel. Those beings are special messengers of God, and I've never aspired to such a lofty role. My comings and goings are much more modest. Friend of small boys. Observer of human suffering. Offerer of assistance and whatever blessings might be appropriate to my station.*

She was chattier than I thought she'd be. "Why have you answered my call? I wasn't expecting you."

*I knew you'd reach out. I was ready. Tell me what you want to know.*

"What's going on! That's what I want to know. I don't understand the first thing about what's happening here. Explain to me what's going on."

*You've reached a point in your life where you must face your greatest test. You must discover who you truly are, Madeleine, and what your true capabilities might be.*

"A test? You're telling me this is a test? I'm being tested for something?"

She smiled. It was like extra golden glow inside the glow. *No, my dear. Others are in dire straits. They desperately need help. You're the one most suitably placed to provide that help. Whether you can, and more importantly, whether you will, is the substance of the test.*

"I don't get it. Are you talking about Joelle? That I need to help Joelle?"

*Alas, no. The time is not right for that to happen.*

"Then what? I don't have a clue what's going on here."

*Your mind is like a beautiful flower, still in bud form. My role, the blessing I bring you, is to—oh, wait. You and*

*I share a great love of human language. "The force that through the green fuse drives the flower, drives my green age." Well, cyan in my case. Anyway, I've been chosen— well, directed—to provide that force to you. This is my benediction, so to speak.*

"I still don't get it."

*You will, momentarily. Please don't summon me again. Believe it or not, you're not the only one who gets headaches from this kind of thing. Goodbye, Maddie. Love well, and be loved.*

She vanished. The glowing light disappeared.

Pain shot through my head.

The lantern went out.

Something skittered in the darkness.

Then it began to happen, and I started to understand the benediction that she'd given me, and what the energy she'd talked about would enable me to do.

# 48

Everything was quiet.

The creatures hanging out with me in the shadows remained still. Waiting, no doubt, for what might come next.

As I rubbed my forehead, wishing the migraine hadn't started up again, I looked around in the darkness. What had the church been like when it was still in use? When it had been a place of worship for people in the township instead of an eyesore and a potential safety hazard?

Before now, I hadn't really given it any thought. But suddenly, for some reason, it seemed important to me.

I'd seen the inside of the new church, which they'd furnished with most of the stuff from here, so I knew what the pews looked like. In this old dump, filled with people, they would have crowded the space, leaving only narrow aisles along the sides and down the middle. The altar would have been in the centre of the little stage up front, the pastor gripping it with both hands as he leaned forward and spoke to his congregation. Behind him, the small choir shifted back and forth on restless feet, waiting to break out into their next number.

I could see it clearly, as though it were a bright Sunday

morning. The pastor was old. His grey hair was a fringe around the back of his head. His neck was long, and his Adam's apple bobbed up and down as he spoke. Some people in the pews made a show of listening, but others stared at the stained-glass windows or down at their hands, or their eyes were closed. The pastor was a widower, so there was no wife in the front row, listening attentively, who would go home to the parsonage with him when the service was over. Right now, he was warning about the evils of free love and psychedelic experimentation, but he was thinking about a model of the *Cutty Sark* he was in the middle of putting together.

Ah ha! The Reverend Donald Dryson, I presume.

A few rows back, a young John Pollock and his wife, Theresa (the French hater), sat side by side with a little boy. Not Matt, though. An older brother. How many years ago would this have been? Fifty, perhaps.

The pain in my head was getting intense. I closed my eyes for a moment, and Dryson's voice faded. When I opened my eyes again, the church was empty. The pews were still there, but the Sunday morning sunshine had faded into a late afternoon glow. A man walked among the rows, putting folded papers into the back racks. The latest church bulletin?

It was the Reverend Seymour Blackburn.

The front doors opened. Blackburn straightened and turned. Jack Tulk walked up the aisle toward him.

"You're gonna want to see this," Tulk said.

Something moved in the doorway, drawing my attention, but there was nothing there. When I looked back, Blackburn and Tulk were gone.

A man sat in a wooden chair at the foot of the altar. He wore ecclesiastical robes, and his grey hair was neatly combed. His legs were crossed, and his glasses were pushed up onto his forehead.

He said to a woman sitting in the front row, "I can't do this anymore. It's too much."

They were alone in the church.

The woman sighed. "The exterminators said—"

"It's not rats or squirrels or whatever, Doris. It's something . . . else."

"James. Please."

"Wilson only lasted here for a year. He wouldn't say anything, but I knew there was something seriously wrong. I'd hoped it was just him, but . . ."

"It's only been ten months."

"I know Doris, and I'm really sorry. But we have to leave. Right now."

"I know. I know. I feel it too."

My headache was steadily bad, a pounding that demanded attention and wouldn't relent until I admitted my helplessness before it. I felt a wetness on my upper lip. The tissue in my hand was wet. Closing my eyes, I groped in my knapsack for another one. There. Ah, lord.

I opened my eyes and saw nothing but darkness.

The images had been so vivid. I wiped my lip and dabbed at my nose. I'd seen very brief glimpses of the past as it had played out inside this building. Were they figments of my imagination, generated from photos shown to me by Reverend B from church records and online websites?

I knew better.

*Where am I?*

Fresh hot fear burned through my head, as though the place in my brain where the headache pounded had suddenly been stabbed with a knife.

*Dark. Where's the light?*

It was a man's voice, whiney and childish.

*I don't know what this place is.*

The same confusion I'd experienced this afternoon with Patrice. Thoughts going in a bunch of different directions all at once. Nothing making sense. Random, unconnected thoughts

*Why am I here? I don't understand.*

"Who are you?"

*You can't find me. You'll never know the truth.*

"You're here right now, aren't you?"

*Please. I can't . . . I keep coming back.*

"Why?"

*That thing. That worthless, faithless bastard.*

"What thing?"

*O the horrible, horrible beast of Satan.*

"I don't understand what you're talking about."

*I'll kill you. I'll hunt you down and tear your flesh from your bones and kill you filthy dead.*

I felt a thrill of fear. "Why? What have I done to you?"

*Not you, fool. Him.*

"Who?"

The voice began to shriek. It rose and fell, up and down the scale, deafening, echoing in the empty church, until it broke off into a ragged sob.

I suddenly began to see chaotic images, a kaleidoscopic vision of faces and colours and shapes and flashing lights. Voices babbled in my head, incoherent, shouting in languages I didn't understand. I covered my ears, but it didn't help. They were inside my head, clamouring mindlessly, smothering me, smothering me, smothering me—

I think that's when I passed out.

# 49

The next morning I was outside raking leaves when Patrice Rogers pulled into the driveway and got out of her car.

We sat on the front verandah steps. She was wearing a very law enforcement-looking navy jacket and skirt suit, with black shoes and her black handbag, and of course her badge was hung around her neck, as usual, in case anyone wasn't quite sure that she was a cop. She didn't seem to mind risking her skirt on the rough surface of the old wooden steps, though. She was more interested in how I was doing.

"Okay," I said. "Better than last night."

"I'm glad you called this morning. I wish you'd waited until I was with you, though. For your own safety."

I shrugged. "I had to see if I could do it."

"Apparently you can."

"Yeah. I guess so."

"Are you still up to trying it again?"

"I guess so. It has to be done."

"Your mother used to say the same thing," Patrice said, looking sideways at me. "When we got to a place where she was going to try to get a reading, it always took her a minute or two to get out of the car. It's not that she was afraid. That's not the right word. Maybe apprehensive is a better way to describe it. Uneasy anticipation. I'd stand around for a while, talking to whoever was on site, and then finally I'd turn around and there she was, right behind me. I'd say, 'Are you okay to do this?' and she'd say, 'It has to be done.' Those exact words."

"Like mother, like daughter."

"I don't know. You said yesterday your abilities are different than hers."

"Now I'm not so sure." I smoothed my skirt, not meeting her eyes. "So far, I've just been contacting dead people. Through the scrying. Now, though . . . I'm hearing people's thoughts."

"You mean, living people."

"Yes. Reverend B. A couple of others."

"Me?"

I bit my lip. "Yeah. Once. Yesterday morning. But just one thing, very short." I met her eyes. "It's involuntary. I'm not trying to hear what other people are thinking. It's intrusive, I mean toward the people whose thoughts I'm hearing, and, well, really upsetting. It drove my aunt literally insane, and I don't want to go down that road. Can you understand that?"

"Yes, of course." She frowned. "Are you talking about a sister of your mother?"

"Yeah. Aunt Nicolette. Joelle's little sister. She was telepathic. She heard other people's thoughts, but it was all the time, constantly in her head, and she couldn't control it. She ended up in a mental institution. She finally killed herself there."

"I'm very sorry."

I hesitated a long time before saying, "I contacted her

last Sunday. During a session. It really threw me. She said I'd have to go into someone's mind to learn the way to be safe. I think, whoever's thoughts I'm hearing in the church, they're alive somewhere, not dead, and I'll have to use this other ability I seem to have. I'll have to go into their mind and stop whatever this is all about."

She smiled. "So, what was I thinking? When you read my mind?"

"Just that you were worried about me," I fibbed.

"I am."

It was my turn to frown. "You don't think I'm psychotic or something? You really believe all this stuff?"

She hesitated for a moment. "Yeah, I do. At one point in my career I would have been calling in paramedic support and having you taken to the hospital, but that was before I met your mother. She changed the entire way that I look at life." She sighed. "I still miss her, so much."

"Yeah, I know."

She didn't pick up on my little joke.

"Did she ever tell you about the first time we worked together?"

"No. I don't think so."

"I was a detective constable, about five years in with the crime unit at that point. I'd seen a lot. It's a tough job. Anyway, we were working a series of robbery homicides in Lanark County. Elderly residents living on isolated back roads, you know, a rural setting—"

"Sort of like this one."

She laughed. "A lot like this one. Minus the church and graveyard, of course. Anyway, some woman had called the detachment office a couple of times wanting to speak to the detectives assigned to the case, and one of my co-workers ended up talking to her. She claimed to know where stolen goods relating to the latest murders were currently located. When he asked how she knew, she told him she'd seen them in a vision. When he suggested that maybe she knew because she was involved in the robberies and should turn herself in, she got a little shirty with him and asked to speak to the sergeant. He hung up on her."

"That would be Joelle."

She laughed. "That was Joelle, for sure. Anyway, she showed up at the detachment office, and I was nominated to check her out and either arrest her or have her committed to the booby hatch. I took her into an interview room and away we went. She wasn't anything like what I was expecting. She was . . ."

"Joelle."

"Yeah. Joelle. The recording of that interview still exists, by the way. I have a copy of it in my desk drawer. But to make a long story short, she'd visited the adult daughter of the victims, who'd told her about a pocket watch originally belonging to her great-grandfather that the killers had stolen along with a lot of other stuff. She showed Joelle a gold ring with a ruby in it that had also belonged to the great-grandfather. Her father had given it to her when she got married. Joelle said she handled the ring for a moment and knew almost immediately where the watch was."

She sighed. "I figured, what the hell, right? We've got nothing but smoke so far on these guys, and my afternoon's free. So I took her for a drive. She led me right to this beat-up old house on Highway Seven just the other side of Carleton Place where these three brothers were living. It was filled to the rafters with stolen property, guns, ammunition, and everything else. Including the watch. Case solved. Just like that. It seemed she had a talent for finding lost property as well as lost people."

You could have knocked me over with a feather.

Joelle and I had talked a bit about the things she did with the police, but not in much detail. With the exception of the Norway Lake case, of course. But all this time I'd had no idea she also had the same ability to find lost objects as her grandmother, Lisette.

There was a lot more crossover between the generations than I'd thought. Which perhaps explained what was happening to me right now.

I stood up. "I'll get my stuff."

"Are you sure, Maddie?"

I noticed for the first time, when she stood up next to me, that she was actually a couple of centimetres taller than I was, which was saying something, since I was taller than most females my age that I knew.

"Yeah, I'm sure." I smiled sadly. "It has to be done."

# 50

A little red squirrel ran like crazy across the floor and disappeared down through a gap in the floorboards as Patrice and I eased inside the church and made our way tentatively up toward the front. Wings flapped somewhere above, but when I looked up, there were only shadows.

Far enough. I took off my knapsack and dropped it at my feet. I'd brought my scrying kit, but I didn't think I'd be using it this time. I sat down cross-legged and took several deep breaths, slowly letting them out again. I wrung my hands, interlaced the fingers and squeezed, rubbed my palms, then crossed my arms in a defensive posture.

"If you feel uncomfortable at any time," Patrice said, "just stop. We'll leave."

"Okay." Again, I wasn't sure what to do, but I had a strong sense that I didn't need to summon Benedicta or anyone else this time. She'd created, well, I didn't know what exactly, but something like an expectation within me that by reaching out with my mind, by concentrating and *really* reaching, that I'd make contact with whatever living person was haunting this church.

If that's the right word. Normally you'd think that a place would be haunted by a ghost, right? Like the ghosts of the women I'd seen in the parsonage. But I was very sure that the man whose voice I'd been hearing was alive. Somewhere. And, since I knew about everyone who lived on Twilight Road from Bennett's Corners on down, it wasn't somewhere close.

Patrice walked over to the far wall and leaned back against it. Partly to give me space to operate, I figured, and partly because she didn't want to sit down on the filthy floor like I was. The skirt suit she was wearing was obviously expensive, and God knew what you had to pay a dry cleaner these days to look after a garment like that.

Marie-Claire's front porch steps were one thing, but this dump could ruin a nice skirt in an instant.

I tried to clear my mind. I closed my eyes, thinking about how tired I was. Exhausted. If only I could get a good night's sleep. Sleep. Sleep. Wait a sec. Was I trying to hypnotize myself? Wrong, wrong, wrong.

I opened my eyes, stopped hugging myself for dear life, and folded my hands primly in my lap. Better. No need to be so scared, I told myself. Everybody seems to be able to think you can do this, so just relax and do it.

Yeah, right. Everybody. Dead people and non-human spirits. Great.

*Where am I?*

"Shit." I jumped as the voice rang in my head. I'd been so distracted by trying to get my nerves under control that it caught me completely off guard.

*This place. This place. Why am I here again?*

"Who are you?" I asked, my voice cracking.

*You again. You. Why do you keep bringing me here?*

"I'm not bringing you here. You're coming by yourself. Who are you?"

*The bathroom stinks. Can't stand the reek of it. Why*

*don't they do something?*

There was no bathroom in the church, of course. "I don't understand."

*I want to look out the window. Why do they close the curtains all the time?*

"There aren't any curtains here."

*Can't breathe. This thing on my face. Damned nuisance.*

"What's your name?"

*My name? My name? Am I Job? Am I Jonah? Or just another worthless, accursed loser? Abandoned with all these other broken souls.*

"Let me help you. Tell me where you are. I'll come help you."

*Help me? Tell me where he is, then. Spawn of Satan. I'll tear apart his flesh with my own hands and feed it to the dogs. I'll kill him filthy. That worthless, faithless bastard. He destroyed me. I'll destroy his worthless soul! I'll—*

Abruptly, it ended. No shrieking this time, thankfully, and no chaos. Just silence. Silence ringing inside my head and inside the church.

I slumped, exhausted.

Patrice stirred. She came over, knelt down beside me, and handed me a wad of tissue.

"Thanks." I dabbed at my upper lip. Blood, predictably, to go along with the migraine.

"Are you okay, Maddie?"

I nodded. "He's crazy."

"I know. I heard."

I frowned. "You heard?"

"Every word." She touched my shoulder. "Somehow you made me hear what was in your mind. Unbelievable."

"Yeah." Welcome to my world, I thought.

"I know. It's not easy for you. Not an easy world for you at all."

I blinked at her. "You heard that too?"

"Yeah. Look, I'm not a novice at this stuff. And I've done a lot of reading on the subject. You must be a full telepath, Maddie. Telesending as well as receiving."

"I guess." I didn't really care. I was too wiped to think about it.

"Like your Aunt Nicolette, from the sounds of it."

I didn't say anything. I didn't want to be like Aunt Nicolette. Not at all.

She patted me again. "The good news is, since I heard everything, I think we may be able to get to the bottom of this."

"Oh?" That got my attention.

She helped me to my feet. "Come on. I've got an idea."

# 51

She took me home and put me to bed. I slept around the clock and got up the next morning, which was Wednesday, feeling better. The migraine was gone, my mind was quiet, and I was hungry. Really hungry!

I ate a huge breakfast and puttered around the house, emptying waste baskets and running a load of dishes in the dishwasher. I went around the living room with a feather duster, swiping at shelves that still held some of Marie-Claire's knick-knacks, her horse clock made by the United Clock Company back when Christ was a cowboy, and her big console television set that now served as a place to put vases of flowers from the back garden in summertime.

I was dusting the multi-shelved glass unit that housed her stereo system when I happened to look at the turntable and saw a record sitting on the platter. In all the time I'd been cleaning this room since her death, I'd never noticed a record sitting there.

I guess I've said before that strange things sometimes happened in Marie-Claire's house, and it usually wasn't wise to ask a lot of questions. In this case, though, it was probably just the last record she'd played before she passed away.

Curious, I lifted the dustcover for a look.

The label had a cool-looking yellow and brown design with the logo of Tamla Records at the top. I frowned at the title: "What's Going On" by Marvin Gaye.

Wow! I had no idea that Marie-Claire had been interested in the Prince of Soul, or that Motown R&B music had appealed to her in any way. I knew who Marvin Gaye was, of course, and I recognized the titles of two of the songs on the side she'd listened to, "Mercy Mercy Me" and, of course, the title track. I'd heard them when I was a kid, because Joelle sometimes listened to the radio when she was doing housework, and I'd always liked them. But I'd never even seen this album before.

Mark and Joelle were not exactly audiophiles. Their record collection had tended toward Christmas carols by Kenny Rogers and Neil Diamond's greatest hits album, inherited from Mark's mom. Stuff like that.

I looked down on the shelf below the turntable and saw the dust jacket for "What's Going On" sitting on top of the cassette deck. I pulled it out, thinking that I should just return the record to the sleeve and put it with the others on the bottom shelf of the unit.

In case you haven't seen this album before, the front cover is dominated by a close-up photo of Gaye, the collar of his leather jacket turned up, his hair, eyebrows, and beard dotted with drops of rain. It was very, very cool-looking.

What the hell. It was too quiet in the house, and I was in a mood for some music. I hit the power button on the receiver, lifted the dust cover on the turntable, and dropped the tone arm onto the record.

*Mother, mother, there's too many of you crying.*

I listened to the whole side of the record while I finished

the cleaning. It was really great. I couldn't help marvelling at the fact that Marie-Claire had been a fan of R&B. It made me feel strange and a little disappointed in myself that I hadn't known more about her when she was still here with me and Quinn.

Later in the morning, I was doing some online reading when Patrice called.

"How are you feeling this morning?"

"Okay," I said. "Better than last night."

I heard the rustling of pages at the other end as she flipped through her notebook. "Yesterday afternoon I started making calls. Well, first I talked to Terri Swift, and when she told me she and Sheckley are neck-deep in another case already, I volunteered to do some follow up for them. Which was fine with her and her sergeant. And my boss. *Then* I started making calls."

She reached the page she was looking for. "What really stuck with me were the things the voice said about a bad-smelling bathroom, curtains in the window, and other broken people. I wondered if the individual might be living in an old folks' home, so that's where I concentrated. I have no idea what kind of range your talent has, Maddie, so I started with the closest ones and worked my way outward."

She found the page she was looking for. "I had to leave a message at a couple of them for the administrator or director to call me back, and it finally paid off this morning. Jack Tulk is a resident at the Pine Hill long-term care facility, where he's been living for the past eight years."

"I don't know where that is."

"North of Kingston. Just before you get to Joyceville. He's eighty-one years old and suffering from dementia."

"Tulk? Really?"

"The dementia's been worsening over the last year or so, and they recently had to put him in a single room. He's been so noisy he was keeping his roommate awake all night and upsetting everyone on the floor. The guy's in rough shape, Maddie. He's mostly bedridden, and he only has very brief periods of lucidity. They made a point of emphasizing that they don't over-medicate residents, that the doctors are particular about what these old folks are given, but he does get a medium-strength sedative when he gets agitated."

"It doesn't sound like there's a lot he could tell us."

"No. It's pretty sad. My father-in-law fought the effects of Alzheimer's for eight years before he died. Every day of every month of every year of that time was very, very stressful for everyone involved. Tulk's mind is probably pretty much gone at this point."

"A dead end."

"I'm going to go down there this afternoon to see for myself. Depending on what I find, I may be able to get a warrant for DNA, blood, and fingerprints, and we can see where it takes us. I'd expect Tulk will be a match one way or the other for forensic evidence we've already collected on Twilight Road, and it'll give the major case manager a basis on which to make her decision on how to proceed."

"You mean charge him with the murders of these women?"

Patrice sighed. "I don't know. If the evidence tells us what I think it will, the court will appoint him a lawyer, and they'll no doubt find him unfit to stand trial. After that, he may be transferred to a different facility, but that'll probably be the extent of it. You can't bring someone to justice to get their due punishment when life has already beaten you to the punch."

"It doesn't seem right," I said. "For those women. And what about their families?"

"I know, Maddie. There's follow-up ongoing right now to identify the remains, where possible, and their families may want more than just closure. But if he's already out of reach because of his dementia, there's nothing anyone can do about it."

I started to wonder whether or not she was right about that.

"I'm going down there," I said.

"I don't think that's a very good idea, Maddie."

"I have to. This is far from over. I have to see him with my own eyes. You know I've been hearing his voice. Somehow he's still able to reach out with his mind, I have no idea how, and contact me. I have to get to the bottom of it. I have to."

She was silent for a moment.

"What time will you be there?" I asked.

"I'm not sure," she said. "I have a couple of stops to make first. Maybe around two."

"I'll see you then," I said, and ended the call.

# 52

As I backed out of the driveway after bolting a quick lunch, I saw the Canada Post truck coming along, so I pulled back in to wait for them to do their thing.

The driver put something in Marie-Claire's mailbox before turning around and heading back up the road. I got out and grabbed it, then shook my head when I saw it was a letter addressed to Reverend B. Occasionally, they made mistakes like this, mixing up mailboxes and whatever, and we had to finish the delivery process ourselves. It was the price you paid, I guess, for the luxury of driveway-to-driveway service out in the middle of freaking nowhere.

Oh well. It was a pretext for calling on her, I figured. Sort of touching base a week after the discovery of the bodies, to see how she was doing. I figured she was probably blaming me for everything that had happened to her since Stephen had flown out of her life and left her stuck here with a wackadoodle next-door neighbour and a bunch of grisly murder victims in her cemetery.

She opened the door with a tentative expression on her face. Was I bringing more trouble into her already-turbulent life? I handed her the letter, explaining that it had been left in my mailbox by mistake, and her expression relaxed a bit. Not much, but a little.

She invited me in, so I stepped into the hallway. We chatted for a moment, inane small talk about stuff I can't remember now, and she looked out at my car in her driveway.

"Heading into town?"

"I'm on my way to Joyceville."

"Oh? What's in Joyceville, other than the prison?"

"They found Jack Tulk," I said. "He's in a long-term care facility. I need to go down and try to talk to him."

"Oh, Maddie." She leaned against the edge of the door. "I don't think that's wise."

"Why not? He's the only link left to what happened back then, and I'm pretty sure he's the cause of all the phenomena we've been witnessing up here."

"Personally," she said, folding her arms, "I think you should just let all of this go. Murdered women and disembodied spirits and ghosts and what not, it's just not the sort of thing a young person like yourself should get wrapped up in. If you were a spiritual person, I'd tell you to pray for guidance from the Lord, but I know that's not how you see the world, so the best I can do is advise you to let this go. Move on with your life."

"So has that been a big help for you? Praying for guidance from the Lord?"

She winced at my sarcasm, and I immediately felt bad.

"I'm sorry," I said. "I didn't mean to be disrespectful."

"I know you're upset. I'm upset, too. I don't see that there's anything to gain by confronting that man with something that happened forty years ago. You said he's in long-term care?"

"Yeah."

"His mental state may not be very good, Maddie."

"I know. Patrice said he's suffering from dementia. Just the same, I need to see him for myself. I need to see if I can communicate with him in person. I've been communicating with him already, from here. From the church. Now it's time for me to put an end to it for good."

"It's likely to be a wasted trip. Not to mention depressing. Are the police sure he's the one responsible for what happened to all these women?"

I explained that Patrice would be going down there this afternoon to assess the situation and decide whether to have a forensics team come in to collect DNA, fingerprints, and blood samples from Tulk. They expected to be able to link him in one way or another to the murders, and then they'd be able to wrap up their investigation.

"Well, there you have it, Maddie. That's your closure right there, isn't it?"

"Not by a long shot. I know I've been hearing his voice. So have you. I need to know why. And I need to know why the women have been reaching out to me for help. Help for what?"

"But hasn't it all stopped, now that the bodies have been found and their souls can find peace at last?"

Shaking my head, I told her about having gone into the church the other night. I described how I'd communicated with the voice and that the next day, after I'd told Patrice what I'd experienced, she'd been able to track down Tulk at the Pine Hill rest home.

"I know it was him. He may be demented and medicated, but he must still have lucid moments in which he travels back here to revisit the site of his horrible crimes."

"Travels. You mean like Quinn's supposed journeys into the spirit world?"

Ah, it was that last qualifier, *supposed*, that hurt the

most. She hadn't needed to tack it on, like a little spacer thing to create a bit of distance between herself and me, but she had.

She seemed to have moved into full denial. None of this actually happened, Belinda. None of this was real. It's okay, God's in His Heaven and all's right with the world after all.

I turned and stepped out onto the porch. "Thanks for everything, Reverend B. I'll be seeing you."

"Wait."

She pushed away from the door and shoved her hands into her jeans pockets. "I can't let you do this."

"Pardon me?" I stared at her. Was she really going to try to tell me what to do?

She muttered something that sounded like *shit* and made a face. "I can't let you do this by yourself."

"I have to. There's no one else who can. Besides, Sergeant Rogers will be there."

"That's not what I mean. Just a minute." She disappeared into the kitchen and came back a moment later with her handbag. "I'll drive."

"No. I can't ask you to—"

"It'll be easier just to go straight down to Joyceville from here. We'll follow Highway Fifteen all the way."

I frowned at her. One moment she was implying that Quinn and I were frauds, that we'd made the whole thing up and somehow tricked her into falling for it, and now she was signing up for what would likely be a very unpleasant and potentially dangerous road trip. How was I supposed to take this?

She pulled out her keys and shook them. "Come on. Move your car, and we'll go."

"Are you sure?"

"No, I'm not sure at all. But I owe you at least this much, Maddie. You've been a good friend. No matter what happens in the future, no matter where I end up, I'll always remember that."

I opened the door, thinking that it sounded as though she'd just recited my epitaph. *She was a good friend.*

Lovely. Well, as Ambrose Bierce said, friendship is a ship big enough for two in fair weather, but only one in foul. Or something like that.

# 53

The drive from Bennett's Corners down to Joyceville took just over an hour, Reverend B being the cautious driver that she was. Once we'd worked our way through Smiths Falls it was all two-lane highway, County Road 15 for the most part, as Reverend B had said. Like any other two-lane highway it was completely insane, traffic-wise, and there was a constant line-up of cars behind us waiting to pass. It was a tension-filled drive, as Reverend B took the 80 kilometre-an-hour speed limit as gospel while pretty much everyone else treated it as a lame joke.

My stress load was already high enough without being afraid of dying a violent death in a fiery car crash, so after a while I tried to block it out and concentrate on the autumn colours lining both sides of the highway. It was a beautiful time of the year, for sure, with streaks and splashes of red and yellow and orange pushing out the green, and scraps of blue sky showing through overhead, but it wasn't really working for me right then. I was very afraid of what I was going to find when we reached the Pine Hill long-term care centre.

For better or for worse, I'm not quite sure which, Reverend B decided she needed to get a few things off her chest. At first she just commented on the colourful scenery and how it always made her think of the New England Transcendentalists and Thoreau and others from that period, for whatever reason. She reminisced for a few kilometres about her days at Wilfrid Laurier and how much she'd loved the fall terms in particular, a fresh start each year with great new courses to dive into and always a few new professors to get to know.

Then she switched to talking about her former marriage, something she'd never uttered a word about before.

"Terry was a widower," she said, staring straight ahead at the highway in front of us. "I met him when I was installed at Cobourg. He was an orchardist. How's that for an interesting word? Apples, twenty acres worth. Spartan, Empire, and Cortland, for the most part. Plus raspberries and strawberries. His wife had died of breast cancer before they'd had any children, and he was very introverted, so it took a while for him to realize it was okay to pay attention to me other than on Sunday mornings."

I laughed softly but didn't say anything. It was a monologue, not a conversation. I could sense her emotions though—sadness mixed with nostalgia for lost times and lost people. I resented her attitude toward me and there was no way around it, but I also felt sorry for her. She was a lonely person and not as self-confident as she pretended to be.

"We dated for two years before we got married. Stephen was born a year later, and I was very happy. A family of my own. It was wonderful. I was twenty-eight. He was thirty-four, and you couldn't have asked for a better husband."

She was silent for a while, gripping the steering wheel tightly. "He never had a chance to know what it was like to be a father and raise a child, though. That winter, after

Stephen was born, he was killed in a horrific pileup on the Trans-Canada in the middle of a blizzard. I left Cobourg with Stephen for another posting the following spring."

"I'm sorry," I blurted.

"It was a long time ago. It doesn't hurt any more; it's just very sad."

Another car passed us, a silver Audi with those blue Ontario plates that were discontinued because they're impossible to read after dark. It rocketed up the road ahead of us as though it were the front half of a police car chase. I looked over my shoulder to be sure, but there were only regular-type vehicles behind us.

"I'm not sure if I told you that I wrote my doctoral thesis on the subject of evil."

"No, I don't think you ever said."

In fact, I'd Googled her not long after she'd moved into the parsonage and found her thesis online at Library and Archives Canada. Its title, *Considerations of Evil and Problems with the Free Will Defence*, had been enough for me.

She sighed self-consciously. "You're probably familiar with the term 'theodicy,' the attempt to explain the existence of evil in the world while also believing in the existence of God, who is omnipotent, omniscient, and omnibenevolent. It's a classic in religious philosophy, in part because it's paradoxical—a benevolent God who tolerates evil in the world he created as an act of love—and also because it causes us to question the whole situation. Why does God permit evil to exist?"

"I've heard of it, yeah." I wasn't really very interested in philosophy. After a while, the arguments and counter-arguments all seemed to blend together into a confusing mulligan stew, as far as I could tell.

"In my thesis I looked at the classic defence of God that he has granted humanity the gift of free will to choose whether to be good or evil. One of the problems with this defence, which we can now see more clearly in our post-modernist world with its distrust of wide-sweeping theories and ideologies, is that there are those among us who are incapable of knowing the difference between good and evil. Psychopaths who are evil by their very nature and cannot make the choice the theologians believe God has given us all. Serial killers who prey on innocent people with complete depravity while totally devoid of emotion."

A black BMW passed us on a very short straightaway, its engine roaring aggressively. The person in the passenger seat stuck their arm out the window and leisurely flipped us the bird.

"I'm running at the mouth, I know. I'm sorry. It's just that this whole thing has always been for me an abstraction, a mental exercise, a neat and tidy academic debate with many sides and many opinions. Good and evil, free will and determinism, theism or atheism. Faith and psychopathy.

"Now I'm faced with the possibility that it's all just bullshit. Complete and total bullshit. There are no fine and noble arguments, no this side or that side. It's time to cut the bullshit. Evil's right there, coming out of the ground next to the house in which I live, and the human being responsible for that unspeakable, horrific evil is still alive, breathing air that God gave to us all in His benevolence, and I'm about to come face to face with him."

"I feel the same way," I said, but I don't think she heard me. I was starting to feel the emotion radiating from her, in waves, building up in my mind with increasing pressure. My head started to ache.

Here it was again, I groaned inwardly. Not just normal

empathy, the kind of situation where you understand someone's emotional state and respond to it in kind. I was suddenly inside her mind, experiencing her emotions with her as they happened.

I fought against it. Why can't I control this? Why can't I just say, "I don't want this; leave me alone" and it will? I struggled to get out of her head. I didn't want to do this. I didn't want to feel her feelings and hear her thoughts as they played out inside her mind. I didn't want this to happen.

"I don't know what to do," she went on. "I really, really don't know what I'm going to do. Will I grab the table lamp beside his bed and crush his head to a pulp? I might. I just don't know."

I saw her imagining herself with the lamp in her fist, bringing it down on some old man's head, crushing his skull like an eggshell.

I fought against it. Aunt Nicolette said I could do this, I reminded myself. So if I can read their minds, then I can control it. Somehow. Right?

I focused on myself, on who I was. *My name is Madeleine. I'm my own person. I am not this person, I am me. I am Madeleine. Madeleine. Maddie, Maddie, Maddie.*

The pressure eased. I realized my eyes had been squeezed shut. I opened them and blinked to get rid of the blurriness.

"Are you all right?" Reverend B asked.

"Yeah. Look, when we get there, you don't need to come in with me. You could just drop me off and go get a coffee or something. Say, for an hour, and then come back and pick me up."

She said nothing, staring straight ahead. It gave me a

few moments to rally. I was back outside her mind; the connection was broken; I was okay.

Okay okay okay.

"It's probably better if you don't come in with me," I pressed. "I'll be fine. I won't be very long. Besides, Patrice is supposed to be there, too."

She shook her head. She drove for a while longer in silence, and then shook her head again. "No. I can't let you go in there alone. Just in case the sergeant isn't there. It's not right to let you face that monster alone."

"Whatever you think, Reverend B."

She laughed without humour. "That's just the problem. I can't think. My mind's paralyzed. I'm so very, very afraid."

I didn't have to be telepathic to empathize with her fear.

I was just as afraid of what was coming as she was.

# 54

"Family or friends?"

The Pine Hill long-term care centre had a reception desk at the front entrance where visitors were required to register and answer a few questions, mostly health-related, before they could get in to see one of their residents. Reverend B and I dutifully took turns with the clipboard, submitted to a temperature check, and answered basic questions about travel outside the country, contact with someone who was ill, and whether or not we were experiencing any flu-like symptoms.

"Mr. Tulk used to live in the parsonage on our road," I said. "I'm researching a paper on the history of the church, and we were hoping he might be able to answer a question or two."

Our tried-and-true cover story. It would take us about as far as you could throw a beached whale, but it was all I had at this point.

"I see." The woman behind the desk wore a name pin that identified her as Denise, Administrative Assistant. "You may not have any luck with him, I'm afraid."

"Oh?"

She shrugged, reluctant to disclose Tulk's personal

health-related information to someone who'd just admitted they were not a family member. "You'll see."

"I'm expecting to meet someone here from the OPP," I said. "Sergeant Rogers. Is she here yet?"

"No." The woman pointed at the clipboard. "You didn't see her name there, did you?"

"When she arrives, can you let her know I'm already here?"

Denise had already turned her attention to an older couple who'd come in behind us. She handed them the clipboard and took their temperatures, ignoring me completely.

Fine.

The facility was a single-storey structure laid out in four intersecting wings with the main entrance, cafeteria, and kitchen at the central hub and resident rooms down each spoke. I led the way around a central atrium filled with comfortable-looking armchairs, most of which were occupied by residents dozing comfortably in the muted sunlight from above. Music played faintly from overhead speakers. Orchestral string stuff from another generation. I spotted a nursing station and headed for it, Reverend B trailing reluctantly behind.

I stuck my head in and waited for the two women inside to notice me.

They laughed at something, and one turned toward a computer monitor while the other glanced over her shoulder at me.

"I'm looking for Jack Tulk's room."

"Family?"

I shook my head. "Former neighbour." Close enough.

She pointed behind me to the north wing. "Down at the end, on the right."

"Thanks."

Having never been inside a long-term care facility before, I hadn't really known what to expect. None of the awful things I'd anticipated seemed to be in evidence, though. The place was clean and tidy. Its age was beginning to show in scuff marks and scrapes along the baseboards of the hallway, but the air currents that met my nose carried the odours of disinfectant and some sort of lemon-scented air freshener.

A woman in a wheelchair was coming up the hallway as I led the way down toward Tulk's room. Her plump hands, adorned with several large rings, gripped the arms of the chair. She moved briskly forward by paddling her feet, like a duck gliding along the surface of a lake. Her hair was neatly permed and dyed reddish brown, and she wore a bright-coloured dress.

As I edged over to the side to give her ample room to pass, she slowed a bit and smiled up at me. "Hello."

Hearing her French accent, I smiled back. "Bonjour, Madame."

"It's a very nice day outside today, isn't it?"

"Yes, it is," I replied.

She smiled again and paddled past me on her way to somewhere important, no doubt. What a sweet, pleasant lady.

As I approached the end of the hall, a PSW came out of the room I'd been told was Tulk's. Tossing bundled laundry into the container on the bottom shelf of her cart, she looked up at me.

"Here to see Jack?"

I nodded.

"You're in luck; it's one of his quiet days today. Family?"

"No," I said. "He used to live on our road."

"Well, he just finished toileting so you'll have to ignore that for a few minutes until the vent fans do their work. And he's dozing, so he probably won't be much for conversation."

"Okay," I said.

"Enjoy your visit."

Yeah. Right.

I watched her wheel her cart up to the next doorway, where she called out someone's name and disappeared into the room. Taking a deep breath, I glanced at Reverend B. Her face was pinched with tension.

"You should wait out here," I told her, "or go back to the lounge area and wait for me there."

She shook her head. "Let's get this over with."

My sentiments, exactly.

Tulk was lying in bed, the covers pulled up close to his neck. His head was turned toward the curtained window, but his eyes were closed. His face was beat up, scarred, and lined, and he bore little resemblance to the mug shot Patrice had shown me. Of course, that had been taken a long time ago, in the seventies. He'd done a lot of aging and had endured a lot of punishment since then. I wondered if it was self-harm that had put those scars on his face and neck, or run-ins with other residents fed up with his noise.

There was a chair alongside the bed, in front of the window, so I walked around and sat down.

Reverend B stayed where she was, just inside the room, in front of the door to Tulk's bathroom.

As I sat down, his eyes opened. They were cloudy and unfocused, but after a moment he licked his lips and looked at me directly.

"You."

"You know who I am."

He said nothing, but the recognition in his eyes was unmistakeable.

I bit my lip. "You know why I'm here."

"Go away. Leave me alone."

"Not going to happen, Mr. Tulk."

He turned his head and, staring at the ceiling, bared his teeth.

"Fuck you," he said.

# 55

Behind me, Reverend B mumbled something about waiting outside. I heard her footsteps receding down the hall as I leaned back and closed my eyes.

Tulk swore under his breath, a muttered string of obscenities that seemed to be directed more at the universe in general than at me. I knew I was hearing the same voice that I'd heard before, the wavering, whiney baritone booming from the church when Reverend B had thought it was burning down:

*Goddamn you! Goddamn you to hell, you worthless, faithless bastard!*

Maybe she recognized it, as I had, and it was too much for her to take.

I was a little more ready to deal with it than she was, I supposed, having already heard it again in the church, alone in the dark, a week ago. We'd even had a conversation. Of sorts.

It had been enough to spook me, though, that he'd recognized me right away, even through blurred vision and the haze of his muddled thoughts. I didn't understand how, but I knew that a link had been established between us, an unwelcome and repulsive connection, one that transcended normal physical limitations, and I had to face it now and deal with it.

Somehow, he'd travelled to Twilight Road, leaving his body here in Pine Hill and returning to the scene of his horrific crimes. Was it some kind of etheric projection?

I thought about Quinn explaining to Reverend B about how we're composed of several bodies, including our physical body, a mental body that contains our regular thoughts and emotions, an etheric body that's composed of energy and straddles the physical and spiritual realms, and an astral body. In Quinn's case it was his astral body that detached itself from the rest of him so that he could travel around. Was it possible that Tulk's dementia was sheering off his mental body and flinging it out, pure raw emotion peppered with flawed fragments of memory, and propelling it without his control or consent back to Twilight Road?

Was I caught up in the pathetic flailing of a once-plastic brain trying to repair the damage, re-route connections, restore sanity? Flailing that had inexplicably leaped out into the psychic realm, like Yeats's falcon, caught in a widening gyre, the centre unable to hold, loosing anarchy upon the world?

I didn't really know for sure. It was stuff that was beyond my experience and comprehension.

Why now, though? Why was this happening to him now? Was it just that his dementia had reached a certain stage? That a particular part of his brain, maybe the part that had held everything down in place during his life, had atrophied and stopped functioning, causing this psychic storm?

And the women. What about them?

Quinn's theory was that the burial of Mrs. Pollock in

June had somehow disturbed the unresolved emotional gestalts of the murdered women who were trapped in the moments of their deaths and unable to make the transition to the next plane of existence. I'm not sure he was using the word "gestalt" in its correct meaning, but I knew what he meant.

Again, I didn't quite understand why this would happen, if it did.

Like birds tied to the ground, unable to take flight, the ghosts of the women were beating their wings and crying out in panic and fear. When I suddenly appeared to them in the portals created by the rippling surfaces of water, they lunged at me, desperate for help. Their fear catalyzed my fear, and my fear made theirs that much worse.

But what was holding them back from passing over to the next sphere of being? Why were they tied down to our physical plane, unable to break free, forced to relive their final moments of horror over and over again?

Did it have something to do with the fact that Jack Tulk was still alive? Had his evil soul somehow trapped them in this world, all this time after their horrible murders? And was their thrashing around at me, their fear and torment, which had been inadvertently triggered by my innate ability to see through portals created on the surface of rippling water, now drawing his crumbling, atrophied mind back to them to inflict renewed torment?

I had no idea. And even if I did understand what was going on, what could I possibly do about it?

I certainly wasn't going to murder him in his bed, that was for sure. No matter how great the temptation might be. I wouldn't, as Reverend B had fantasized, grab that lamp off the bedside table and smash his head to a pulp. Maybe his death would release the women and put an end to this whole nightmare, but—

*There's something you must understand, Madeleine,* Aunt Nicolette had said. *You will need to go into his mind to learn the way to be safe.*

I hadn't understood what she meant at the time. In my confusion, I'd thought she was talking about Quinn. Now I knew she was telling me I would have to share the thought processes of this abomination in front of me, this demented, evil old man, to find out not only how to ensure Quinn's safety going forward, and mine as well, but also to do something to free the women Tulk had murdered.

Oh, crap.

Although I hadn't brought my bowl with me, because I wasn't trying to communicate with a dead spirit but with someone who was still living, I'd brought along my silver leaf charm because, well, it had felt like an important thing to do.

I opened my eyes, sat up, and took it out of my pocket. I ran the horsehide lacing through my fingers, trying to swallow my fear.

Had this symbolic charm, a leaf from the Tree of Life, really protected the sun god Ra when he'd battled Apep, lord of darkness and the serpent of chaos?

I was about to go into battle myself, and I sure hoped it would help.

"On what slender threads do life and fortune hang," Dumas had written.

Oh, yeah. Absolutely.

I put it around my neck, closed my eyes again and, like a novice scuba diver, slowly eased myself down into strange and dangerous waters.

# 56

Darkness, streaked with intermittent light.

Shapes flowed into other shapes, faces appeared and disappeared, hands rose and fell.

I was in a very disorienting and surreal place.

It was a shock to be completely immersed in Tulk's mind. I'd moved directly into his thought processes; my consciousness was somewhere inside his cerebral cortex, about to use his neural networks as though they were my own. When Aunt Nicolette had said, *You will need to go into his mind*, I wasn't sure whether or not she was being this literal about it.

Apparently, yeah. She was.

I floundered around, trying to get my bearings. I was aware of his presence all around me. I felt like I was drowning in his identity, in his gestalt. I fought to retain my self-awareness as Maddie Hubbard.

"I'm me. I'm myself. I'm Maddie. Maddie. Maddie."

I visualized myself in my own body, as though the image of my full and complete self were an avatar in an online app. I looked down and saw that I was wearing my favourite dress, the dark blue, ankle-length one with small grey flowers and four white buttons on the front. Using this likeness of myself, I metaphorically began to walk.

In a few moments I reached a half-lighted area that seemed to contain nothing. Ahead of me, I could hear a faint sound, intermittent, up and down in pitch. Almost like someone breathing. Tulk?

*Maddie?*

A voice whispering in the back of my head.

"Patrice! Is that you?"

*Maddie, I can hear you. Are you all right?*

"Sure, no problem."

*I'm sorry I'm late. I was held up. You look like you're asleep or meditating. What's going on?*

"Stay back, Patrice. This could be a bit dangerous."

*I don't like this. What are you doing?*

"I'm doing something that might be stupid, but it has to be done."

*Whatever it is, I want to help. You need me, Maddie. I can feel it.*

"Stay back, Patrice, but stay close."

*I will. I'm right here, sitting next to you.*

I walked through the half-light until I found myself in a bedroom. Not the bedroom I was in; this one was smaller, with furniture more suited to a child. Looking down at myself, I saw that I was in bed. I was a small boy. My head was turned to the right on the pillow; light from a streetlamp streamed through a gap in the flowery curtains.

Voices came to me from the next room. A man and a woman, arguing. Something hit the wall on the other side and shattered. I flinched, afraid.

*What's happening, Maddie?*

"Did you see that? Hear that?"

*No. I could just tell that something scared you.*

"You need to disengage. Stay back. I'll call you if I need

you."

*All right, but I'm not moving from this room.*

She was gone, but I sensed that she was not so far away that I couldn't call out to her again and make her hear me if I needed her. I thought perhaps she could be like Ariadne, at the other end of the ball of golden thread that would help me escape from this labyrinth after I dealt with Tulk once and for all. Hopefully if I got into trouble I could use the connection to her to find my way back out of his twisted, damaged mind.

The child's bedroom suddenly shredded into strips of coloured light, like a photograph thrown into a blender, and was replaced by gloom. Back inside my own avatar, I inched forward. I was in something like a short passage. Eventually it ended at a T-intersection. I went right, and around another corner.

Was I following pathways in his brain? Pathways disrupted by the devastating forces of Alzheimer's disease, cells and connective synapses destroyed by whatever it was, plaque or whatever, that brought about the advanced cortical atrophy that prevented accurate memory retrieval, screwed up cognitive functions, and reduced someone like Tulk to a fluttering, screaming wreck of a human being?

Had the child in bed been him? Had I shared an early memory of his in which he'd cowered in his room, listening to his parents fight?

I realized this was going to be a very unpleasant experience.

⌖

A long stretch ahead of me. As though I'm in a clinic or something. In a corridor. I look down and see myself in trousers and a man's black cap-toe shoes. Behind me, the doctor. He says to someone beside him, "I want to watch his gait. Loss of balance is an indicator of the onset of Alzheimer's."

Resentment floods through me. *Fuck you, asshole. Do you think I'm fucking deaf and can't hear you? On the way back from this little stroll I'll kick your fucking brains out.*

⸎

A hailstorm. Blinding, stinging sheets of ice and freezing rain and bitter cold.

A street in some town. Winter. A messy sidewalk; poor footing. Slipping and stumbling. My face and neck inadequately covered. Freezing, numb flesh. I looked down at myself: a soaked car coat and different shoes, brown and scuffed, turning up at the toes. Just ahead, the front entrance of the bus station. Keep moving.

Time to leave. Time to get the hell out of here. She told her mother, and the shit hit the fan. Questions about the other girl being asked again, the teenager. A brief flash of the dumpster into which she'd gone, afterward. I'm surprised that the body had never been found. No corpus delicti there, but in this instance now the kid was a witness and, although a known problem child, the possibility that she might be believed was too great to risk.

Big, heavy doors that slide open when I reach them. Looking behind, I see a few people on the sidewalk, but just strangers in winter coats and hats, huddled against the storm. No pursuit; not yet. Inside, people sitting on benches or standing around, waiting. Whatever the next bus out of town is, get on it. Just hope to hell the weather doesn't screw with the schedule.

Nothing back in my room worth worrying about. Some

clothing, a few books. Nothing that can't be replaced from a Sally Ann in the next town for a few bucks. Tap my pocket; wallet's there.

I walk through the open doors and head straight for the ticket window.

⟞⟝

Blankness. Gloom. A dead end? A wall of dead cells in front of me?

Back in my own avatar, I turned around and retraced my steps. Tulk's memories were coming at me randomly, not in chronological order or even by direct association. Much as he would be experiencing them, probably. I still heard the sound of breathing. Asleep?

⟞⟝

Water. Warm water, soapy. Sitting on a plastic chair in a little shower room. Naked. A woman rubbing my shoulders and arms with a big sponge. Two other women standing behind her, talking about someone's kid. Doesn't like school; doesn't pay attention. Learning disability?

The woman sponges my left leg, then my right. "Up we get, now."

One of the others steps around, and they ease me up off the chair. The woman sponges my genitals, then turns me around and sponges my ass.

Time was, this would have had a different outcome, wouldn't it?

Too goddamned tired now to care.

⟞⟝

Crappy little room in Regina. Sitting on the edge of the bed, eating take-out Chinese. Reading the newspaper. Nothing about North Battleford. The police questioning had been intense but unfocused; the girl had talked but it must have been too confused, thanks to the drugs.

Finish a can of beer and open another one. Toss aside the newspaper. Oh yeah, the stupid free church newsletter. Flip through it. The usual brainless crap. I turn to the little classified section at the back, and hey now, look at this. Trustees in a little obscure dump called Bennett's Corners, Ontario, looking for a pastor. This could be perfect. Time to get the hell out of Saskatchewan. Clean up the CV; write a great letter; send it to the post office box address at the bottom of the ad; grab the next bus east.

Fold the newsletter carefully. Set it aside. Finish the Chinese; grab my wallet from the dresser. Check the billfold; still almost thirty bucks. Drug store at the corner should still be open. A pad of stationery, a new pen, an envelope, and a stamp. Save enough for the bus ticket.

Check my look in the mirror before heading out. Rough, but presentable. The ladies do love the mutton chops, though. Kind of an Alan Bates thing.

⌒≈⌒

With sudden horror, staring at the mirror, I realized I wasn't looking at the reflection of Jack Tulk. I was confronted with the rakish, grinning features of the Reverend Seymour Blackburn.

# 57

I pulled myself out and ran, but there was nowhere to go. Everything around me rippled and convulsed, a chaos of shapes and forms and colours and shadows. The breathing sound I'd been hearing became ragged coughing, punctuated with hoarse and feeble cursing.

*You. What the hell.*

I stopped running and turned around. "I know who you are."

*What do I care.*

"You're Seymour Blackburn. Everyone thinks you're Tulk, but you're not."

*That's what they call me. Jack Tulk. I'm Tulk!*

"No, you're not. You're Blackburn. You were supposed to be a holy man. A pastor. Educated. Intelligent. What happened to you?"

*Holy man. Ha ha ha! Jesus H. Christ, what boat did you just get off of?*

"I—"

Lightning storm. Flickering, blinding light. No sound at all. Oxygen sucked from the air. I pushed forward.

<hr />

Sitting at a bar. On a stool at the end, trying to make a half glass of beer last another twenty minutes. Guy beside me sneering at photographs of hockey players on the wall above the shelves of hard liquor.

"Frontenacs. Buncha goddamned losers."

I pay for his next shot. He goes through his story. Just released from the Kingston Pen; stuck in a halfway house downtown. Trying to find a job, but not too hard.

"Not much tail in here tonight." Looks over his shoulder.

Never ask what they went in for, that's the rule of thumb, but he feels like bragging. Six in a row before they caught up to him. Students, mostly. The easiest. Careless; overconfident; not thinking about their safety when they really, really should have been.

Young and soft.

Easy pickings.

"All done now. Rehab's the thing, man. Straight and narrow. Know anybody who wants to give a guy a helping hand?"

Effortless enough to offer him a job. Drive home with him sleeping in the back seat. A project; a good deed to show the trustees, the old bastards. Why the hell won't they like me? God knows I turn on the charm whenever I can. Scabby old pricks.

I'll string them the usual bullshit: "We can all take a hand in reforming the sinner. Show him the way to accept Jesus into his heart and repent his transgressions, and we'll be better children of God for it."

Secret anticipation. He'll talk about who he did, and how he did them.

Can't wait.

Recoiling, I felt sick. This man's twisted, perverted thoughts were like a toxin filling my mind, poisoning me. *Aunt Nicolette, what am I supposed to do? Joelle, help. Marie-Claire, help me. Please. Tell me what to do.*

They're all pissed at the idea of Tulk as sexton, but the chickenshits are afraid to deny my request and have me turn around and quit on them. They dread the thought of another long search for a replacement sucker. Pastor, I mean. So they screw up their courage: Tulk it is. I brought him up here, and now I'm sorry I did. Churlish and lazy bastard. They complain, and I keep telling them that criminal rehab's a marathon, not a sprint. Like I believe it myself.

Loud noises upstairs; overhead, coming from his attic bedroom. Investigate and find him in bed with a corpse. The recently buried Mrs. Jane Goodman, age forty-nine, heart failure. Lovely. In life and in death. The repulsive bastard laughs at my disgust. Laughs at my anger. Invites me in. We fight. He beats me badly; leaves me bleeding on the floor. When his rage and his pleasure finally subside, he agrees to return Mrs. Goodman to her grave.

I help, under cover of darkness.

We both know he's now the one in charge.

I was Maddie. Maddie Maddie Maddie.

I had to get away. I had to get away, get away, get away. Panic. I couldn't catch my breath. I tried to run, but I was almost paralyzed with horror. I didn't realize, not really, that such depravity could exist in the human mind. I'd read about that kind of stuff, sure, but it was like an academic abstraction or something, compared to reality. It was like something in Reverend B's thesis: "God is the creator of all things. God created the capacity within man for evil; therefore he must also have created the capacity to transcend evil and do good works." Sure, but this was real. Real, palpable, blatant evil!

I had to escape.

I tried, but I couldn't break free. Something was holding me there.

*Oh God, he wants forgiveness.*

This one he picked up at the train station in Smiths Falls. I don't ask for a name. Barely look at her. This one he kills first, because he tends to prefer them that way. Beginning to agree with him.

I groaned, unable to escape. Forgiveness, he wanted forgiveness, he wanted forgiveness. From me. From me! He must have truly been demented if he thought that was going to happen.

Not this one, please. Tulk, please. Sweet and kind, like a small, gentle animal. Could fall in love this time. Finally. So sweet! Oh no! His hands around her neck. No! No more, no more. Stop!

His laughter like acid in my brain. Bastard!

Alarm clock on the bedside stand. Big and solid in my hand. Swing it with all my strength and drive him off her, down onto the floor. Scalp laid open; blood flowing. Bastard! Still moving.

Blind rage. Hit him again and again and again and again and again.

Fire in my head goes away.

His head is a crushed pulp.

She's gone.

Front door crashes.

Run! Down one flight of stairs, the other flight of stairs, out the open door. Wait! Oh please, please wait!

Ahead of me, she runs.

Down the dark road, bare feet stumbling on gravel, crying, sobbing. Catch her, try to pull her back. Beating my face, arms, chest, nails scratching, biting. Hit her. She won't stop. Hit her and hit her and hit her and hit her and hit her and hit her.

She sags to the ground. Oh God, no. Dead.

Heavy to carry. More than I thought she'd be.

Digging, digging, digging. Moonlight, but hard to see. Hate this. Hands ache. Back hurts. Should have brought a flashlight. No Tulk this time to do the dirty work. Bury her close to the others. Crying. Whispering meaningless prayers.

Back inside for Tulk. His turn to taste the dirt of the

grave.

Drag him down the stairs. Curse him, spit on him. Hate this bastard. Hate him! Down the main staircase and out the door.

Oh God, no strength to dig another grave tonight.

Sit in the darkness and cry. Cry and cry and cry.

Strange shape in the moonlight, at the back. Some monster come to destroy me. I deserve it. Deserve to be torn to shreds, my soul thrown into the eternal flames of hell.

Ah, God. Wait. Wood chipper. Clearing brush at the back of the cemetery. Rented for a week. Tulk refused, so the trustees paid a man.

My heart stops pounding. Idea.

No; absurd.

No, not absurd! Exactly what to do!

Back inside and upstairs. Closet. Old suit. No, not the jacket; trousers and a flannel shirt. My socks, my shoes.

Outside; so dark. Where's Tulk? Oh my God, I— Trip over him and fall down. Cursing, swearing, pain in my elbow. Worthless, faithless bastard!

Struggle to dress his naked, obscene body. My clothes. Me! My wallet in his pocket.

No one will hear. House on the other side of the church still only half-built. Wood chipper still has gas. Start it up and drag Tulk over. Hands first, then the head. Not yet; where's the off switch? Damn the dark; where is it? There. Okay. One last tug, into the threshing blades; arms consumed, flesh and blood spattering me; his head's pulled completely in; hit the button to turn it off.

Job done?

Into the parsonage; find a flashlight; back outside.

O God, please help me.

Horrible, obscene mess. Don't throw up. Struggle to keep it down.

Head almost completely obliterated. Hands gone; no fingerprints for identification.

Job done.

Find his keys and wallet upstairs. A duffel bag; pack a few things; take his truck.

Gone.

# 58

I struggled to block him out. I didn't want his memories invading my mind. I didn't want his thoughts taking over my thoughts, becoming mine. Wildly I fought back, trying to push away from him. Trying to escape.

I cried out for my mother to help me, but Joelle wasn't there. I screamed for Aunt Nicolette, but she wasn't there either.

I was alone against this monster.

What would they do, if they were here? If it were them? What would they do? They were older, more experienced, stronger. Joelle. Aunt Nicolette, please!

Maddie.

My name's . . . Maddie.

Maddie Maddie Maddie Maddie Maddie Maddie Maddie Maddie.

*Forgive me!* he begged.

"NO!" I screamed. "No forgiveness!"

*Mary, forgive me!*

"Go to hell!"

*Elaine, forgive me!*

"NO!"

*Maddie, forgive me!*

He was right in front of me—pale, wavering light, a horrible sulphuric stench, ragged, phlegm-clogged breathing. *I cannot die before being forgiven! I cannot!*

"Die, you foul, poisonous bastard!" I screamed. "Die!"

*You goddamned bitch! I'll kill you with my bare hands!*

He screamed so loudly I thought my mind would explode. He screamed and screamed in mindless rage, the rage of madness, the rage of dementia, and I turned and ran.

I ran and ran and ran.

His mind was an endless maze of random memories and dead ends blocked by the destructive plaque clogging his brain. I stopped running. I was lost, disoriented, confused.

*I'll kill you with my bare hands, you worthless, faithless bastard! Where are you, Tulk? Show yourself!*

"You killed him already, Blackburn!" I shouted.

*No no no, I don't remember that. Christ, I'd remember that. Where is he? I'll kill him filthy dead!*

It was true. I could sense it in his thoughts. The memory of what he'd done still evaded his conscious thoughts. But I'd seen it; I'd experienced it directly from where it was recorded in his brain, so I knew it had happened. He'd bludgeoned Tulk to death in that awful, accursed bedroom and stuck his body in the wood chipper to make positive identification impossible.

His mind, in its torment, was continuously casting out, flying back to Twilight Road, searching for the man who'd completed his corruption, tempted him into ultimate sin, and violated the one woman he'd thought he could actually love. He wanted forgiveness, was begging for it, but first he wanted revenge. He wanted to kill a man he'd already murdered.

It was sick, twisted, perverted.

Blackburn began to gibber.

Flickering light; voices; images of people.

Me!

In the parsonage attic, staring down through a rippling surface as a woman called out to me. He'd been there, watching. He was the horrible presence Reverend B and I had sensed hanging over us, suffocating us.

Seymour Blackburn!

Me, again!

Falling as the ground shook, watching the satellite dish topple from the roof of the parsonage, listening to Reverend B scream about the piece of engraved stone that had flown past her head, nearly killing her. Blackburn had been there, hunting for Tulk, angry and lashing out.

Me, once again!

Sitting cross-legged in the dark, wiping blood from my nose, surrounded by the ruins of his former church, defiant in my fear. He'd been confused, uncertain as to why he was there. Then he'd been swept up in his hatred of Tulk and had raged at me in the absence of his nemesis.

His gibbering now turned to low moaning. It was a horrible sound, the groaning of a suffering animal. I couldn't stand it. I wanted to escape, get out of here, leave this madness behind. I couldn't. It was overwhelming me. Drowning me.

*Maddie? Maddie, where are you?*

"Patrice? Is that you?"

*Maddie, stop this now! Let me help you.*

"No. Stay away. He's insane. He's driving *me* insane."

*I can hear a lot of this, Maddie. So could Reverend*

*Northrop. She left. But I'm here. Let me help you get out of there.*

"No! It's too dangerous!"

*Don't panic. Settle down, Maddie.*

Her words began to echo so that they were difficult to understand.

*Don't panic!* Echo-echo-echo.

*Follow the sound of my voice!* Echo-echo-echo.

"I don't know where you are!" I cried. "It sounds like your voice is coming from everywhere at once."

*Itisn'tMaddie.* The words were beginning to blur together.

*I'mrighthereintheroomwithyou.*

"What? What did you say?"

*Calmdowncalmdowncalmdown.*

*Don'tpanicdon'tpanicdon'tpanic.*

"I can't understand what you're saying." I had to calm down. "My name's Maddie Hubbard. Maddie Hubbard."

I repeated it over and over, like a mantra, barely able to hear myself over the deafening clamour of Blackburn's ranting, which had completely ceased to be language and was now raw noise, endless screaming, insane raving.

*This way, Maddie,* Patrice called out, her voice no longer distorted. *Over here!*

I ran in that direction.

*Over here!* More faint this time, coming from behind me.

*Over here!*

"I'm trying! I don't know where to go!"

*Over here!*

"I'm trying to find you!"

*Here.*

It was Blackburn, majestic in his madness, looming

over me, surrounding me. Words began to tumble from him, obscene, random, meaningless; shouted words that beat at me like blows.

*Maddie! Up here! Come on!*

"Where? Where?'

*Worthless!*

"Leave me alone!"

*Come on, Maddie! You can do it!*

"I'm trying!"

*Faithless!*

"Die, you bastard!"

*Here Maddie, here!*

"I'm coming!"

*Bastard!*

I fell. I crawled.

A woman screamed. I screamed back, frantic.

*Die, damn you! Die!*

I lost myself in his madness.

# 59

On the second Tuesday in April, the weather had taken a turn for the worse. The sky was the colour of wet slate. Snow mixed with sleet angled downward, threatening to cover once again the dead grass and pavement that had finally revealed itself as winter receded over the past few weeks.

Devlin's schedule had cleared up when Maddie Hubbard cancelled this morning's session, freeing him to go for a walk. Beverley was on the phone with her editor, wrangling about something or other, so Devlin threw on his winter coat, boots, and fedora, wrapped a scarf around his neck for protection against the unpleasantness of the gusting wind, and slipped out the front door.

Turning south down Kilmarnock Road, he crossed the single-lane swing bridge over the Rideau Canal. Huddling inside his coat, he looked down at the empty lock with its random puddles, dead leaves, and a few stray sticks. The canal system wouldn't be open to boater traffic until next month, and in this weather it was difficult to picture pleasure craft waiting patiently in the locks to pursue their leisurely cruise along the waterway.

Devlin was a walker, though, and adverse conditions

didn't especially bother him. He normally got out in the early hours, before his sessions began, and he liked to walk about four kilometres, round trip. It was good exercise, and it gave him time to think about what would be coming up in his day. It gave him a chance to get his thoughts in order and to make whatever decisions might lie in front of him.

Today he could only think about Maddie Hubbard. Truthfully, she'd been on his mind all week. After everything she'd told him in their last session, and the way in which she'd talked about it, maintaining eye contact for the most part and not hesitating to admit her fear when it had threatened to overwhelm her, he felt himself wanting to believe her story, wanting to accept the entire idea of entering another man's mind to learn the truth about his identity and his past behaviour.

He couldn't, though. Not without compromising his training and his experience as a professional. The dilemma rasped away at his conscience.

He cleared his throat and spat into the ditch. Damn! He was in a spot, and he didn't know how to resolve it. Every fibre of his being screamed that Maddie was telling him the truth, while everything he knew and trusted as a clinical psychologist urged him to conclude that she'd suffered a break from reality last fall and was delusional.

She believes she's telling the truth, and she's quite sincere about it, but she's only relating an elaborate delusion that has taken root in her disturbed mind.

That was the appropriate diagnosis, and he needed to decide what further treatment she would need in order to deal with her delusional state. This was what he should be doing. Instead of running through the story in his mind again and again, trying to believe it.

He reached the front entrance of Kilmarnock Orchards,

which was where he normally turned around to head back home, giving him his usual four-kilometre round-trip stroll. This morning, however, he adjusted the scarf around his neck and kept going.

Beverley had confided to him that she'd grown rather fond of Maddie. She'd been drawn to her shyness, her pretty plainness, and her polite manner, and she'd been pleased to see her gradually emerge from her near-catatonic shell as the weeks progressed.

Devlin felt the same way. Maddie was likeable, she was someone you rooted for to succeed, and she had a bit of a fighter in her that forced you not to smile when you saw it flashing behind the natural reserve and understated demeanour.

Damn!

He followed the dogleg in the road and continued south down Kilmarnock Road until he reached what the maps called Wolford Chapel. On his left was a large auto repair business. Cars parked in the yard had taken on a thin coating of snow, but it was already melting off and sliding down the windshields into white ridges covering up the wipers.

On his right, as he continued to walk, he passed the Wolford Rural Cemetery. A few metres beyond that was the little church that gave the spot its name. A small white frame structure with a tower and steeple in front, it was an example of what the old church on Twilight Road might still be if it had been taken care of over the years.

The cemetery was established in 1805 and seventeen years later, in 1822, the chapel became the first church to be built in Wolford Township and one of the oldest on the Rideau River system.

Devlin stopped as he drew even with the double-doored

entrance. He stared at it for a moment, lost in thought.

A car horn tooted behind him. Devlin moved off the road into the space kept cleared by the sexton for people to walk into the church. He turned and waved at the driver. It was a neighbour of his.

This winter he and Beverley had, for the first time, attended an evening Christmas Eve service here. It was one of two occasions every year when the church was used, the other being Easter Sunday, and they'd decided, almost on a whim, that it would be a nice way to celebrate the holiday. The pastor, Reverend Will Hart, was an acquaintance, and the handful of people attending the service were all locals familiar to them, so they didn't feel that much out of place.

Afterward, they'd declined an invitation to a little party being hosted by the pastor's cousin in Jasper and had driven home talking about adding the yearly service to their own private Christmas rituals, all of which to this point had been secular and very quiet.

He turned around and started back up the road, retracing his steps while reading the names on the headstones in the cemetery: Pearson, Haskins, Brown, Chipman, Johnston.

It looked peaceful in there, the snow falling quietly on the granite, marble, and fieldstone markers. Involuntarily, he imagined unmarked graves at the back holding the remains of murdered women. Grimacing, he turned away, concentrating instead on the slushy surface of the road in front of him.

*Different church, Dennis.*

*Different reality?*

He briefly considered giving Reverend Hart a call, maybe to set up a meeting to get his perspective on the possibility of life after death. He rejected the idea after a few paces. Hart was a nice guy, but very straight-laced. Devlin had never seen even the slightest evidence of imagination or humour in the man.

Should he call Dr. McGarrigle again? Maybe quiz him further on his own experiences with the supernatural?

Devlin considered the idea for about half a kilometre before deciding against it. He'd already bothered David enough with the subject, and there was nothing further to be gained by talking in generalities. And it was quite possible that the young Dr. McGarrigle *had* been pranked by the ghosthunters after all and that the whole thing was meaningless beyond that.

Not to mention the fact that the particulars of Maddie Hubbard's case were locked inside Devlin's well-trained, professional head, never to be revealed.

He shivered, and it suddenly occurred to him to wonder if Maddie had been reading *his* mind all the time she'd been coming to him over the course of the winter. Had she been fully aware of his skepticism, his doubts about her mental balance? He'd been so absorbed in what she was saying that it hadn't crossed his mind, but now he began to run through the various sessions, trying to remember what he might have been thinking at given moments and whether or not it might have upset her or caused her to doubt his sincerity.

Oh, lord. It was a hopeless exercise. He'd thought what he'd thought, and if she'd been aware of it, it was all water under the bridge now, wasn't it?

Anyway, she'd kept coming back to him, week after week, and had shown steady improvement, so it mustn't have been all that bad.

By the time he reached home, he'd managed to convince himself that things were all right, that he probably hadn't alienated her or upset her in any way. Her cancellation of their session today was likely unrelated to anything he'd inadvertently revealed to her.

Good heavens, did he actually believe she could read minds?

He sighed and shook his head.

As he hung up his coat and kicked off his boots, Beverley came out from the kitchen with a cup of coffee in her hand.

"You look like you could use this," she said, giving it to him.

"Thanks. How'd it go with Abigail?"

Beverley grinned. "How does senior editor sound?"

"Congratulations! I'm proud of you."

She kissed his cheek. "I heard your cellphone ping while you were out. E-mail."

"Thanks. I'll go check on it."

"Probably fan mail from some flounders."

He laughed. In his office, he sipped the coffee and booted up his computer. When he logged in and opened his e-mail account, he saw that he had a new message from mhubbard101x@outlook.com.

He opened it immediately, wondering why Maddie had chosen to write him this morning instead of sitting down with him in person to continue their conversation.

# MADDIE

# 60

Dear Dr. Devlin,

I hope you don't mind if I wind up our sessions by e-mail instead of in person, but I think it's better this way.

I know you have a lot of doubts about everything I've told you, and I know I'll never be able to convince you of the truth of what happened, but that's all right. You've seen that I've made it almost all the way back to where I was before the "trigger event" that started everything last fall, and I'm pretty sure I can cope with anything the future will bring without further assistance or new meds.

No offence. You've been terrific. I'm just ready to stand on my own two feet again. That's all I mean.

You've been wondering, I'll bet, whether or not I've been able to read your mind all this time. You can't see me sitting here typing this, of course, but I'm laughing out loud. Don't worry. When I regained consciousness in the hospital that particular ability had temporarily disappeared, but once it came back it didn't take me long to figure out how to control it.

Unlike poor Aunt Nicolette. For whatever reason, I'm luckier than she was. I can make use of this ability on my own terms, and it won't drive me insane.

Hopefully.

I should backtrack a little, I guess. I don't know how much you know about what happened after I went to see Jack Tulk, or Seymour Blackburn as it turned out. I don't remember a lot, I admit, but apparently I passed out as I was trying to follow Patrice's voice out of that vile bastard's head.

Reverend B had left the building while I was fighting my way out. She *had* been aware of what was going on between me and Blackburn, as Patrice had said. Marie-Claire was right after all—I did have the ability to make her see and hear what I was experiencing in my own mind. As well as Patrice, obviously.

Nurses ran into the room and a doctor was called when they couldn't get me to wake up. I was taken by ambulance to the hospital in Kingston, and I guess it took me several days to come out of it.

I learned later that Blackburn had suffered a massive heart attack right then, while Reverend B was on her way out to her car and Patrice was running down to the nursing station for help. He was dead by the time they got to him.

I've been trying to remember the last moment I experienced in his mind, as the madness overwhelmed me and temporarily drove me insane as well, and I think it was when he had the heart attack and realized he was dying. Even though it almost killed me at the same time, I was glad to have been there for that one.

His last-minute pleas for forgiveness hadn't worked. Now he would have to face the consequences of his evil actions in the next reality, whatever that might be for him.

I know Reverend B would say that vengeance belongs

to the Lord, but if you'll forgive me for descending into slang for a moment, Dr. Devlin, "Payback's a bitch, ain't it?"

Happy to have helped things along to an appropriate conclusion.

Plus, his death released me from the labyrinth of his insanity. Otherwise, I'm not sure I would have made it out.

Because Patrice was in attendance and on duty when Blackburn died, she gave a statement to the coroner explaining the reason for her presence at the moment of death, the nature of the assistance she was providing to the investigating detectives involved in the Twilight Road case, and her doubts about the true identity of the deceased. Fingerprints and DNA evidence proved that he was indeed Seymour Blackburn, not Jack Tulk, and an autopsy ruled that the cause of death was cardiac failure. In other words, the heartless son of a bitch was killed by a heart attack.

Thankfully, Patrice left me out of her account of things, other than to mention that I'd also been in attendance at the time of death. I wasn't in any shape to give a statement, and the coroner decided, after compiling all the other evidence, that one wasn't needed from me.

Thankfully.

They buried his body in Kingston under his real name. No one has bothered doing anything about the grave on Twilight Road with the marker identifying it as the final resting place of the Reverend Seymour Blackburn. No one cares that it's actually Jack Tulk's corpse rotting there.

As for Reverend B, well, she's already disappeared over the horizon, bound for parts unknown. Aunt Brigitte told me she resigned her position, packed her stuff, and left while I was still in a coma. She didn't even try to come around to see me in the hospital.

Whatever.

I don't know where she went, as I say, and I'm not going to try to find out. I guess she's had more than enough of me for one lifetime, and frankly I've had more than enough of her.

If you were sitting across from me right now, Dr. Devlin, you'd ask me how I feel about that, wouldn't you? So okay then, I'll tell you.

I feel let down. I thought she was my friend. In some ways I guess I thought she was like a replacement mother, someone who'd be there for me when I needed her.

Looks like I was wrong about that one, wasn't I?

I feel a little resentment too, I suppose. She kept denying, denying, denying everything despite experiencing most of what I was experiencing, and she ended up making me feel, I don't know, somehow inferior because I didn't have a doctorate of divinity or a pulpit from which to preach the "truth" or whatever. So I guess on some level I resent her ability to leave, to turn her back on it and walk away, pretending none of it ever happened.

Denial is a convenient remedy for the faint of heart, isn't it? Well, it's a luxury I can't indulge in, unfortunately.

There's some sadness too, though. I feel sorry for her. Nothing in her life would have prepared her for what happened, and she really didn't have any defences to put up against it once the proverbial shit started to hit the fan. While I, on the other hand, grew up with this kind of stuff. It made a difference when it came to surviving.

I survived.

You bet I did.

Who knows what she's going to do with the rest of her life? I guess I'll never know.

In just over two months I'll turn twenty-one, and the money Mark left for me in trust will be transferred into my bank account. Quinn and I have talked a lot about what we're going to do. This summer we'll take that trip to India I promised him, and we'll stay there for a couple of months so he can absorb as much of the culture and the mysticism as possible before we come back to Canada and make a fresh start.

After that, although we're grateful to Aunt Brigitte and Uncle Robert for letting us stay with them after I got out of the hospital, we're going to move to Toronto for a few years. I'm transferring to the U of T to finish my bachelor's degree in English, and Quinn's picked out a school he wants to attend in a predominantly Hindu community, so we'll rent a condo there for a few years until things settle out. There's a guru who lives in the city that Quinn's already been in contact with. He's agreed to tutor Quinn once we get settled.

After that? Who knows.

There's one more thing I need to tell you about. Bear with me for another few minutes, okay?

On Sunday I went over to the parsonage with my knapsack slung over my shoulder. The coroner had given the police permission to release it as a crime scene. Matt Pollock was there, having finally gotten around to fixing the plumbing in the downstairs bathroom, and when I told him I'd kind of like to have one last look around the place, he was his usual shaggy-dog self.

"Sure, Maddie. Feel free."

The parsonage had been provided to Reverend B furnished, as part of her deal with the trustees, so most of the stuff was still there. I wandered around a little, feeling crappy about everything, and then I finally worked up the courage to go upstairs.

To the third floor.

Everything up there was also pretty much as I remembered having seen it the last time. The small side table and two chairs still sat in the centre of the attic space. The door leading into the hidden room was once again securely padlocked, the police having finished with their forensic goings-on. A stack of gyprock leaned against the wall, waiting for Matt to nail it over the door and seal up that awful room once again. This time, hopefully, for good.

I'd read in the local paper that the Bennett's Corners church was being permanently closed and that the head office in Toronto, or whatever church organizations call it, had dismissed the trustees and was making arrangements to put everything up for sale. I guess Matt was still being retained as sexton in order to get a bunch of repairs done. Can't sell a nice old country house with a downstairs bathroom that doesn't work properly, can you?

Or an upstairs attic room with a history of grisly, horrible murders.

I sat down at the table and unpacked my knapsack: brass bowl; sippy cup; blue-lace agate pebble; silver leaf pendant.

This was another step in gaining some sort of closure, I guess. Not only as far as the haunting of the parsonage itself was concerned, but also my scrying ability and its place in my life. Part of what you've helped me accomplish during our sessions, Dr. Devlin, is to accept who I am, *what* I am, and embrace it.

I'll never go public with it the way Joelle did—that's for darned sure!—but I won't hide it away and not talk about it the way Marie-Claire did. There's a middle ground there somewhere, and I'm going to work very hard over the next while to find it and get settled in.

Who knows, maybe Quinn's Mumbai guru will have a few sage words of advice for me, too.

Anyway, I went through the ritual and dropped the pebble into the water.

Nothing happened.

I tried again and again.

Nothing.

I knew that my scrying ability was still there. I could feel it. If I went back to the house and tried in my own kitchen, chances were I'd find someone to talk to. Maybe Marie-Claire again; I'm pretty sure her spirit is never far from me and Quinn.

Maybe Aunt Nicolette, although I'm not so sure about her.

But here? In the parsonage? Right now?

Nothing.

The women were gone.

Their ghosts had moved on, now that Seymour Blackburn was dead. They'd crossed over to the next plane of existence, their spirits freed of Blackburn's malevolence for all time, and they didn't need to communicate with me any more.

Hopefully.

One thing I've been grateful for is that I never contacted the ghost of Jack Tulk at any time. Not while the women were pleading for my help, and not this time, either. I have no idea where his essence would have gone, and I really, really don't want to know.

Hopefully some place where he'll have to pay the full price for his depravity.

I packed up my stuff and went home.

I'll never set foot inside that place again. Ever. And it

feels good, a huge relief, to know—yes, with the certainty of clairvoyance—that that's the truth.

I'm fully aware that there's one thing I never talked about with you that I said I would, and lo and behold, I'm not going to talk about it now, either.

I promised I'd talk about what had happened when I tried to contact Joelle, and why it was so awful and traumatic that I vowed at the time never to scry again. Unfortunately, that's one promise I'll have to renege on, at least for the time being.

Maybe the day will come when I can talk about it. That'll probably be the day I make the attempt to find out where she is and what has to be done to rescue her.

But that's a story for another day.

Don't you think?

Thank you so much for all your help, Dr. Devlin. Words can't express the debt of gratitude I owe you. Please pass along my thanks as well to Mrs. Devlin, who was always so patient and kind, even at the beginning when I wasn't much more than a zombie and didn't even answer when she tried to talk to me. I'll always remember her for being so sweet and considerate.

And don't worry about the mind reading now, really. Apparently I have to be within spitting distance of someone before I can hear their thoughts, so there's no danger I'll pick up on what you're thinking after you read this.

Unlike Aunt Nicolette, whose ability worked no matter where she was. Which was why she and I were able to communicate while she was in the hospital and I was at home, an unsuspecting little kid with an invisible friend. And I guess that unlimited range, or whatever you'd call it, was probably why it was impossible for her to control it. Imagine being vulnerable to the incessant internal yammering of thousands and thousands of people all at the same time, from almost anywhere, at any time of the day or night.

I couldn't handle that, I know.

By the way, don't be afraid to talk to your mentor again.

What Dr. McGarrigle experienced in the old farmhouse, the girl he saw who told him he shouldn't be there? That was definitely the spirit of someone trying to warn him away.

Not a prank.

Far from it.

Just saying.

Love and my very best wishes for the future,

Maddie.

# ACKNOWLEDGMENTS

The following resources were helpful to the author in the writing of this novel: Robynne Boyd, "Do People Only Use 10 Percent of Their Brains?" *Scientific American*, Feb. 7, 2008. https://www. scientificamerican.com/article/do-people-only-use-10-percent-of-their-brains/ accessed Feb 17, 2022; Maria Miceli and Cristiano Castelfranchi, "Reconsidering the Differences Between Shame and Guilt," *Europe's Journal of Psychology*, 2018, Vol. 14 (3), 710-733; Candace Savage, *Crows: Encounters With The Wise Guys.* Vancouver: Greystone Books, 2005; Brad Bulin, "Ravens and Wolves," *Yellowstone Quarterly*, Spring 2020, 16; Hans Dieter Betz, ed. *The Greek Magical Papyri in Translation, Including the Demonic Spells.* Chicago: The University of Chicago Press, 1986; *Three Books of Occult Philosophy Written by Henry Cornelius Agrippa of Nettesheim*, trans. James Freake, ed. and annotated by Donald Tyson. Woodbury, MN: Llewellyn Publications, 2009; Richard Kieckhefer, *Forbidden Rites: A Necromancer's Manual of the Fifteenth Century.* Pennsylvania State University Press, 1998; Armand Delatte, *La Catoptromancie Grecque et ses dérivés.* Paris: Librairie E. Droz, 1932; Tom Harpur, *Life After Death.* Toronto: McClelland and Stewart, 1991; and Flavie Waters, "Auditory Hallucinations in Psychiatric Illness," *Psychiatric Times*, Vol. 27, No. 3, Issue 3, March 2010.

Many thanks to my dear cousin, Sandra Vanalstyne, for her unflagging support and for encouraging me to finish this story.

Once again, thanks to my best friend, life partner, and editor-in-chief, Lynn L. Clark.

# ABOUT THE AUTHOR

**Michael J. McCann** lives and writes in Oxford Station, Ontario, Canada. His crime novel *Sorrow Lake* was a finalist for the Hammett Prize for best crime novel in North America.

A graduate of Trent University (Peterborough, ON) and Queen's University (Kingston, ON), he served as production editor of Criminal Reports (Third Series) and law reports co-ordinator for Carswell Legal Publications (Western) before spending fifteen years at the Canada Border Services Agency as a project officer and national program manager. He's married to author Lynn L. Clark. They have one son.

If you enjoy supernatural fiction,
you'll want to read the chilling story
of a tormented boy's ghost
trapped in this world!

**The Home Child**

Lynn L. Clark

ISBN: 978-1-927884-00-3

**The Plaid Raccoon Press**

Ask your local independent bookstore
to order it today!

Is supernatural suspense your thing?
Don't miss these two exciting novellas
by the author of *The Home Child!*

**The Fire Whisperer & Circle of Souls**
Lynn L. Clark
ISBN: 978-1-927884-05-8

The Plaid Raccoon Press

Ask your local independent bookstore
to order it today!

**A deadly struggle between good and evil in a cul-de-sac at the end of a quiet street. Who will prevail?**

**The Accusers**

**Lynn L. Clark**

**ISBN: 978-1-927884-07-2**

**The Plaid Raccoon Press**

**Ask your local independent bookstore to order it today!**

Simon wanted to be left alone,
but They had other ideas.
Michael J. McCann's debut novel

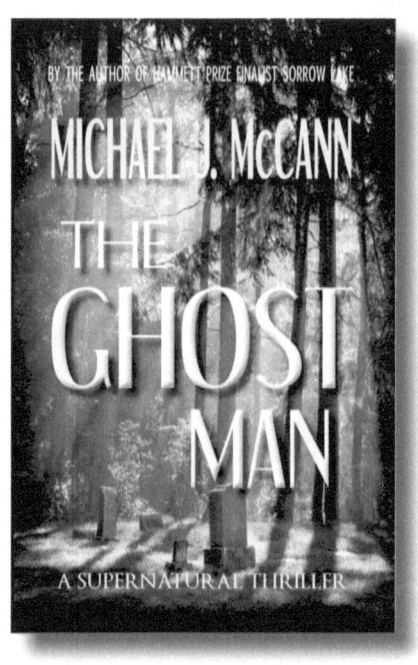

**The Ghost Man**

Michael J. McCann

ISBN: 978-0-9877087-6-2

**The Plaid Raccoon Press**

Ask your local independent bookstore
to order it today!